BLACKWATER RISING

Anne B. Jones

Indigo Publishing Group, LLC

Publisher	Henry S. Beers
Associate Publisher	Rick L. Nolte
Associate Publisher	Richard J. Hutto
Executive VP	Robert G. Aldrich
Editor-in-Chief	Joni Woolf
Designer	Scott Baber
Print Studio Manager	Gary G. Pulliam
Print Studio Assistant	Chris Bryant

Library of Congress Control Number: 2008931953

ISBN: 978-1-934144-36-7
1-934144-36-3

Indigo Publishing Group books are available at quantity discounts with bulk purchase for educational, business, or sales promotional use. For information, please write to: Indigo Publishing Group, LLC, 435 Second Street, Suite 320, Macon, GA 31201, or call 866-311-9578.

Dedication

Blackwater Rising is dedicated to my friend and mentor, mystery writer Anna Ashwood Collins. Her untiring interest and encouragement were the wind beneath my wings in completing this work.

Blackwater Rising is set on the Georgia Coast. In some cases, place names, geographical features, and historical information have been changed to accommodate its story. All characters and events are fictional.

The Georgia Coast

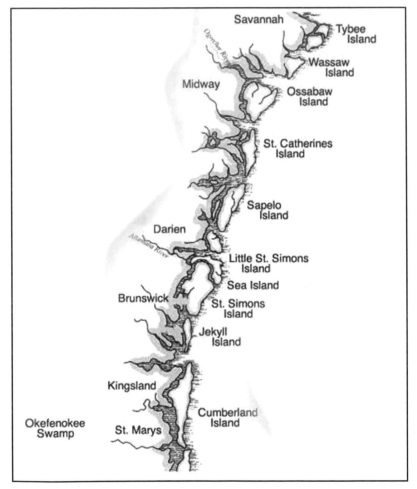

Acknowledgments

Black Water Rising is dedicated to my friend and mentor, Anna Collins for her advice, support, and faith in me.

I am in deep appreciation to Anna Collins, Sue Morrison, the late Ron Laitsch, Andrea Parnell, Chief Doering of the Glynn County Police Department, Carl and Jackie White, Cec Murphy, George Baker, Helen Cahill-Ruffner, Rosemary Daniell and the "Zona Rosa" group, the Glynn County Police Department, Brunswick Police Department, Gwinnett County Police Department, and the Henry County Police Department. There are many others whose contributions made *Blackwater Rising* a reality and whose encouragement has supported me in my writing endeavors. These include Karen Krider, Susan Abken, Susan Larson, Michael Shields, Carmen Adams, Barbara Bird, Eddie Van Buren, Mel Suddeth, Jim Smith, Judy Neal, Vicki Hunter, Andi Kulp, Kathy Socha, Carey Knapp, Frankie Willis, Estelle Ford-Williamson, Brenda Bozeman, June Dalton, Totsy Walker, Darlene Chamlee, Bobbie Sanders, Jackie Miles, Sisters in Crime, the Generations Gallery, The Writing Group in the Village at Indian Springs, Flint River Writers, Georgia Writers, Atlanta Writers, and the Harbor Shores Book Club. Special thanks go to my mother, Holly Barksdale, and my husband, Sidney Jones.

I thank God for the never failing support of my faith and the doors that have been opened through my turning my writing over to Him.

Once to every man and nation

Comes the moment to decide,

In the strife of truth with falsehood

For the good or evil side;

Some great cause, some great decision

Offering each the bloom or blight,

And the choice goes by forever

"Twixt that darkness and that light."

. . . Though the cause of evil prosper,

Yet the truth alone is strong;

Though her portion be the scaffold,

And upon the throne be wrong;

Yet that scaffold sways the future,

And, behind the dim unknown,

Standeth God within the shadow,

Keeping watch above his own.

Adapted from "The Present Crisis"

James Russell Lowell, 1818-1891

Prologue

The body moved closer to land with each succeeding wave, the incoming tide pulling it shoreward as if by an unseen hand. Floating on top of the water, it snagged a large mass of seaweed. Bloated and discolored, it could have been mistaken for a large dead fish had it not been for its dragging arms and a head covered by a matted mass of mud and hair.

Several hundred feet lay between the body and the swimmers at the water's edge. Walkers roamed the beach, pawing through the piles of debris dotting the sand. A recent violent storm had missed the barrier island, but its rain-swept winds and tidal surge had taken their toll. A wide variety of objects deposited on shore attracted shell collectors and other treasure seekers.

Sweat dripping from her face, a woman placed a handful of sand dollars on her blanket and walked to the ocean. Adjusting the straps of her string bikini, she waded into the water, dodging the waves. She moved slowly, deeper and deeper, until the cool dark water surrounded her. Standing waist-deep, she braced herself against the incoming tide, dug her toes into the sandy bottom and turned to face the beach. A small fish bumped against her and a clump of sea grass scraped her back. Reaching behind her, she flung it aside. Small pieces of worm-eaten wood drifted past her as she backed slowly outward and shaded her eyes with her hand to avoid the glare of morning light. The wave action lifted and lowered her as the ocean seemed to rise around her.

Suddenly, the sky darkened and the air turned cool. A chill ran through her as the sun slipped behind a cloud and she felt a large object graze and rest against her shoulders. Startled, she turned, faced the corpse, and screamed.

1

Police Lieutenant Jackson Ryder stepped out of his car and glared at the chaos before him where cops were struggling to control the crowd. Determined to see the body, onlookers pressed against the circle of yellow and black tape protecting the crime scene.

Ryder smoothed the front of his shirt, adjusted its collar and ran his fingers through his thick brown hair, before walking toward his colleagues.

"The Rock's here," muttered one of the officers.

Ryder heard the comment and sighed. He'd had the nickname since high school, where he'd been the county's star lineman, famous for being immovable. The label followed him to the University of Georgia where he was proud to have a scholarship and be part of the college team. As a freshman, he rode the bench, but he was starting by his sophomore year.

"Too good to be true," he'd thought, and he'd been right. A torn ligament in his leg ended his dreams, his dreams of a professional football career. Dejected, he'd quit college and returned to Brunswick where he enrolled in the county's police academy. After twenty-five years in the department, he was still haunted by what could have been. His divorce, two years ago today, was the only thing that hit him harder.

Despite the career change, the nickname "Rock" stuck and acquired new life. As his brotherhood of cops replaced his teammates, he transferred his passion from football to police work. His leg, reinjured in a scuffle with a crack dealer, bothered him now. Stopping to rest, he pulled a stick of gum from his shirt pocket, unwrapped it and stuck it in his mouth. His shoulders drooped further and he walked slower, as if pulling a weight behind him.

"Ryder," a loud voice called.

He ran his hand across his brow.

The voice called again, "Over here." As Ryder headed toward Officer

Andy Collins, he was joined by local diver Danny Wong.

"This is the fourth floater this year," said Wong, "all of them women."

"Anyone report her missing?" asked Ryder.

One of the cops shook his head.

"She couldn't have drowned far from the beach," said Wong, "or the tide wouldn't have brought her in." He looked back at the body. "This one's been out awhile."

Ryder cussed under his breath as he walked closer. "Helluva lotta damage." He stared at the body. "She'll be hard to I.D." Wong and Ryder were inside the circle now where the pungent smell of decaying flesh turned Ryder's stomach. He swallowed hard.

"I see you're treating this one seriously." Wong eyed the photographers shooting the corpse from every angle.

Ryder grimaced. He looked at a sobbing young woman, huddled beneath a blanket. "What's with her?"

"The body hit her in the back," said Collins, lowering his voice. "Everybody on the beach heard her scream. They thought a shark had her. The lifeguard pulled her in and then pushed the body onto the sand. Not a pretty sight."

"The crabs dined well," muttered Ryder.

Wong studied the body and looked at Ryder. "This is no coincidence."

"Hold on," snapped Ryder. "We don't know anything yet. We're just not taking any chances. We're going to do this one by the book."

Ryder's thoughts drifted back to the first victim's body, found by a beachcomber. Predators had gnawed her hands and her skin was bloated and torn. Sharks had recently attacked two swimmers and the medical examiner thought she'd been bitten too. The police checked up and down the coast, but there were no missing person reports fitting her description so she was buried in a pauper's grave at Old Pirate's Point.

The second body was identified as Charlotte Thomas, a teacher, who spent summers in her parents' cottage and most of her spare time sailing. A storm had also occurred the week she was found. In that instance, the medical examiner believed she'd lost control of the boat and was hit on the head when it capsized. Contusions on her shoulders could have occurred when she fell. Satisfied with his opinion, the department closed the case.

Vicky Laker was a different story. Known to stay out all night on Saturday and confess on Sunday, she was a party girl who liked to see and be seen in bars. Rumored to use cocaine, she had acquired what the locals called a "dark side" reputation. Her journey along the Intra-Coastal Waterway ended at the Starboard Marina, where a restaurant overlooking the site provided a view for an inquisitive diner. Seeing movement at the water's edge, he leaned over the railing of the restaurant's deck and peered directly into Vicky's face.

Her arm was caught on the remains of a large wooden boat embedded in marsh mud. As the tide went out, it left her body suspended and twisting as the current flowed past. No one was surprised at her death, but again, there were bruises. She'd drifted three to four days, and was wearing the clothes she had worn the previous Saturday night. Now, there was another one.

Ryder became aware of Wong's voice, "Your crew wants to know if you're ready to move her."

Ryder looked at the questioning glances before him, gave a dismissing wave, and walked away. The team was loading the body onto a stretcher as he cranked his battered old Crown Victoria.

"How 'bout some coffee?" asked Wong, as he opened the passenger door and slid inside. "I've got some things I want to share."

"Papa's?" suggested Ryder.

"Sounds good to me, Jack." Wong settled into the ragged seat and sneered at the car's grimy interior. "This wreck must be as old as the department."

"Still runs good," said Ryder, defensively. "No use to change something if it ain't broken." He lapsed into silence and steered toward the island's village. The road snaked through an assortment of old cottages, spotted here and there with contemporary homes. Oak trees and palmettos lined the street, allowing an occasional glimpse of the Atlantic.

Traffic increased as they neared the center of the island where a hodgepodge of bars, restaurants, and souvenir shops competed for tourist dollars. Summer was turning the normally quiet resort into a circus. Loud radios, raucous groups of teens, and the political debates of older generations blended into a cacophony of noise along the strip. Papa's, a small café frequented by locals, was an escape from rowdy visitors, a place for catching up on island news.

They settled into a booth by the window where a short pudgy waitress took their order. Within a few minutes, she returned and placed a mug of coffee before each of them. She reached into her apron pocket, pulled out a handful of sweeteners and creamers, and piled them in the middle of the table before leaving again.

Ryder shifted his weight, adjusting the position of his aching leg.

Sipping quietly, each waited for the other to begin. Wong broke the silence. "Something wrong?"

"Naw," said Ryder.

"Been a long time," said Wong softly.

"You reading minds now?"

"I know you. We go back a long time."

"Been two years since Sheila left…"

"You've come a long way." Their eyes met as they shared unspoken memories and understanding. Wong was the most respected oceanographer in the southeast and a top-rated diver. Known for his research and Asian resolve, he moonlighted in boat repair and maintenance, untangling shrimp nets for locals and fixing propeller blades on tankers at the port. He helped the Coast Guard with search and rescue, but more importantly, he was Ryder's friend. Their bond was sealed on a day when they were in high school. Wong, the target of racial harassment, had been jumped by a gang of rednecks. Ryder had come to his aid, fighting them off single-handed. Wong repaid the favor by tutoring Ryder in math, helping him keep up his grades for the football team. Later, when Ryder had tried to drown the pain of divorce in Glenlivets Scotch, he had hauled him to AA meetings.

After a few moments, Wong brought them back to the present. "Give me the scoop. I've told Becky and the kids to stay off the water until things cool down."

"I haven't a clue as to what we've got," confided Ryder, as he leaned forward and ran his finger along the rim of his cup. "I'm not holding out on you. If I knew anything, I'd tell you. The first bodies were all screwed up, could have been sharks. God knows there are enough out there."

"Especially near the pier," Wong agreed. "Between the fish and the shrimpers' bycatch, the ocean's a floating smorgasbord. You can see them from the air. Ever been over St. Simons Sound in a plane?"

"Never had cause."

"It might be worth your time."

Ryder began again. "Nothing looked suspicious at first, no reason to think anything was out of the ordinary. Then, we saw the last ones. Had bruises on their shoulders like they'd been held under and drowned. Hell, we don't need this. The sharks are enough of a problem. We're playing it low so's not to cause panic."

"And avoid the press getting in it," interjected Wong.

"Ain't that the truth. The Chamber of Commerce gets squirrelly when there's shit during tourist season." He gestured out the window toward a passing police car. "As you can see, things are cranking up. The chief's called John Ames at FLETC*. They're sending us one of their instructors, a profiler named Dr. Lindsay. She's coming in today to look at the files." He sighed.

"You're not pleased?"

"Not a matter of being pleased or displeased. I don't have time to play politics, nursemaiding some PhD." Ryder pushed his empty cup aside.

Wong looked at him. "Give me information on locations, dates, weather conditions, water temperature and body-weight and I'll plot the tidal drift so we can tell where the bodies went down. That may give us some answers. Remember the drowning at Hampton last year? The guy who fell from the dock on the Hampton River? You were surprised when I found his body a few hundred yards away near Pelican Spit."

"Pelican Spit," repeated Ryder. "I knew you were guessing on the tides, but I never knew how you did it."

"I didn't guess; I calculated where it would wash up by a number of factors, where he went under and, like I said, weather, water temperature; also time of year, fullness of moon and the position of the inlets. Bodies rarely travel far from their point of origin. This time, I'll go in reverse. I'll backtrack."

Ryder raised an eyebrow. "And then?"

The waitress reappeared and poured more coffee into their mugs.

"It isn't foolproof," Wong continued," but I can get a general idea. Sometimes there are things that interfere. Bodies hang up on debris, like Vicky Laker, or they're pushed farther out or closer to shore by waves from passing boats."

He paused to sip his coffee. "I can tell how long a body's drifted and where it's been, partly by deterioration. Types of predators also help pinpoint the path. Sometimes bodies wash ashore and back out again"

"Wouldn't be surprised if that was what happened today," said Ryder. "This one looks like the remains of a seafood buffet."

Wong grimaced. "It stayed close to shore or the crabs couldn't have gotten it. Types and sizes of bites tell the kinds of fish it encountered. It isn't likely she's been out past buoy one. Think about it. All the bodies have come ashore within a one-mile radius." He paused and shot Ryder a questioning glance.

"O.k. Danny, you're on."

*Federal Law Enforcement Training Center

They paid their bill and Ryder drove Wong back to his car. The crowd was dispersing and the evidence techs were gone. A few trailing pieces of tape were all that remained of the scene.

"When we get Frost's report," said Ryder, referring to the medical examiner, "I'll be in touch." He swung the car around and headed to his office in mainland Brunswick.

2

More victims. Another killer. The call had come yesterday at 9 a.m. Police were sure it was murder and were calling her to help. Dr Catherine Lindsay breathed deeply, leaned back in her chair and stared at the computer in front of her. She'd known the call would come, had prayed it wouldn't. She would soon be riding again on an emotional roller coaster, one she was trying so hard to avoid. Filled with apprehension, she allowed her thoughts to traveled back in time.

It had been three years since her life had spun out of control. Three years of rebuilding, focusing on her work and trying to forget, but there was no forgetting her past. Each time she'd almost found peace, another case came.

She closed her eyes, trying to block the images, her muscles tensing as she grasped the arms of her chair. Forcing the painful thoughts from her mind, she stood and walked to her bedroom where she exchanged her jeans and top for a suit, tidied her hair and straightened her shoulders. She glanced in her mirror and let out a sigh. Her armor was on.

*****

Ryder was working at his desk when Catherine Lindsay entered his office. He looked up and stared. The woman was not what he'd expected. Her long blonde hair was swept upward into a loosely held bun, framing an oval face with well-defined features. Carefully groomed, she wore a blue suit with a paisley scarf that accented her large blue eyes. She looked around appraisingly, before resting her gaze on his. Criminal Justice major? The woman looked like a model. He stood and offered his hand. She shook it firmly as they exchanged greetings.

"Sit," he said, waving her toward a chair.

She moved toward it, then, stopped abruptly, eyeing its contents.

"Just move them," he said, brusquely.

She gathered a pile of files from the seat, placed them on the floor and tried again.

"Can't get caught up," he muttered as she sat down.

"I know the feeling."

"So Miss, uh, Doctor…"

"My colleagues call me Lindsay," she interrupted.

He paused. "Lindsay, welcome to the case, that is if we have a case. How much has the Chief told you?"

"Not much. I've been involved in a project in Washington the last few days and flew back last night. The medical examiner thinks several drownings are related?"

"Looks like it." He pulled four files from his drawer, held them out to her and watched as she slowly flipped through them. "At first, people thought it was a shark, but if it is, it's a mighty strange one."

She looked up, and caught him staring at her. "Just what exactly do you do?" he asked.

Her face reddened and she clenched her jaw. Was he questioning her credentials?

"Hey, I didn't mean anything by it, just curious about your background."

She summarized her experience as a street cop and her climb through the ranks of the NYPD. Recruited by the FBI, she'd stayed with them four years before changing to the Georgia Bureau of Investigation. A year ago, she'd accepted a job as an instructor in the Behavioral Science unit at FLETC.

Ryder raised an eyebrow, hoping she'd provide more details. He'd heard rumors she'd left the FBI abruptly, but no one knew why. Consistently on the mark in identifying and predicting the traits of violent criminals, she'd earned her colleagues' respect. She'd worked in the same capacity for the GBI, before teaching at the center near Brunswick.

The FLETC complex provided training for almost all federal law enforcement branches, with the exception of the FBI, and its extensive and demanding program could make or break recruits. Located in the confines of a former World War II naval base, it housed an extensive database and a forensic center.

Since arriving, Lindsay continued to work with the GBI as a consultant, but this was the first time locals had asked for her help. Ryder understood his chief's desperation, but he resented the intrusion of having an outsider on the case.

As she closed the last file, he asked. "Well?"

"There are similarities," she said with interest, "Too many to be accidental."

"All the vics are female," said Ryder, "Each time, the drowning occurred away from the beaches, but still near shore. We thought the first was attacked by a shark, but she may have had marks we didn't see."

"Using water to get rid of bodies is common. Using it as a modus operandi is not. When will you hear from the medical examiner about the last one?"

"With Frost, could be an hour, could be two days." He looked her straight in the eye and his voice grew serious. "Lindsay, I'm forming a task force. I want you to put us on the right path and tell us what type of guy is doing this and why. I'll give you two homicide detectives. Sam Morrison knows the county inside out. Andy Collins came on the force four years ago. Like me, he started out on the streets, but he got through college and shortcut the ranks." He paused. "And there's Danny Wong. His family immigrated here in the fifties. He lives on Goat Man's Run, a marsh island near the channel bridge. He knows everything about the ocean and tides. Hell, he can predict a hurricane. If you want to know anything 'bout the water, just ask him."

She closed the folders and placed them on his desk. "I need copies of these and I'd like to meet with the others as soon as possible."

He punched a button on his phone and a woman appeared at his door within seconds. She touched her puffed platinum hair with long red fingernails and smiled.

"Dix, this is Dr. Lindsay. She'll be working with us the next few weeks. Dr. Lindsay, my secretary, Dixielee Boatright." The woman's eyes narrowed as she nodded at Lindsay.

"Dix will be glad to help you," he said handing the woman the files. "Yes ma'am, she keeps us on our toes around here." He smiled at the woman appreciatively. "Make us a hard copy of the file, Dix, and give us one on disc." She beamed at him, then shot Lindsay a sidelong look as she left.

"I'll set up an office for you here," offered Ryder.

"No," Lindsay said quickly. "Thanks, but it's easier for me to work at home."

"Your choice but, anything you need, just..."

She looked at her watch, "I have a class from one to two. I'll return for the files before three."

"If I'm not here ask for Dixie. I'll call the others and set up a meeting."

"Helluva looker," he mumbled to himself after she left.

He stared at the files she'd placed on the floor and the clutter around him. Keeping up with his job was a battle. The constant calls, problems and paperwork took all his time. Maybe that was good. It sure as hell beat dealing with his personal life. The "3 Ds," debt, divorce and drinking, had almost destroyed him, but, he'd made progress since he'd stopped drinking, and the bills were almost paid. Now, if he could find a good woman…. His thoughts flicked momentarily back to Catherine Lindsay.

3

He gradually awoke from a drug-like sleep. He'd dreamed again last night. Breathing a painful sigh, he huddled in the bed he'd slept in since childhood. It was always worse when he dreamed. His night terrors had never subsided from the time they first began when he was small.

He pulled back the curtain covering the windowless alcove in which his bed was enclosed. The narrow bunk no longer fit his 5'10" frame. To sleep, he had to lie on his side, his knees drawn up towards his stomach, finding comfort in the fetal position.

"Brauner, Brauner," he silently mouthed the name. It was his now, since its original owner no longer existed. His mind drifted back to the day he first saw Parks Brauner, his first day of high school, the beginning of a painful black journey from which he'd never emerged.

His school guidance counselor had told his father to have him try out for team sports; get involved in a group activity. Following the counselor's suggestion became a mandate his father demanded fulfilled.

At the beginning of the school year, he had trudged through the halls to the locker room and into the gym, where a large group of boys were gathered around the football coach. Reading from a list, the coach called out the name of each student. Suddenly, he stopped. "Timmie Mullis?" he said incredulously, pausing between syllables. "You're trying out for the football team?" The other boys snickered as he blushed and nodded.

"Little Timmie's trying out for the team," a student said sarcastically above the boys' laughter. Timmie hesitated, before walking forward and joining the others whose names had been called.

"Parks Brauner," The coach continued, looking up with a pleased smile.

Parks responded, "Yes Sir" as he approached the coach, and extended his hand.

"Ralph's son," said the coach, "I've been expecting you." Timmie stared at the boy, envying his confident smile and swaggering walk.

That scene was rooted in his memory like a festering boil. It symbolized his new beginning and the death of his father's dream. For days afterward, he watched Parks constantly, practicing his walk and speech, even the combing of his hair. Despite his father's prodding, he never made the team, but he observed Parks throughout his high school years. By the time he was a senior, he knew Parks Brauner as if he was a part of him, which in fact he was, as he, no longer Timmie, had made him so.

He learned a lot during those years as he followed other students without being detected, copied their behaviors and made them his own. He learned the ease with which one could assume the identities of others and even acquire their belongings. Over time, he stole a few pieces of Parks' clothing, a jacket placed near a door, a cap and an old pair of running shoes, found in the trash by the Brauners' home. It paid to watch and wait. Sometimes at night, he spied on the Brauner family sitting at their dining table. Their house was near the beach, a few miles from his, and he watched them often during the summers when blinds were raised to let in the breeze. That it backed up to dunes made surveillance easy. He frequently caught glimpses of Parks, working out with weights in his garage or practicing for track and football by running along the shore. In time, Parks became a quarterback and captain of the football team. When he was a senior, he dated the homecoming queen, a cheerleader named Beth Davenport. Once when Parks was away, Timmie managed the courage to speak to her. Rolling her eyes, she turned on her heels and strode away. He stood for what seemed an eternity, watching her long blonde hair as she faded into the distance. Later, he saw her with several friends, whispering and laughing as he passed them.

God, how he wanted her. Lying in bed at night, he thought of her. For months, it was the same. He would lie transfixed as he felt himself swell and harden. But, every time he reached down to touch himself, to bring his yearning to completion, he was interrupted by the memory of Parks' taunting voice, blotting out his thoughts of Beth, intruding on his most private moments.

Beth, her real name was Bethany. The name echoed over and over in his mind. Bethany Anne Davenport. He watched her too, in a painful gut-wrenching pattern. Her house, a short distance from Parks', also backed up to the beach. Directly behind her bedroom, a large dune with thick clumps of sea oats provided safe vantage.

Sometimes, he'd follow her, observing her movements and gestures. He knew her clothing by heart and could guess what outfit she'd wear, if he knew the occasion. He'd acquired several souvenirs. It had taken time and patience, but they were all worth it. He still had her broken gold anklet that had dropped by her desk in class. Seated behind her, he was able to slide his foot forward and then bring it back by his side, the chain covered by the sole of his boot. Picking it up had been easy. He simply dropped his pencil and reached down, grabbing them both.

The challenge was the lock of her hair. It had taken several days and constant attentiveness. Gradually, he'd moved his desk closer to hers until she turned so that part of her hair rested on its edge. He quickly snipped a lock with a small pair of trimming shears he'd hidden beneath his coat-sleeve and then dropped the lock and scissors down his arm, buttoning his cuff behind them.

Rolling his legs over the side of the bed, he sat for awhile, thinking as always of Beth. He gazed around the room until he saw the woman's sandals, gave a short sarcastic laugh and then reached down and picked them up. Clutching them to his chest, he returned to his bed.

4

Shortly after two, Lindsay returned to the Glynn County Police Station to pick up her copies of the files. She noticed Dixie Boatright watching her approach from her desk outside Ryder's office. The woman held out the folders and a disc before Lindsay could knock on his door. "Let me know if you need anything else, honey."

Her jaw tightening against the patronizing endearment, Lindsay managed a nod as the woman returned to her work. She slipped the disc and folders into her briefcase and went back to her car. The ten-year-old Porsche looked new as it gleamed in the sun, its silver paint meticulously polished. She sighed appreciatively as its engine caught and roared with power. Since she had no afternoon meetings, she headed home.

Crossing the tall series of bridges connecting St. Simons Island to the mainland, she soared over the picturesque landscape of water and marsh. No matter how many times she saw it, she never tired of the scene. Land, water, and marsh formed patterns in every direction, their color and design changing constantly with season and tide. When she'd first come, she'd planned to stay a year. She lowered her windows, breathed the salt-filled air and knew she would never leave.

On the island, stately trees spread moss-draped branches over the roads. Her A-Frame cottage was nestled in a wooded lot near the beach, allowing glimpses of ocean between clusters of oak and pine. She was anxious to be inside, where she could listen to the soothing tempo of mellow jazz as she studied the files.

She pulled into the shaded drive and parked beside the short walkway leading to the entrance. Opening the door, she walked into her living room and was comforted by the sight of bookcases lining each sidewall. Filled with familiar and treasured volumes, they gave her a sense of continuity and belonging. The back wall was glass, except for its center, which held a massive tabby fireplace with a wide hearth. Navajo rugs, a leather sofa and a recliner were accented by Mimbres pottery and Native-American paintings. She'd kept the house as clean as the day she'd bought it with everything neat and orderly.

She kicked off her heels, changed into jeans and went into the kitchen. A cup of coffee would settle her thoughts. She fixed the coffee and took it with her to the living room where she dropped on the sofa and opened the files. She gazed now and then at her bookcases, their contents divided into sections, each a part of her life, Psychology, Criminology and an assortment of mystery fiction. The books provided security, pages in which she immersed herself to escape loneliness and despair.

Lindsay forced herself back on task, scanned each folder's contents, then, methodically, went through them again. When she finished, she sat still while her mind played over them. Did a shark kill the first victim or had she been murdered? The drownings were an aberration. Most serial killers used their hands, overcoming their victims' strength to prove their power. What type of person chose water as a weapon? These killings were a conundrum, out of character.

She shifted restlessly and looked through the files again, searching for details she might have missed. Were the bruises on the victims' shoulders from holding them down? Why choose the ocean? Was he trying to hide them? Were the bodies always found? How many had washed out to sea? The use of water was puzzling, as were the victims. How did he choose them and what did they have in common? Two were still unidentified. Were they prostitutes? The thought was discomforting. From what she'd read in the files, it seemed unlikely, yet appearances could be deceiving, as she well knew. The doorbell rang, jolting her from her thoughts. She put down the files and hurried to answer it.

"Hotter'n hell out there." Her neighbor Patty Crandall walked in as soon as the door was opened. "Just thought I'd let you know I won't be running with you in the morning. Beau's got a new client. Some guy from Atlanta brought his wife down to pick out a condo. They're looking in the half-million bracket, so we're wining and dining them. I probably won't see bed 'til way after midnight."

She held out a plate filled with cookies. "After dinner, they're coming by the house for coffee and desert. Molly baked a few extra for you."

Lindsay smiled. Patty's housekeeper, Molly, had looked after two generations of Crandalls. Now, she included Lindsay as part of the brood.

Lindsay took the cookies to the kitchen. "O.K. to sample now?"

"Go ahead, but don't pull out any for me. I've eaten six already."

Lindsay grabbed a cookie and followed Patty into the living room where she was eyeing the files. "Whatcha been doin?" asked Patty.

Lindsay was accustomed to her friend's curiosity. "Working on a case for the local police."

Patty's brown eyes grew wide. She started to pick up a file, but quickly withdrew her hand. "I know. I know. I can ask but can't touch. Doesn't have anything to do with those drownings does it?"

Lindsay nodded.

"You think those women were killed? Gawd. Who would do such a thing?"

Lindsay sighed. "That's what we're trying to find out." She moved the files to her desk. "Want some coffee?"

"I'd rather have a Diet Coke. I've spent half the day in the kitchen by the stove with Molly."

Lindsay poured the soft drink into an ice-filled glass and placed it on the kitchen counter.

"Guess I interrupted you, huh?" said Patty, picking it up, taking a sip and plopping down on a bar stool.

"I needed a break." Lindsay returned the bottle of remaining Coke to the refrigerator before joining her.

"I can't stay long anyway. I've got to go home and finish cleaning, get the house spiffy for our guests. And," she said, grimacing and touching her long auburn hair, "do something with this incorrigible debutante do."

They chatted a few minutes before Patty finished her drink and rose to leave. "Wanna run Wednesday?"

"Sure," said Lindsay. She walked Patty to the door and watched her disappear down the path through the woods toward her house. Lindsay had grown fond of her during the past year. Beneath her chatty southern-belle demeanor, the woman had depth. She was honest, decent and caring, three characteristics Lindsay valued. After she left, Lindsay went back to the files and loaded the disc Dixie Boatright had given her into the computer.

The next morning, her alarm went off before dawn. She pulled on shorts, a T-shirt and running shoes, hooked her cell phone to her pocket and walked through her backyard to the beach. Taking the path through a break in the pines, she picked up speed; then, dodging shells and driftwood, she raced beside the incoming tide. Bubba Joe Odum, another neighbor, jogged a few yards ahead of her. Overweight, his uncoordinated body listed from side to side.

"Mawnin', Miss Lindsay," he gasped.

"Take it easy," she warned. "Remember, you're just starting. It's going to take time to get into shape." His answer trailed off in indistinguishable agreement.

Rounding the curve of beach known as Gould's Inlet, she paused to watch the sunrise. Ahead, the sky was a vivid pink, spilling into the ocean. With the coming of post-dawn light she saw movement further ahead. Strollers zigzagged along the shore, searching for shells from the night tide. How could such a peaceful setting be a murder site? Her mind racing along with her body, she went over and over the files. As she ran, her cell phone beeped. It was Ryder wanting her to meet with the task force at nine. With determination and purpose, she turned and headed back home.

5

He fought to pull himself to consciousness. Like so many dark nights, this one had been a return to the source of whom and what he'd become. Lying still, he listened for night sounds under the rustling and whistling of the wind. Clouds raced across the moon, illuminating his room like a fast blinking strobe. His thoughts mimicked the light as memories flashed, then receded into blackness, his mother's screams, his father's fist, the day of the senior picnic. His mind stopped at the scene passing before him. He could see as clearly as if he were there, re-enacting the unfolding events, the drama that had enabled his rebirth.

He'd dreaded the outing the first time he'd heard of it, had planned not to go but curiosity forced him. He couldn't bear the thought of not being there, not seeing them together.

When the day came, he felt inadequate and unprepared. Gathering at Neptune Park near the old pier, the students ran to the beach as their teachers began grilling hot dogs and hamburgers. The football coach patted Parks Brauner on the back as he pointed to the "No Swimming" signs near the pilings and cautioned the students to stay out of the water. Several boys set up a volleyball net in the sand and marked off a court.

Timmie watched from a distance. He sat on the side of a large pile of rocks extending into the tide line, his body covered by a long T-shirt and a loose-fitting knee-length swimsuit. Despite his attire, he was painfully uncomfortable, conscious of his thinness and undeveloped physique, the paleness of his legs against his dark pants. The sharp rocks cut into his skin, but he remained there, held by the sight of Parks and Beth, the glare burning his eyes as he watched their every move.

"It's hotter than the devil's dick," yelled Parks.

The other boys laughed and several girls giggled.

"Speak of the devil," said Beth, with a sidewise glance at Timmie.

"What's the matter Timmie-poo?" asked Parks. "Afraid of the water?" The others laughed at him.

"Better be careful, Beth," warned a girl. "That devil's dick is after you."

"He better cool it," said a male student.

"He doesn't need to cool his dick," taunted Parks. "He doesn't have one."

Timmie sat, unable to move, his eyes riveted on Beth in her skimpy two-piece suit, and the muscular movements of Parks. Frozen in place, he watched for almost an hour, ignoring the scathing remarks sent in his direction. He watched and waited, observing them pour vodka into cans of Seven-Up, forgetting him in the heat of their game as their senses were dulled by the alcohol.

After a few hours, the sky became overcast and the air became humid and thick. A strong gust of wind blew the ball into the sea where the tide swept it away, driving it farther and farther out of reach. Parks raced into the water and swam after it. Immediately, the current swept him outward.

"He'll have a hard time getting back," yelled one of the boys.

They watched until he was several hundred yards out, then, gasped in horror as his arms flailed and his head bobbed on the surface.

"Help him," cried Beth. "The current's too strong."

No one moved.

Turning, she looked at Timmie and an inner tube abandoned in the sand.

As if hypnotized by her gaze, he jumped down from the rocks, picked up the tube, and waded into the water.

"Hurry," she screamed.

Clinging to the tube, he shoved off with his feet and kicked rapidly. The strength of the water, combined with his frantic exertion, brought him closer and closer to Parks, who'd allowed the ball to drift into the distance as he fought to stay above the water.

Within minutes, Timmie was beside him. He rested briefly and the current pulled Parks farther away. A sense of power surged through him as Parks reached for him, only to be defeated by the riptide. It became a game. He would kick and paddle furiously, almost within Parks' grasp, then stop, allowing the current to pull them apart.

He watched the terror in Parks' eyes as the water swirled around him. Gradually, Timmie tired and decided to end it. He watched as Parks used the last of his energy, futilely propelling himself toward the inner tube as Timmie inched away. Their eyes locked as Parks mouthed "Why?", before slipping beneath the waves.

Never realizing the truth, the others praised Timmie for his courage, his valiant effort. Parks' parents thanked him in person, presenting him with the watch they'd selected as a present for their son's graduation. Through it all, Timmie felt a euphoria he'd never experienced, and a power that was his for the taking.

6

At 9 a.m. Lindsay tapped on the door of Ryder's office, turning just in time to see Dixie Boatright walking past with a malevolent stare.

"C'mon in," Ryder said as Lindsay entered.

Papers, gum wrappers, and Styrofoam cups littered the surface of his desk and there were dark circles under his eyes as if he hadn't slept. Two more chairs were somehow squeezed into the room and Collins and Morrison were already seated. The chair she sat in yesterday remained clear, its files still stacked on the floor where she'd left them.

Ryder offered her a cup of coffee and couldn't help watching as she sat down and crossed one shapely leg over the other. God, the woman was beautiful!

After brief introductions he pointed to a portable whiteboard propped against the wall behind him. "I've outlined the characteristics and patterns of each case," he said. "So far, the only things they have in common are they're female and they drowned. Some had marks or bruises on their shoulders and they were all fully or partially clothed."

"Do you have the medical examiner's report from the last one?" interrupted Lindsay.

"Just got it this morning, same marks, nothing much different from the others." He cleared his throat, and continued. "According to Danny Wong, they were either killed close in, then dumped off-shore, or taken out and drowned beyond the second buoy. And," he paused, "there's no I.D. on the last vic, no missing person report, no abandoned vehicle."

He looked at Collins. "Check everyone working at the marinas and the docks. Talk to the shrimpers and people who live near the boat ramps." The young black detective nodded and Ryder turned to Morrison. "See what you can find in the village. I have photos of the vics for each of you, but hell, we still haven't identified the first one. We don't have much."

"I thought the first one got bit by a shark," Morrison grumbled.

"Could have been, there're a lot of 'em out there, but we're grouping her with the others until we know more." Ryder gave Lindsay an expectant look. "I'm hoping you can give us direction."

"We're definitely looking at the work of a serial killer," she began. "These killers usually attack their victims on land. They dump the bodies, or bury them when convenient, except when they want to taunt. Most follow rituals and develop patterns. They may return to the same place over and over. The burial or dumping site is an important part of their plan. It can be symbolic. That may be what we're dealing with here, a ritualistic death and burial at sea. Although these bodies have been found, in each case he took them offshore. If the killer's familiar with the area, he knows generally where the bodies will surface and if the current can bring them back. He proved that with the first one."

"These bodies," repeated Collins, "You think there are more?"

"Could be, "said Lindsay.

"He can't possibly know when or where they'll wash up," argued Morrison. His chair creaked as he shifted, rearranging his bulk. A tall man, with a ruddy complexion and thinning gray hair, his potbelly hung over his belt.

"Not exactly," she agreed," but he may have a general idea and may be in the vicinity, waiting."

"According to Wong," interjected Ryder, "A body will typically sink to the bottom and return to the surface after a relatively short period of time, sometimes after three to seven days. The body doesn't usually end up far from where it entered the water."

"News travels fast, when something goes down," said Collins. "If he's anywhere on the island, he could be at the scene in minutes."

"Good point," said Lindsay. "It may be part of his plan and increase his sense of power. He may be watching the tides, guessing when the bodies will surface and mingling with the crowds when the bodies are found."

"I sure as hell hope there's not another one," said Ryder, "but if there is, we'll be in the crowd too and ready to finger him."

Lindsay nodded approval. "These guys like to see the results of their crimes. They get high on the follow-up, watching people's reactions and seeing them struggle for answers. It makes them feel in control and lengthens the drama."

"That's all we need with tourist season starting," snorted Morrison, "a sea full of sharks and a damn serial killer movin' in."

"He could have been here for years," said Lindsay, "gradually working his way up to larger crimes."

"Dumb bastard," muttered Morrison.

"He's not dumb," she countered sharply. "Serial killers are usually bright. This one's cold and calculating. He gets high from committing and reliving the crime, and," she turned to Ryder, "from making the police look foolish."

Ryder grimaced.

"He gets his feeling of power by taking it from others," she emphasized, "and being in control."

Morrison gave her a steely look, glanced at his watch and sighed.

"What? You got an appointment?" snapped Ryder, glaring at him.

Morrison said nothing, and Lindsay continued.

"The point is, if he goes for long without getting caught, he feels omnipotent. He'll get cocky and that's when he'll make mistakes. He's also likely to screw up under stress. Exercising control over what happens means everything. If things go out of control, he'll get anxious. He may shorten the time between kills, trying to gain control again."

"What the hell does this have to do with our catching him?" asked Morrison. "Sounds like you've been watching too many TV shows. Is this what you're teaching in your classes at FLETC?"

"My classes have ended for this session," she said coolly," but, to answer your question, yes, this is part of what I teach. The more we know about him, the easier it will be for us to find him. As I was saying, we need to be wary. We're not dealing with an amateur."

Morrison grumbled under his breath and Ryder shot him a reproving glare.

The meeting broke up and Morrison hurried out the door, but Collins lingered. "What makes weirdos like this?" he asked.

"There are a lot of theories," said Lindsay. "Most have been beaten and abused in childhood."

"Beating a child who misbehaves can produce a killer?" He chuckled. "If that's true, I ought to be a psycho. My mama's belt kept me in line."

She shook her head. "It's not that simple. Many people are abused as children and don't take it out on others. If a child knows he'll be punished, he'll toe the line, just like you did. There's a difference between parents who are merely strict and those who produce psychopaths. The latter are often unpredictable and their children may not know what sets them off.

That's why the children become so difficult to handle. They can't associate consequences with behavior. Adults may vent their anger on them for no reason, or threaten them and never follow through." She paused and noticed Ryder quietly listening.

"There are other factors such as temperament and brain damage. It could be a combination, including teasing and taunting by bullies. Instead of adults being the abusers, it's their peers. Analyzing serial killers, any type of human predators, is like putting pieces of a puzzle together. There are many factors, but they all interconnect."

Collins listened silently and then asked, "Women get bullied too. Half of our cases involve child abuse or domestic violence. Why don't we see female serial killers?"

"We do, but it's rare. Sometimes the bullying is in the form of sexual harassment, even assault but, in general, women don't externalize anger like men. It's not as acceptable in our society. They're more likely to self-destruct through bad life choices or suicide. They may be abusive toward people close to them, but rarely strangers. It's simply cultural conditioning. Most women are taught to stay close to home and not show anger in public but male aggression is considered normal. It's encouraged in warfare." She glanced at Ryder. "and especially in sports and police work."

His eyes narrowed.

Lindsay continued, "Abused children learn to turn off their feelings and manipulate others because it means their survival. That's why they develop into psychopaths, individuals with little, if any, conscience or empathy. You can see it in their treatment of animals and people they see as weak. Manipulation is a form of control, a way to exercise power and dominate, and if it goes unchecked, it increases and becomes more daring."

"Like in rape and murder?" said Collins.

"They're the ultimate examples of power over others."

"We'll find the bastard," said Ryder. "He's no Houdini, and he doesn't have power over us."

"Water," added Lindsay," is one of the strongest forces on earth. The killer increases his sense of strength by making it deadly."

"At least we're not dealing with slice and dice," commented Collins.

They looked up as Danny Wong appeared in the doorway. "We may have another one," he said breathlessly. "That's why I'm late. I heard people talking at the pier. A man is in the intake room filling out a missing person report."

Lindsay followed Ryder and Collins to the lobby where a young man was leaving.

Ryder stepped in front of him and introduced himself and the others.

"I'm John Blake," the man said nervously. "My sister, Susan Adams, is missing."

Ryder's cell sounded. Pausing briefly to look at it, he signaled Lindsay and Collins to take over as he walked away.

"Let's go where we can talk," she said. "We need to ask you some questions."

Collins led them into an interview room where they sat in chairs facing each other across a narrow table.

"Start from the beginning," said Lindsay.

His words gushed out as if a dam had broken. "My sister is staying at the Shoreview Inn on St. Simons, been there a month. She usually calls every night, but for three nights she hasn't and we can't reach her by phone, not even her cell phone."

He paused to catch his breath. "This isn't like Susan. This isn't like her at all. She always lets me know where she is. Brenda, that's her friend, Brenda Brown, is worried too. She drove down from Atlanta yesterday. When she knocked on Susan's door, no one answered. Mr. Parker, he's the manager. Mr. Parker said he hadn't seen her since Tuesday and here it is Friday and there's no sign of her or her car."

"Where's Brenda now?" asked Collins.

"She's at the motel, rented a room to wait; says she's not leaving until Susan shows up. I flew in from Atlanta this morning."

"Oh," he said, reaching into his pocket and removing his wallet. "I have a picture. Perhaps it'll help."

He withdrew a small snapshot of an attractive blonde woman holding the hands of two small children. A tall, thin man stood beside her, looking into the distance.

"That's her husband Brandon and her children, Laura and Jean."

"Has Susan done this before?" asked Lindsay.

"What?"

"Susan, has she ever gone somewhere without telling anyone?"

"No, that's the thing. She would never leave without telling Brenda or me. And, she'd never go where she couldn't be reached, not without the kids."

"Tell me about her," said Lindsay.

The man looked down and his shoulders drooped. "She's had a horrible year. Her husband left her for a younger woman and she's raising the kids by herself. The divorce will be final next month. She's been under a lot of stress so Brenda and I encouraged her to get away. We thought it would be good for her to spend time on the island. The kids are with their grandparents."

"Is she suicidal?"

His face looked pained, "Oh no, not Susan. She's not that type of person. Besides, she'd never do that to her children."

After John Blake left, Lindsay and Collins returned to Ryder's office to share the information he'd given them.

"Collins, you and Morrison check around the motel," said Ryder, "up and down the strip. Jog some memories. See if anybody's seen her."

Lindsay held out Susan's photo.

"Collins," said Ryder again.

The detective stopped.

"Check her room. Get her license number and put out an APB on her ride. And," he added, handing him the picture; "Be sure to make copies of this."

7

Collins and Morrison had ordered the hotel manager to allow them into Susan Adams' room. Finding nothing unusual, they were about to leave when Lindsay and Ryder drove up. Seeing their lieutenant, the two men walked to Ryder's side window.

"Find anything?" asked Ryder.

"Zero, zip, nada" said Collins "place is neat as a pin."

"The lady wants a look-see," said Ryder.

Barely hiding a sneer, Detective Morrison held out a plastic room card to Ryder as he and Lindsay got out of the car. In an aside to Collins, he muttered, "Bigshot broad thinks she'll find something we missed."

"Room 219," said Collins, "three doors down on the left."

Susan Adams' room was neat with no signs of struggle. Clothes hung in a small closet with its door ajar. The bed was made and a pair of slippers protruded from beneath it. A night table held a lamp and a stack of books, the top one spread open, cover side up.

Lindsay caught her breath as she read the title, *Living Alone: Becoming The Person You Want To Be*. She, too, was reading the book. She suddenly felt a kinship with Susan and her pain. The woman must have been lonely. She turned away, gazing about the room. It felt empty even with Ryder's presence.

They searched the bathroom where makeup was lined behind the sink and towels were evenly spaced. Bras and panties hung from the shower bar, where they had been placed to dry. The area was comfortable, but impersonal, as were the usual rentals the island offered. As they examined the bedroom, Lindsay moved to a small desk by the window. On its top was a basket of shells, grains of sand spilled around it. The first drawer held paper, pencils and a journal.

She flipped through the pages. Entries had been faithfully recorded for several weeks. The last was Monday and read "The motel is like a prison. I have to rejoin the world. I can't keep reliving the past. It blocks my vision, walling me in. I want to feel again, to experience life to the fullest. Like Father R. said, I can't give up. There are things I have to do. Well, today is the day I will-----." The sentence ended abruptly, as if the writer had been interrupted.

"Oh, Susan," Lindsay said softly, "Will what? Who is Father R., and what did he tell you to do?"

"What?" Ryder turned toward her with a frown.

She thrust the journal into his hand without answering as she walked to the closet to examine its contents and then thumbed through several hangers holding dresses, jeans and skirts. Continuing her search, she sifted through a basket of magazines. *Time, Cosmopolitan,* and *Island Singles* were mixed with an assortment of supermarket tabloids. On the floor by the basket were letters from friends wishing her well, an unopened pack of notepaper and a CD player with several CDs lying beside it. She opened and closed the drawers of a small chest and searched through piles of underwear, shirts, shorts, and socks.

"No bathing suit," she commented. "There are walking shoes and heels but no sandals or beach clothes." She surveyed the room. "No sunglasses or suntan lotion either."

"So?" shrugged Ryder. "Maybe, the lady doesn't swim."

"Or, she went to the beach and took it all with her," countered Lindsay.

"I'll have Morrison question people along the pier."

"Wherever she is, she didn't plan to stay." Lindsay eyed the cosmetics and a bottle of Prozac marked 'One a day'. "Her nightgown's under the pillow and her robe's on a door hook."

"Let's go," said Ryder. He thumbed through the journal and dropped it on the table. "There's nothing here." They headed for the street, momentarily blinded by the brightness of the sun.

Lindsay spent the rest of the afternoon at home, organizing data and files. It was evening when she finished. She made a peanut butter sandwich and sat in the darkening living room as she ate while her mind flitted back and forth from victim to victim, searching for a link. As she thought about Susan, her expression hardened. She walked to the kitchen, put her plate in the sink and went to bed.

The next morning, she made a pot of coffee before her run. Still puzzling over Susan Adam's journal, she sat at her dining room table, reviewing the files, and sipping her coffee as morning light filled the room. Finally, she rose and placed the mug on the kitchen counter, slipped out the back door and ran to the beach. The sun was up and the tide was low. Running close to the dunes, she avoided the wet sand and pools of water. As she approached the inlet, she saw Bubba Joe, arms flailing and running faster than usual. As he came closer, he yelled and signaled to her. She ran toward him, leaping over the tidal pools. Stumbling, he stopped and waited for her, still yelling and pointing down the beach. When she reached him, he grabbed her arm. Eyes wide and mouth gaping, he frantically pulled her back the way he'd come. As they retraced his steps, he caught his breath and tried to calm down. Still grasping her arm, he dragged her to the edge of the water and pointed.

"I f-found it," he gasped, wrapping his arms around his chest as if he had chills. Lindsay followed his gaze to the bloated and disfigured remains of a woman. The body was lying on its stomach, head toward the ocean, arms extended as if the encroaching tide was pulling it back to sea. Unlike the last body, it had not floated long. Lindsay recognized the woman's features, her long hair now in a ponytail and held in place by a bright green band. She was wearing a yellow bathing suit, its straps cutting into her skin. A small gold earring hung from one ear.

Lindsay quickly unhooked her phone and called Ryder and then turned back to Bubba Joe. "Go up to the road. Wait until the police come and guide them here."

Bubba Joe stayed rooted to the spot, as if in a trance, his eyes still fixed on the corpse.

Lindsay grabbed him by the shoulders, and turned him to face her. "Go now," she said sternly.

He blinked at her and then trudged away, picking up his pace as he followed the winding shoreline and then cut through a path to the road. After he disappeared, she walked carefully around the corpse, studying it from every angle. She was sure it was Susan. Despite the bathing suit, she was convinced Susan hadn't planned to go swimming, not wearing the fragile gold watch now tightly binding her wrist.

She noted several darkened areas under the back and sides of the woman's neck. The pattern was there. If someone had held her beneath the water... She positioned her own hands over the body. The marks coincided with the shadows of her fingers. Seeing a runner heading toward her, she bent down at an angle, blocking the body from view. He glanced at her curiously, as he ran past. After several more minutes, a group of people, led by Ryder, tromped down a path through the dunes.

8

John Blake and Brenda Brown identified Susan Adams' body and, after lengthy questioning by Ryder, left for Atlanta to be with the woman's parents and children.

The woman's small motel room had remained locked since the initial searches and Lindsay decided to return. Just as she entered the lobby, a man stepped up to the desk. The manager handed him some towels and turned to her with a questioning look.

"You're back," he said uneasily as she flashed her ID.

Lindsay nodded. "I need the key card for room 219."

"Something wrong?"

"No, I just want to take another look."

"When do you think the room… ?" he began.

"I'm sure Lt. Ryder will let you know when he's finished. Shouldn't be much longer."

"I hope not, we've been turning people away. All the other motels are booked solid, and…"

"As I said, Lt. Ryder will let you know." The sharp edge to her voice stopped him in mid-sentence. He quickly turned and retrieved the key card from a shelf on the wall behind him.

She took it and turned towards the door.

"I don't mean to sound uncooperative ma'am, it's just that, well I've got a business to run and this being our heavy season…" He let the sentence trail, leaving it unfinished as she left.

The room seemed emptier than before. The afternoon sun shone through the blinds, casting alternating light and dark stripes across the carpet. "We missed something," she thought as she looked through the contents of the drawers and closet a second time. She reached for the journal, seated herself near a window and began reading. Thumbing through the last days of Susan's life, she sensed hopelessness and confusion. The woman had struggled for emotional survival and her words reflected her despair. For a few minutes, Lindsay sat as if paralyzed, her mind filled with memories from her own past. How had Susan handled her pain? What had she done that could have led to her death? She pulled her thoughts back to the present, picked up the journal again and turned the page.

"Laura and Jean are my only joy, but I need time to myself, to think, to pull myself together. Please God, help me find peace." What had Susan found? Certainly not the type of peace she'd craved.

A pounding on the door interrupted her thoughts. Looking through the peephole, she saw a tall man, dressed in a suit, holding a small suitcase. She jumped back, startled, as he pounded louder.

"Who is it?" She asked.

"Dr. Lindsay? The manager told me you were here."

"Who are you?"

"I'm Susan's husband. Let me in."

Lindsay partially opened the door and stared at him.

"Dr. Brandon Adams," he said, thrusting out his hand. His handshake was loose and sweaty. "When John called I caught the first flight down. I thought he'd still be here," he said impatiently.

She let him in, and motioned him to a chair.

"He said Susan drowned, that it wasn't an accident. Surely, she wasn't.... I mean, it was an accident wasn't it?"

"We've just begun our investigation," said Lindsay. "You may be able to help us. When did you last speak with your wife?"

"We weren't exactly on speaking terms. I tried to get her to stay in Atlanta and just calm down, but she was so damned headstrong about coming here."

"So, you haven't seen or talked to her in the last week?"

"No, not in a week, not in two weeks."

"When did you last see her?"

His face reddened. "Surely, you don't think I had anything to do with Susan's death."

Lindsay started to speak but he interrupted, "I didn't know she was still down here. We haven't lived together in months. Her friend Brenda called me last night but I didn't think anything was wrong. This morning when John called, I thought there was a misunderstanding. I thought she'd turn up, that she was trying to scare me."

"Was she likely to have done that?"

"What?"

"Scare you to get your attention. Has she disappeared before?"

"No, no, but we're going through a divorce. She doesn't, didn't want to accept it. Damn, I didn't think it would turn out like this. What am I going to do with the children?"

He shifted his weight from one side of the chair to the other and pulled at his fingers, unconsciously cracking his knuckles. "When Brenda asked if I knew where she was, I thought she was home. I had to call all over to find the kids."

"You found them?"

"What?"

"The kids, you found them?"

"They're with her parents." He hung his head dejectedly and then looked around the room. His gaze stopped at the sight of the journal. He reached for it, but Lindsay quickly held it aside.

"We haven't finished with it," she said. "Everything will be given to you when we complete the investigation." He continued to eye the journal uneasily.

"Tell me about Susan," Lindsay said gently.

He shrugged. "What can I say? She was decent, a good person; a good mother. Ask anybody. She went to church every Sunday, did volunteer work."

"Did she have any enemies?"

"Enemies?"

"Was there anyone who had a grudge against her, who might have wanted to hurt her?"

"Susan? You must be kidding, and she wouldn't want to hurt anybody. Quite the opposite, like I said, she was a good wife and mother. She went out of her way to help people."

"So," Lindsay measured her words, "she tried to make the marriage work."

The words stung and his face darkened. "Susan wasn't the problem. She was a stewardess when we married, worked while I went to med school. Not many med school marriages make it, you know?" He looked at Lindsay, seeking understanding. Finding none, he looked away.

"O.K., O.K., like I said, Susan wasn't the problem. Med school pressure was intense. With my studies and her work, we led separate lives. By the time I set up practice, things had changed."

"Things?" Lindsay continued to press.

"Things." He repeated. "Look, we weren't the same people. I'm not the same. It's hard for people to understand, but that's what happened."

"Was it hard for Susan?" she asked.

"What are you driving at?" he demanded angrily.   "What does our marriage have to do with her death?"

"If you were the person closest to her, you are the person most likely to help us," she said calmly.

"I'm trying to tell you we weren't close, not anymore. I don't understand how this has any bearing on what happened to her. I'm on a tight schedule. I wouldn't have come down if there wasn't another doctor on call and I don't have time to play your question and answer games."

Lindsay gave him a cold look, "I can assure you, Dr. Adams, this is not a game."

For an instant, he looked frightened but then he quickly composed himself. "I need to call Jennifer," he mumbled, standing.

"Jennifer?"

"Uh, Jennifer, she uh, oh hell, what difference does it make now?"

"Jennifer is your girlfriend?"

"She's my fiancé," he said, his face reddening again. "I need to let her know where I am." He turned toward the door.

"Sit down," she said in an icy tone. "I haven't finished." He glared at her as he returned to his seat.

After an hour of additional questioning, he left, having added little useful to the case.

Lindsay pictured him rushing to Jennifer and the warm comfort of her embrace, a stark contrast to Susan's body, now in the morgue. Returning to Susan's journal, she noticed what she'd previously thought was one page was actually two folded together. Carefully, she ran her finger between them, pulling them apart. The second page held a list of names and telephone numbers. At the bottom, Susan had drawn a small heart. Beside it were the numbers 8783588. What could they mean? She took a pen and small tablet from her purse and copied the page. Sighing, she slid the book into her pocket. Surely, there was something she'd overlooked. She glanced around one last time and left.

9

The next morning, Lindsay parked in front of the tall brick structure housing the medical examiner's office. Over a hundred years old, the city hall's appearance was dark and foreboding. Now used for an assortment of government agencies, its ancient architecture and checkered past attracted a continuing flow of antique lovers. Four tour buses were parked at the curb, emitting heavy diesel fumes. One group of sightseers gathered around an historical marker on the building's front lawn, while others walked the few blocks west to the riverfront. Lindsay checked her watch. 10:30. Already the tourists were wiping their foreheads with handkerchiefs.

"I've only been out here ten minutes and I'm sweating like a faucet," complained a large woman with a New Jersey accent. "It's too damned hot."

"I do declare," said their guide in an exaggerated drawl. "Just listen to you. We southern women don't sweat. We glisten. But, you're right, it's hot enough to give one the vapors."

Another time Lindsay would have laughed at the tour guide's embellished southern accent, but not today. She hurried past the buses, their idling motors humming an off-key quartet. Turning onto the concrete walkway, she looked up at the old bell tower atop the second story. According to legend, in the early days the bell served to alert the community to danger. There was no bell now. During the early fifties, it was removed, not from the tower, but from the mayor's office to which it had plummeted. Luckily, he was out of the room at the time and remained unharmed.

Lindsay slowed her pace. The building's stark brick exterior had been softened by the wear and tear of coastal storms. "Old Brick," as it was called, had become a prized building material bringing a high price at auctions after structures were razed. Many expensive island homes were made of it. Lindsay grimly passed through the wide double doors into a dimly lit foyer, its walls covered with dark tongue and groove paneling, its floors pale gray marble. A few rays of morning sun came through high windows casting patterns on the walls. A sign with the letters M.E. had been taped to the front of a corridor to the left of a long curved stairway and the odor of antiseptic permeated the air. She followed the smell to a barely open door at the end of the hall, pushed on it and entered.

"Dr. Lindsay, I presume," a voice rumbled, so close it startled her. "I'm Dr. Frost."

A balding, bulbous-nosed man stepped from behind the door. Lindsay towered over the short squat figure whose round face was fringed with a scraggly gray beard.

He chuckled. "I didn't mean to scare you, but Dix told me you were coming. I was oiling the door hinges. Hearing its squeaks and groans gives people the creeps. Old buildings have their idiosyncrasies and this one's got quite a few. If I'd been here as long as this one, I'd be moaning too." He adjusted a pair of gold-rimmed spectacles on his nose and peered at her as if waiting for agreement.

"I---," she stopped, interrupted by a loud noise and the chatter of voices as two medics wheeling a gurney pushed into the room.

"Old man Tanner," drawled one of the men. "Probably his heart stopped; after all, he was ninety."

"Why'd you bring him here?" demanded Frost. "Wouldn't the funeral home have been more appropriate?"

"Been dead about two days. Stuff missing from his house. His neighbor thinks his yardman took it. Probably found him dead and helped himself." He scratched his head. "The chief says you better check him just in case its foul play."

Frost sighed as they transferred the body to another gurney and rolled theirs out, "I thought the pace here would be slower than my old job in Boston, but lately, it's about the same, one body after another, and these women." He shook his head and pushed the gurney into an adjoining room while Lindsay waited impatiently. The morning was getting away and so far she'd accomplished nothing.

When he returned his face had darkened. He put the oil can on a nearby shelf and paused. "As often as I see it, I can't get used to senseless death." He motioned her into a small dressing closet where they took off their shoes, climbed into disposable surgical suits, then put on booties and masks and pulled on latex gloves.

Lindsay understood his caution. There might still be evidence on Susan's body and they couldn't risk contamination. As they walked into the autopsy room, she felt an overwhelming sadness. Its modern interior contrasted with its antiquated surroundings. Fluorescent lighting reflected from stainless steel tables and sinks. Metal cabinets stood against white walls, their glass doors displaying an array of equipment and tools. Squares of black and white vinyl covered the floors. Lindsay shivered in the cold air and then stopped abruptly as she saw the woman before her. Susan Adams' body looked like a vandalized mannequin, her torso bisected by incisions, her skin ashen gray. Her tangled hair appeared as if it were attached to a neglected, battered doll.

"Ryder said you knew about this," he said, pointing to the dead woman's shoulders.

Lindsay fitted her hands above the marks as she had done at the beach, "The bruising must have occurred prior to or at the moment of death," she commented.

"Correct. The marks were made when she was held down, very forcibly from what I can see. She was alive when she went under. Her lungs were full of water, so death was from drowning."

"Was she…?"

"Yes," he said, reading her thoughts. "There's tearing of the vaginal membranes and internal bruising."

Lindsay thought of the lonely woman, struggling to get her life in order. She seemed so small and vulnerable in death.

"We've completed the toxicology reports," said Frost. "She had eaten little food on the day she died but there are traces of Valium. The hyoid bone's still intact so she wasn't strangled and there wasn't enough Valium to have knocked her out, so I believe she was conscious when she drowned. The damage on her shoulders extends well below the cutaneous membrane. It took a lot of pressure to push her down and there was probably a struggle." Frost moved the body onto its side. "As you can see the contusions are more pronounced on her back where the killer's fingers dug into the skin."

"If he held her that tightly, he must have left evidence," said Lindsay hopefully.

He shrugged "None that I see. Either it was washed away by the water or "Valium is a controlled substance. Prescription records?"

"I don't mean to discourage you, but the prescription may not be recent. Most physicians have changed to Prozac or related medications. Herbal remedies are also popular. Not as much Valium out there now."

"Mama's little helper," she murmured.

"I beg your pardon."

"Mama's little helper," she repeated. "In the sixties and seventies, sedatives, such as Valium, were drugs of choice for women. Doctors prescribed them to treat their patients' nerves. It was easier to take pills than face unhappy marriages and low-paying jobs."

"What better way to eliminate problems than anesthetizing the patients." he agreed, shaking his head.

For a moment, neither spoke.

"There's one more thing," he added, pointing to the woman's wrists and ankles. "Ligature marks under the skin and almost undetectable rope burns."

"She was bound?"

"I'm sure of it. Take a look."

Lindsay could barely make out the discolorations, distorted by the swollen skin.

"What I can't understand," he said, "is why he removed them if he was going to drown her."

"It didn't fit into his plan," said Lindsay. "If she was already incapacitated, there was no point in holding her down. She'd automatically sink to the bottom."

Frost shook his head again as they walked back into the dressing room, "A horrible way to die."

"Horrible for the others too and any who follow."

"You think there'll be more?"

"It's a game to him Dr. Frost, one he's not going to stop."

The doctor was silent as they pulled off their disposable coverings. His mind preoccupied, he didn't respond to her thanks and farewell.

Lindsay walked back to her car and was relieved to see the buses were gone. She was in no mood for carefree tourists.

10

"You're right. It's a serial killer, no question," said Ryder, who had called Lindsay to his office after receiving Frost's report. "I want to nail this scumbag." He pointed to the front page of the morning paper and growled. "Damn media's got wind of the case. Hell, we're even getting calls from Washington." He tossed the paper across the desk and rubbed his aching leg.

"Blackwater Killer" screamed in large type from the headlines.

Lindsay scanned the article and pushed it back to Ryder who continued to glare.

"Jeez, I wish something would pop on this case. Gotta hold a press conference this afternoon. Now the word's out, the island folks are scared. Tourist Bureau wants to play it down but the locals won't buy it. They don't want any more floaters and they're afraid to go swimming."

"Remember Jaws." Lindsay said wryly. "Stay out of the water."

Ryder scowled. "Ain't no joke." He pressed a button on his phone and Dixie Boatright entered, her hot pink nails matching her polyester pant-suit. She arched her brows as she looked at Lindsay, noting her beige lizard pumps and matching linen dress and then turned toward Ryder and ignored her.

"Dix, make Dr. Lindsay a copy," he ordered, handing her Frost's report.

The woman took it and hurried out, returning a few minutes later.

She handed the copy to Lindsay, placed the original on Ryder's desk and looked at him expectantly, "Anything else?"

"No."

"Thank you," Lindsay began but the woman was gone, leaving the scent of a dollared-down version of Seduction cologne behind her.

"Ryder, you know the killer's going to strike again soon."

"I don't need more evidence to tell me that, I can feel it."

She rose to leave. "Something more I can do for you?"

He hesitated. "No, nothing now, just keep in touch."

He moved to the doorway as she left, longingly watching her walk away.

"Interested?" asked a voice.

Ryder jumped, and then turned to see Wong smiling mischievously and walking toward him.

"C'mon, let's grab a bite to eat," the diver said suppressing a laugh. "You're blushing like you've got a fever."

****

By late afternoon, Lindsay was home, too restless to work and unable to concentrate.

After changing clothes, she ate a bowl of canned stew and sat staring at the front of her computer. She picked up the phone to call Patty, put it down and picked it up again.

"Lindsay, what's up?" She must have looked at her caller I D.

"How about a run on the beach?" As unsettled as she felt, exertion might help.

"Not for me," said Patty regretfully. "Beau-re-gard's client has picked out a condo and he made me promise to help his wife plan her decor. Gotta leave in ten minutes. Whew, make that five, gotta run."

"I'll give you a rain-check," said Lindsay.

She stared at the computer again. By sheer will she forced herself to work for the next four hours. Finally, she closed out the files and decided to go for the run and a change of scenery. As she ran along the narrow road towards the village, she tried to clear her head. The late afternoon light cast dappled patterns through the trees, drawing her gaze down side streets as she passed. She noticed a man running parallel to her, one street over. Shaded by massive live oaks, the area was blocked from the sun. Thankful for a diversion, she watched for him at each intersection, catching glimpses as he darted by. Dressed in dark clothes despite the heat, he blended in and out of the shadows as he ran. She picked up speed, challenged by his pace, letting it dictate her own.

She approached the first strip of shops and turned to look for him again, but he was no longer there. She ran onward, circling at the pier and turning back, thinking she'd catch up with him, wondering where he'd gone.

Back home, she returned to work, determined to accomplish something.

Remembering the telephone numbers from Susan's journal, she took the tablet from her purse. Using the internet, she found three numbers were from Atlanta, Susan's parents, John Blake, and Brenda Brown. The local numbers included a take-out restaurant, a beauty shop and St. John's Episcopal Church. She fed the information into her computer and faxed the information to Ryder, adding the unidentified numbers, 8783588 and a reproduction of the accompanying heart. When she finished, she called Frank Felder, a former FBI colleague.

"Frank, we have an unusual case," she began.

"So I've heard," he interjected, "been expecting your call."

"I'm sending you the info. If you tap into the Violent Criminal Apprehension Program data base, we may get a match."

"Not likely, Lindsay. I don't remember any like these. The drownings are odd, but we need other signature factors."

"I know it's unlikely, but…"

"What the hell," he interrupted," I'll give it a shot."

There was silence on the line.

"Lindsay?"

"Yes."

"I miss you. If you ever want to come back…"

"Thanks Frank," she said, her voice choking. She quickly placed the receiver back in its cradle.

Thursday, it rained continually, forming huge puddles around Lindsay's house. The storm intensified as the day wore on, the wind howling through the trees, tearing away moss and small branches. She sorted through stacks of papers compiled by the task force. They'd questioned marine workers, shrimpers and clerks. A few shopkeepers recognized Susan's picture but recalled little about her.

The storm subsided by late afternoon, leaving the air hot and humid. Determined to get her daily run, Lindsay rubbed her eyes, rose from her chair and changed into shorts and a T-shirt. She stuffed a ten dollar bill in her pocket, locked her door and started a slow repetitive pace. Changing her usual route, she ran on Frederica Road toward the island's northern end. The run gave her a sense of power as she drove herself harder. Skirting the inland marsh, she continued beyond the most populated areas. As she passed a narrow overgrown path, something moved in the shadows and a figure sped past. It was the runner she'd seen near the village. His muscular body seemed automated. He ran smoothly with his chest out and back straight and his elbows held close to his side. Challenged by his speed and the effortlessness of his stride, she accelerated. Maintaining a wide distance behind, she followed him deep into the island's interior.

Tabby ruins broke through the landscape, the remains of Spanish missions, a colonial fort and old plantations. The soil was mixed with the shells of Native-Americans and ancient pottery shards. Distracted, she momentarily forgot about the other runner. Rounding a curve, she stopped. "Where is he?" she wondered aloud. Did he know she was following him? Feeling as if she were being watched, she warily retraced her path.

Pangs of hunger reminded her she hadn't eaten. She returned to Frederica Road and, after a few minutes, spotted the sign for Barney's. The restaurant was almost empty with only stragglers from the noonday crowd. Sipping beer and munching on popcorn, they talked in low tones. "These are locals," she surmised, noting the relaxed look of old-timers, comfortable and accustomed to each other. She slid onto a stool at the bar and eyed the menu.

The bartender wore a bright red apron with "Josh" stitched on the pocket. He rubbed a spot of grease and looked at her questioningly.

"Soft-shell crab sandwich with fries, please."

"We have a special on Red Barker Beer."

"Thanks, but I'll have lemonade." She scanned the faces of the customers nearest her. Barney's wasn't listed in Ryder's files. Were the police just concentrating on the tourists? If it was known as a hangout for locals, it could have been overlooked. It was unlikely Susan came here but it should be checked. Maybe someone would remember her. Lindsay finished her meal, paid the bartender and left.

It was almost five by the time she reached her cottage. She showered, changed into clean clothes, pocketed Susan's photograph and drove back to the bar. The early evening crowd filled the booths and talk was loud and animated. As she entered, the bartender wiped his hands on his apron and smiled at her. "Back so soon? Ready for that beer?"

"Have you seen this woman?" she asked, holding Susan's picture before him.

"Susan Adams," he said, instantly interested. "Heard about her on the news. Such a shame, a real nice lady. She started coming in a couple of weeks ago, always sat with Father Reed."

Lindsay's eyes followed his gaze to a corner of the room where a priest in a wheelchair was talking with a young woman.

The bartender laughed at Lindsay's puzzled look, "Strange isn't it, a priest in a bar, but that's just like Father. He says the people who really need help don't go to church so he goes to them. Sometimes, he's in the taverns at the pier, sometimes here. I guess that's how he got to know Susan."

He turned to wait on another customer and Lindsay walked to the priest who looked up expectantly with a welcoming smile on his face.

"I'm Catherine Lindsay," she said, extending her hand.

"David Reed," the priest responded with a firm grip. Releasing her hand, he looked into her eyes. "Something's troubling you. Please join us."

"I was just leaving," said the woman. "See you next week?"

He nodded and as she walked away, he turned his attention back to Lindsay.

She studied him appraisingly. His voice was gentle but firm. Thick brown hair covered his head, trailing over his collar to the base of his neck and heavy eyebrows accented his large brown eyes. A short beard, beginning to show streaks of gray, framed his straight nose and firm chin. His arms were large and muscular. As she lowered her gaze, she saw he had no legs. Realizing she was staring, she flushed and looked away.

"You knew Susan Adams?" she asked, sitting in a chair across from him.

His eyes clouded and his expression turned sad as he nodded. "Were you a friend of hers?" he asked.

Lindsay showed him her identification. "Special investigator," she said. "I'm working on her case. As you may know, her drowning was no accident."

He glanced up at the TV over the bar and then looked back at her as if searching for answers. "I heard about what happened on the news. She was a troubled soul," he said softly, "but I can't imagine anyone wanting to harm her. Do you have any idea who did it?"

"I'm hoping you know something that can help us."

He shrugged. "What can I tell you? I knew her for such a short time. She was going through a difficult divorce and I gave her moral support. She was discouraged and depressed when we met, but I'd noticed a change. She said she'd met someone and was tired of holing up in her hotel room."

"Met someone? A man?"

"She didn't say. She called to tell me she wouldn't see me Tuesday and said she'd explain later. She sounded rather cheerful."

"Did she mention a name?"

"No, we only talked a minute. She called me here, shortly before our appointment."

"Appointment?"

"I began seeing Susan on a regular basis, every few days. I'm a psychologist as well as a priest." He paused "There's no effective psychological treatment that ignores the soul."

"You do psychotherapy in bars?" she asked incredulously.

"It's where I usually meet my subjects. I don't charge," he hastily added, "and I only give support and guidance."

She remained silent.

"Those who need help most are first to deny it. Bars are full of people who try to end their pain by numbing their body and stopping their symptoms. They don't recognize their spiritual needs and they aren't likely to be found in spiritual settings." As he looked at her intently, Lindsay shifted uncomfortably in her seat, disturbed by his words.

"Was Susan treating her symptoms?" she asked. "An alcohol problem? Drugs?"

"Perhaps at first; but nothing illegal," he hastened to add. "She was taking them by prescription."

"She was reading a book," began Lindsay.

"*Living Alone: Becoming The Person You want To Be,*" he interrupted. "I gave her the book but that's not why you're here."

"No, I'm here to learn all I can about Susan and find her killer. Anything you remember may give us a clue."

"I've probably said too much already. There are issues of confidentiality and I really don't think there's anything I can tell you that will help."

"Confidentiality in bar room conversations with a woman who is now dead? Susan was not the first victim and if the police don't get some answers, more will die."

A woman appeared by the bar, waved shyly and walked toward them.

"May we talk another time?" asked the priest. "Tomorrow morning? Here's my card. I'll be in my office at St. Martin's by nine."

"I'll be there," promised Lindsay as she slid the card into her purse.

11

Unlocking the front door, Brauner carefully entered his house. Heavy curtains darkened the interior of the first floor, casting shades of gray about the rooms. He was confident no one had come. The threads he had taped across the doors and windows were still held tightly in place. No one could have entered without disturbing them.

He slammed his right fist into his left palm. He must be more careful when he was running. Not seeing the woman, he'd headed straight into her path. Surely, she wouldn't remember him. Why would she? Why had she been running so far from the main roads? He'd only gotten a glimpse of her, but he felt certain he hadn't seen her before, or had he? The other day when he was running near the strip? Was that her? He shook his head. She wouldn't have had a reason to follow him.

He moved into the hall. He shouldn't waste valuable time worrying. There was too much to do. Climbing the stairs to the second floor, he flexed his arms. An hour of working out lay ahead. At the top of the stairs, he turned down a hall leading to a large room. Bodybuilding equipment lined the walls. The room was divided into sections marked with numbers and filled with barbells and exercise machinery. Charts measured each day's accomplishments and a CD player sat on top of a long, low bookcase. The shelves were filled with boxes of meticulously catalogued recordings. There were motivational CDs of every description.

He thumbed through them, pausing at a box labeled "Personal Power." Pulling it out, he withdrew a plastic case. "Side 1 Taking It All" was emblazoned in red and black print. Under the title was a smaller subtitle, "Personality and Persuasion." He inserted the disc into the CD player, turned up the volume and began his routine.

Slowly, with discipline and control, he picked up the first of the weights, then progressed through each area's ritual, still listening to the tape. When he finished the last section, he turned off the CD player, replaced the CD in its case and box, and noted the day's workout on one of the charts. Carefully, he removed his clothes and shoes, dropped them into a basket by the door and stepped into an adjoining shower.

As usual, he began with water as hot as he could stand it. He filled a washcloth with soap and lathered every part of his body before rinsing. Abruptly, he turned off the flow of hot water, replacing it with cold. After a few minutes, he ended the ordeal, stepped from the stall, pulled a towel from a rack and dried.

He examined himself in the mirror covering one wall of the room, ran his fingers through his short black hair and then smoothed his brows, focusing his dark eyes on his angular face, its narrow nose and tapering chin.

He moved his palm over his chest and across and down his abdomen, his lips curling with satisfaction at his reflection. The "Timmie" he once knew was gone. In his place was a strong muscular man, what some women called a "Hunk." Giving a short laugh, he lowered his hand and began to stroke, slowly, back and forth, until he was fully aroused; then walked down the hall to his bedroom. Opening the closet, he removed a key from the hem of a jacket where a row of stitching had been torn. Taking a metal box from the shelf, he unlocked it and pulled out a knotted lock of hair. Holding it against himself, he began to rub gently, then more forcefully, but his focus was interrupted by thoughts of Parks' arrogant voice. Despite his attempt to block it, the taunting intrusion continued.

He sat on his bed and turned on a small CD player. As heavy metal rock reverberated through the room, Parks' words echoed in his mind above the music, "You wormy little queer. You think any girl would go out with you?" Hearing Parks' laughter over and over, he turned the music louder and stroked himself harder. Unable to come, he wiped tears from his eyes and turned the volume as high as he could. Finally, he was able to drown out his thoughts of Parks and concentrate on images of Beth.

After he finished, he replaced the hair and key, returned to the shower and washed again in the hot and cold water. After he'd carefully dried himself, he returned to his bedroom where he opened a cabinet and withdrew one each from the stacks of folded jeans and dark-colored T-shirts. He took briefs and a pair of socks from a drawer, straightening the remaining clothes before moving back to his closet, where he pulled out a fresh pair of running shoes and sat on his bed to put them on, doubling the knots as he tied them.

12

The next morning, Lindsay stopped at police headquarters on her way to meet Father Reed. Dixie Boatright glared at her as she passed towards Ryder's office. "Why don't you just tell me what you need and I'll give him a buzz," she said with a condescending wink.

Before Lindsay could answer, Ryder appeared at the door looking tired and disheveled. Upon seeing her, he straightened his tie and tucked his rumpled shirt more tightly inside his trousers.

"Are you busy?" she asked.

"Oh sure," he said. "I'm squashing crime left and right like bugs on a windshield."

She ignored the sarcastic remark.

"It's O.K., Dix. Dr. Lindsay can come in."

The woman returned to her work without comment.

"Nothing's changed," he said, as they sat down. He pushed half of a donut from the top of a file into the trash and then opened his desk and withdrew a package of Big Red gum.°

"Wanna stick?" he extended the package to her.

"No thanks." She waited as he tore the wrapper, unwrapped a piece of gum and stuffed it into his mouth.

"The lab reports are in. Here's your copy." He handed her a file with a computer disc attached.

Lindsay slid them into her brief case, and noticed ink marks on his wrist.

"My palm pilot," he grinned, "helps me remember things."

"Brandon Adams's alibi checks out," he continued. "He was with his squeeze, unless she's covering for him. Hope you can come up with something. Heard from the Feds?"

"I checked VICAP. So far, no matches. I have a contact who's calling the coastal jurisdictions. If he finds anything suspicious, he'll let us know."

"How about profiles?"

"Southern killers don't always fit the mold, and this one's m.o. is different. We're breaking new ground."

"Yeah, well my turf can sure as hell do without it."

"I have some ideas," she added, "but I need more information."

"Time's passing." said Ryder. "If a murder's not solved in the first twenty-four hours, chances are it isn't going to be and look at how many we've got. There'll be another vic if we don't get some action."

He pointed to a Loran map tacked to the wall behind his desk. "I've plotted the time frames between the murders, if they are all murders. The map shows where the floaters were found. Danny Wong is backtracking the weather, currents and water temperature, trying to pinpoint where the bodies were dumped." He paused as he thought of Wong.

Divers rarely chose to work in the murky black water of the South Georgia coast. Stained by the mud of surrounding marshes, the saltwater looked more like that of an inland river. Wong had lived near the water all of his life, was accustomed to it. Experience had taught him the nuances of the tides. He knew the water and its ways like the back of his hand and Ryder had learned to rely on him. Lindsay cleared her throat to regain Ryder's attention.

"We're still chasing leads," he added. "Same old routine, we need something to pop."

"I've met a local who knew Susan," she interjected.

Ryder brightened as she told him about Father Reed.

"I know Reed. I'll go with you."

"I can handle it. Are you going to be here all morning?"

Ryder eyed the piles of paperwork on his desk. "Hell, I may be here all night. Stop by when you finish. I want to know what he says."

Driving away from the station, Lindsay marveled at the graceful turn-of-the century homes lining the streets of Old Town Brunswick. According to locals, the urban renewal of the seventies had destroyed most of the waterfront buildings and many of the old neighborhoods. Later, preservationists had become almost fanatical in their zeal for saving what remained of the Historic District. Their progress had resulted in the deteriorated dwellings of the poor alternating dramatically with the opulence of restored Victorian mansions.

She caught sight of St. Martin's towering over Gloucester Street, headed toward it and pulled into a nearby parking space. The church's stately vine-covered exterior and peaked roof were a symbol of stability in an area of transition, but its stained glass was covered with Plexiglas and its massive double doors were securely locked.

he pressed an intercom button.

"Dr. Lindsay?" the priest's voice echoed.

"Yes, I'm a little early." She hadn't completed her sentence before she heard the click of the door's lock releasing.

She entered the church foyer where she inhaled the smell of darkened time-seasoned oak. Passing through an archway into the sanctuary, she walked across plush red carpeting. Rows of pews with red cushioned seats faced a white altar and a large gold cross. The top of the altar was covered by a richly embroidered tapestry, as were two matching lecterns. Above it was the most beautiful stained glass window she had ever seen. To the right, a ramp led to the altar. Viewed from the inside, the building's vibrantly colored windows were breathtaking. Wooden beams crossed the ceiling at perpendicular angles framing the scene. Transfixed by the beauty of her surroundings, she stood at the end of the long middle aisle.

"Lovely isn't it?" said a voice beside her.

"Oh, I didn't hear you come in."

The priest moved closer, his wheelchair noiseless on the thick carpet.

"I didn't want to interrupt your thoughts, or your prayers," he said gently.

Unsure how to reply, she made no comment.

"Are you all right?" he asked.

"Yes, I, I'm fine," she said, averting her eyes from the cross, embarrassed at being observed. "I want to ask you some questions about Susan."

"I don't think I know anything useful, but I'll be glad to tell you all I can. Come with me." He turned his chair into a hallway beside the ramp.

She followed, growing increasingly uneasy as they entered an office adjoining a small apartment.

"It's easier for me to live where I work," the priest said matter-of-factly. "Our congregation is kind and generous. They remodeled these rooms when I came. This was the church nursery before it was moved to the Sunday School Building."

She scanned the room in surprise. A display case with Pueblo pottery was pressed against a wall. Hung above it was the most beautiful Navajo rug she had ever seen. Its intricately woven pattern of reds and oranges contrasted with a brown and gray background giving the impression of fire. Sand paintings and a series of Native-American prints adorned the rest of the walls. Low bookcases were placed at intervals and several rocking chairs were in front of an old stone fireplace, modernized with gas logs. The similarity between the priest's small home and her own was striking.

Reed wheeled behind a long table with raised legs and gestured for her to pull up a chair. As she sat, she noticed papers and books littering the floor.

"Dropped the darn things when I heard the buzzer," he explained pleasantly.

Bending over, she scooped them up and placed them neatly on his desk.

"James Deer," she said aloud.

"You're familiar with him?" inquired the priest. "He's my cousin."

"Really! I've read all of his books," said Lindsay. "I've been looking for his new one."

"It'll be out soon."

"We like the same author and this room reminds me of my home."

"My grandfather was Navajo," he explained. "We spent a lot of time together when I was young. Unfortunately, this is all I have left. Much of what my family had was lost or stolen. Collectors offer a lot of money for artifacts and many people like Native-American décor. Unfortunately, it usually has little to do with our actual heritage."

She felt her cheeks flush.

"I'm sorry. I shouldn't have said that. I'm afraid I've become too sensitive about the issue. When my father was alive, there was a lot of anti-Indian prejudice. He changed his name from Deer to Reed because he thought it would be more acceptable, help him get a job. Now, it somehow seems appropriate, with all that's happened to our culture."

"Looks can be deceiving," said Lindsay, touching her hair. "My grandmother was Cherokee. She died when I was small. I used to stay with her in a cabin in the Cherokee Mountains."

"The Southern Appalachians."

"Yes, as they're now called, the Appalachians. The décor you refer to gives me a sense of kinship. I don't have much to remember her by."

"What about your heritage of beliefs? Don't you feel a kinship there?"

Lindsay looked puzzled.

"I don't mean to offend, especially in my position as priest. It just seems sad that people identify with external symbols, rather than seeking true community with their past."

She didn't respond.

"I enjoy James Deer's characters," he said, taking her cue and changing the subject. "You must like detective stories, too. Not surprising in your line of work."

"I've always enjoyed mysteries," she said, relieved at the conversation's turn, "starting with Nancy Drew when I was young, but yes, I like James Deer's characters. He deals with real Native-American issues and I've learned more about our heritage, and its problems."

"Perhaps, that was his intention. History books are rarely accurate and controversies cost sales. Few people take the time to learn the truth but mystery readers can be fair game for education."

"By mysterious means," said Lindsay thoughtfully.

"By mysterious means indeed," he repeated.

"Speaking of which, we're facing a real-life mystery," said Lindsay. "No one seems to know anything about Susan Adams' death and you're the only local I've met who knew her."

He looked at her with piercing eyes that seemed to penetrate her soul. Had he been trying to lead her away from the subject on purpose? So far, their conversation had been interesting but unproductive.

Meeting his gaze, she phrased her words carefully. "Tell me everything you can remember. The smallest detail may help, no matter how unimportant it seems. When did you first meet Susan?"

"Four weeks ago today while I was in Barney's. A few of the locals were rowdy, playing practical jokes on each other and drinking. Susan was by herself, seated on a stool at the bar. She looked sad, so I approached her."

"You just went over and started talking?"

"Yes, women aren't usually guarded with...," he hesitated and then continued. "Not only am I an Episcopal priest, but as you can see my physical condition is non-threatening." His muscular arms contrasted with the useless stumps at the end of his thighs, covered by trousers with ends tucked under.

Lindsay waited expectantly for him to explain.

He gestured toward what remained of his legs. "Vietnam. In an instant my life was changed." He waited for her to comment but she stared down at her hands.

"The disabled, Dr. Lindsay, suffer from many misconceptions. We're treated as if we're invisible, as if our thoughts and feelings don't matter and since we're seen as non-sexual objects, women aren't afraid of us. As a servant of God, I use this to my advantage. It isn't easy. It isn't easy now. You're very attractive but I know you have no such thoughts about me. You're surprised we have interests in common and read the same books."

She started to speak but could think of nothing to say.

"Josh says you're a runner; so was I. Now I must confine myself to swimming. I only run in my dreams."

She looked at him questioningly, waiting for him to continue but he again changed the subject.

"To summarize, Susan's story is one I've heard many times. She lived for her husband and children. Her devotion was unquestionable, but unappreciated. The more she tried to please and appease him, the less interest he showed. Eventually, she discovered he was having an affair. When she confronted him, he asked for a divorce."

Lindsay detected bitterness in his tone.

"It was traumatic," he continued. "She felt she'd been used and discarded. When her husband asked for the divorce, it was more than she could bear. Her marriage had fallen apart and she wanted time to get her bearings and think. Susan left her children with her parents so she could come here. She spent most of her time walking the beach and reading self-help books. Mostly pop-psych," he added, with disdain.

Lindsay opened her mouth to comment, but the priest went on. "She was trying to heal herself in the only way she knew. I served as a listener, loaned her better reading material and suggested she keep a journal. The last time we talked she was less withdrawn and said she'd met someone. When I asked her about him, she said she would tell me about him the next time we met. If only she'd told me more. I should have…" His voice trailed off.

"There's nothing to be gained by blaming yourself," said Lindsay. "It won't help her and it can't help you. You couldn't have known what would happen."

"No, but I should have warned her to be cautious. She was such a pretty woman and very vulnerable." He was quiet a few seconds and then shook his head. "That's all I can tell you."

Lindsay gave the priest her card. "If you think of anything else…"

"I'll call you," he assured her.

She hurried out of his office and through the sanctuary, avoiding the altar and its large gold cross.

The priest listened for the sound of her car and then withdrew a picture from a drawer in the side of the table. A young woman with long blonde hair posed beside a sand castle on a deserted beach. The photograph was torn down the middle so that her partner was no longer seen. The only evidence of his presence was a muscular arm around her shoulders.

Sighing, the priest stared at it for several seconds before putting it back in the drawer and resting his head in his hands. Another minute passed before he unfastened the collar above his black shirt, and threw it aside. It symbolized the imprisoning darkness that still overcame him.

13

When Lindsay returned to Ryder's office, he was huddled over his desk, sorting papers into folders. As she entered, he gave her a questioning glance.

"The priest wasn't much help," she said. "We already knew the woman was depressed and getting a divorce. She was lonely, read a lot and walked on the beach. She'd recently made a new friend, probably male, but Reed doesn't have a name. Other than that, he says he knew little about her. No one seems to know anything."

"Wrong. The killer knows; we just haven't found the maggot. Collins and Morrison have come up dry, too. We're meeting again this afternoon, three sharp. Put something together. Paint us a picture. I want to know this guy better. How does he lure these women?"

Lindsay shook her head and told Ryder goodbye, drove home, changed into shorts and headed down the path through the dunes. The beach was almost empty. Questioning the priest had left her with a gnawing hollow feeling. The ocean would help. It always did.

The tide was out, exposing a wide wet expanse of mirror-like sand. She ran faster and faster until she was out of breath. As she slowed, she noticed the uncomfortable feeling was gone. She pulled off her shoes and socks and walked, leaving a line of footprints behind, her head bent in thought.

All of the victims were alone, out of the mainstream. The first was not reported missing, never identified. She stared at the sea. It seemed dark and threatening as she envisioned bodies floating toward shore with sharks and other predators following. Had the first woman been attacked by a shark, or by a man? Which was more vicious? Was reasoning the only thing that set them apart?

harlotte Thomas was a part-time resident. No one knew when she came and she had no friends in the area. Had she died by accident or murder?

Vicky Laker was an alcoholic. Even though she was local, few knew her well. Her relationships were short and sexual and only with men.

The fourth victim remained anonymous. Then, there was Susan. Lindsay caught her breath. There was the pattern, lonely, unattached women who wouldn't be missed, at least not for a while. The time span gave the killer an edge and their lifestyles gave him anonymity. The ocean provided a perfect crime scene, no blood, no weapon, no clues.   She thought of Father Reed waiting in bars and pictured the powerful muscles in his arms. Was he a savior or a predator?

She shivered.

"The priest," she said aloud. Could it be?

She turned back, headed for home, dressed and returned to Ryder's office.

"Hell, I've known Reed for years," he said coolly.

"But, is it possible?" she countered. "Does he have access to a boat?"

Ryder stared at her. "He's got a boat and he can swim, but he can't walk. The guys at Starboard Marina built him a ramp so he can roll his chair onto the dock. He drives a van with some sort of hydraulic gizmo, some kinda lift that he parks at the edge of the boardwalk, close to his boat."

"So it's easy for him to slip in and out," she interjected, her face darkening. "He goes out alone?"

"Sure, he can handle the boat," admitted Ryder. "At high tide, it's even with the dock and there's a gate in the boat's railing so he can roll his chair on board." He sighed and gave her an exasperated look. "He's a priest for God's sake. I'm telling you. The guy's not a killer."

Lindsay was silent.

"He swims from the same gate," Ryder continued, "and holds onto the railing to get in and out of the water. The boat's controls have been lowered and since there's no cabin, he's free to move around."

A mental motion picture formed in Lindsay's mind.

Ryder scowled at her. "I know what you're thinking. You're wrong. What about your profiles? There's no way Reed fits."

"You're wrong," she said. "Do you know his background? What makes you think a physical disability would preclude sociopathic behavior? It might increase his need for power, especially over women."

"Like I said, it's not David Reed."

"But…,"

"We're meeting again at three o'clock," he said, dismissing her.

Lindsay stared at him.

"Three o'clock," he repeated. She abruptly turned to walk out of his office and almost bumped into Dixie Boatright, who was standing outside the door. Ignoring Ryder's opinion, she hurried to her Porsche, maneuvered out of the parking lot and went back to St. Martin's where she impatiently pressed the intercom twice.

"Who is it?" asked Reed over the intercom.

"Catherine Lindsay," she answered. "I thought of something else."

A period of silence followed before she heard the lock release. She hesitated uncomfortably at the cross before walking down the hall. Reaching into her purse, she was reassured by the feel of her Glock 9 mm automatic. She paused, listening at the door to his office, straining to hear any sound.

"Dr. Lindsay? Are you there?"

She cautiously opened the door. He was still sitting behind the table which was covered with papers. Settling into the chair closest to him, she saw his puzzled look and decided to catch him off guard. "Father Reed," she said slowly. "Where were you last Tuesday?"

His expression showed confusion. "I was here. I'm always here on Tuesdays unless I have an appointment."

"Your boat...?"

"It's being repaired, why?"

"When did you last go out in it?" she pressed.

"It's been at least two weeks, but ...?"

"Who can verify that?"

"My boat broke down three weeks ago, didn't even make it past the marina. Joe Kelly, the boat mechanic at Starboard, looked at it that afternoon. He's had the motor torn apart ever since."

A startled expression crossed his face. "Surely, you don't think I had something to do with Susan's death? Why? Am I that abnormal?" His voice rose angrily. "You believe because I'm physically deformed I'm mentally deformed as well?"

"I..."

"Say it. How do you see me? As a weak, sexually repressed individual who's channeled what power he has left into hurting others? How would I have carried it out? I have strong arms. I can swim and run a boat, but am I that big a threat? Are you so repulsed by me you assume I'm a murderer?

A monster?"

His words were suddenly fueled by bitterness and rage. Just as quickly, his anger subsided and he fell into silence.

Lindsay was conscious of the weight of her gun against her side as she watched his reaction. Several minutes passed.

"Please go," he whispered.

She remained seated, watching him carefully. He met her gaze and then looked away.

"I'm sorry," he said, regaining his composure. "I know you're just doing your job. I shouldn't have taken it personally." He swept his arm across the top of his thighs. "I'm still dealing with it. I thought I was handling it."

Lindsay sat wordlessly, feeling the intangible barrier that had risen between them.

"How did it happen?" she asked, beginning to relax.

"I was on a Navy SEAL team in the Mekong Delta. Our mission was to destroy the supply line. We used to say "They had it by day, we had it by night'." He laughed sarcastically. "We'd been watching the unloading of a sanpan. It was almost midnight so we moved down the trail to set up an ambush. I was with three other men behind the point man, and...," His voice lowered and he took a deep breath. "One of the men stepped on a mine. All three were blown to bits. I was the only one who survived and I wished I'd joined them. You'd think after this length of time..." His cheek muscles tightened and he laughed bitterly.

"Time may pass," she said sadly, "but memories don't change."

"You're right. Time passes and some things heal, but it doesn't change reality. I'd like for it to at least change my outlook."

She looked away.

"Look at me," he said in a demanding tone. As she turned back to face him, he wheeled his chair from behind the table and moved beside her.

"Are you uncomfortable with me?"

"No," she answered weakly.

"Don't I at least deserve your honesty? Is it not enough for me to carry my own burden without taking on the judgments of others? God knows we were all faced with that after the war. The fighting ripped us apart. Was that not enough to give? Some of us left parts of our bodies as well as our spirits, if we left at all."

He sat quietly for several seconds before resuming. "Dr. Lindsay, I'm not an old wrecked car without an engine. I'm not an empty shell. I'm a human being like you, the same person I was when I was able to walk. I still have hopes, dreams and feelings. I'm not a thing turned into a monster."

Stunned by his bitter words, she sat rooted to the chair.

He grasped her hand. "What do you feel? Flesh and blood. My hand is as warm as yours."

The feel of his hand against hers oddly comforted her.

Releasing her, he rolled closer, again took her hand, and gazed into her eyes. They sat, eyes locked. He reached over with his other hand, and lightly brushed her cheek with his finger.

Momentarily disoriented, she remained seated, unable to move.

"I better leave," she said suddenly rising from her chair. "I have work…"

She walked quickly out of the office, shutting the door behind her. As she passed the altar, she felt a surge of dizziness and slipped into a pew. What had happened to her? Was she reacting to the priest? The church? Kneeling, she looked at the cross and tried to pray but words wouldn't come. Hot tears ran down her cheeks and her hands were shaking. She rose and hurried to her car where she sat a long time in silence before starting the engine. She felt off-balance and confused, as if she was losing perspective and, despite Reed's anger and alibi, a nagging doubt tugged.

14

He paced restlessly, back and forth in his bedroom, his mind in torment. Finally, he tried to sleep. As he lay in bed, his thoughts jumped back and forth from past to present, triggering memories. One seemed always with him.

When he was twelve, he had slipped into an adult theatre through a side door, where terrified of discovery, he sat motionless in the dark, stunned by what he saw. It was the first time he'd seen a naked man and woman, the first time he'd seen a woman taken by force and his first experience with his own sexuality.

At first, his feelings frightened him, but in the end he'd been consumed by an explosion of pleasure. Identifying with the actor, it was as if he were overcoming the woman, feeling her struggle. He'd watched as the woman fought, struggling against the weight of the man until her strength was gone and she lay exhausted. He gloried in the sense of power he felt as an onlooker.

Picturing the scene in the months that followed, he tried to recall the look on the woman's face. Was she in ecstasy or pain? At night, in his fantasies, he reenacted the scene.

Years later, the fantasy remained. But, then, it was Timmie who subdued her. She would fight, but always succumb, unable to resist his strength. Each time, he experienced a frenzy of pleasure and release, imagining many sexual encounters with the woman. He always controlled her and she obeyed his every command.

When he was fourteen, he began approaching girls in his class, but they rebuffed him with ridicule and laughter, mocking his lack of social skills. As his pain changed to anger he returned to his fantasies. Yearning for more, he stole pornographic magazines from stores, particularly those with graphic and violent pictures. He kept them all, hiding them beneath his dresser and bed where he had them still, their paper yellowed, their edges frayed. With the passing of years, his desire increased, his hunger turned into insatiable want and his frustration changed into fury.

15

The task force filled the conference room by Ryder's office where they listened attentively to the profile Catherine Lindsay had compiled. "We're dealing with an organized killer," she began. "There was evidence of bruising on some of the victims. The cause of death is drowning and we know they were held down."

"Why go to the trouble to drown them?" asked Ryder. "There are easier methods of murder."

"The method is important," said Lindsay, "because it's part of a ritual. Otherwise, he would have just rendered them unconscious and thrown them in."

"The method's so important," said Morrison sarcastically, "they float right back to shore."

"That's the point," said Lindsay coolly. "Since water represents life and the womb, the killings may be symbolic. They may have religious significance and relate to baptism or rebirth. Whoever discovers them bears witness."

"What the hell's religion got to do with it?" Morrison interrupted, "Just give us the facts."

Lindsay glared at him and continued. "If the killer had a traumatic childhood sanctioned by a perverted use of religious doctrine or if someone was treating him cruelly, in the name of religion, he could turn against God and become perverted himself."

Morrison was frustrated. "I don't get it. Religion is what we need. If more people went to church…"

Lindsay sighed. "There's a difference between religion and spirituality. Some people have a legalistic approach to their beliefs. They use religion to justify their actions and punish others. It has nothing to do with spiritual faith."

"Get on with it you two," Ryder urged impatiently. "We haven't got time for a theological debate."

"You're saying this guy's killing people because he's religious?" asked Andy Collins, ignoring Ryder's comments.

"No," said Lindsay firmly. "I'm saying there may be a religious component to his rituals. The FBI's never encountered this type of killer. We're mapping new territory and it's important to explore every angle."

"Great," snorted Morrison, "we're guessin' without facts, just dealin' with a friggin' theory."

Lindsay glared at him again and looked to Ryder.

"Enough," he ordered. "Stop the bickering. We're on the same side."

"At first, I thought he might be killing the victims in one place and moving them to another," continued Lindsay, "but, they show no sign of post-mortem bruising or aberrant lividity. He takes them out, drowns them and leaves."

"Wong's charted the path of the floaters," interjected Ryder, nodding to the diver who walked to the Loran map now taped to a flip chart on a portable easel.

"In many ways," said Wong, "the bottom of the Atlantic is like land above sea level. If something blows onto our doorstep and we want to know where it's from, we look at wind patterns. If we can determine which way the wind was blowing, we can figure where the object started and retrace its path. With the ocean, we look at current, tide, water temperature, and weather. Geographical features such as undersea ridges and drop-offs are also a factor."

He pulled a red marker from his shirt pocket, made a large circle on the map and drew lines from it to the areas where the bodies were found. "He took each of them to the same general area, less than a mile from shore."

"But the bodies were found in different places," objected Collins. "Vicky Laker was around the southern tip of the island."

"There was a storm in the early hours of the morning before she was found. The water was probably rough when he took her out. She was carried seaward by the current until the tide turned and then she was swept into the channel. Considering the distance and the boat traffic, the body drifted only a short time before it washed in."

He returned to his seat and Lindsay continued the profile. "Since they're all coming ashore, we know he wants them to be found. That's a statement about his personality. He wants others to see what he's done so he can vicariously relive the experience."

"He must be a frequent flyer," quipped Morrison. "Hell, he seems to know the area better than we do."

Lindsay ignored him and went on. "The pattern of bruising suggests he's forcing them underwater, gripping them by their shoulders and using his weight to hold them down. There's evidence of drugs but not enough to prevent a struggle. He likes the fight, the action of pushing them under while they're still alive. It enhances his feeling of power."

"He'd have to be one hell of a strong dude to get them out of the boat and keep them under," added Collins.

Lindsay nodded. "He's muscular with powerful arms and may be a body-builder or have a physically demanding job. We have no evidence from the first victims, but Susan Adams was sexually assaulted."

"We're dealing with a friggin' animal," snarled Morrison.

"But a clever one," added Lindsay. "He's smart. He's also angry, depressed, mobile, and carefully selects his victims."

"How?" questioned Wong, turning to Ryder. "How does he decide whom to target?"

"Your guess is as good as mine," said Ryder. "Maybe he meets them on the beach, in bars. How the hell does anybody get a date these days?" He glanced at Lindsay and blushed.

She saw his discomfort and smiled. "The women had similar features, height, weight, and hair. He's got a pattern for his crime and his victims. If we can find out how he selects them, we can bait and trap him."

She paused. "We also know he'll follow the cases once the bodies are discovered and come to the crime scene."

"If there's another vic, we'll have a couple of undercover guys in with the onlookers," said Ryder. "Most of them know the islanders. They can eliminate them."

"Not necessarily," Lindsay warned. "Just because this hasn't happened before doesn't mean he wasn't here. It's common to begin with less serious crimes and he may have been incarcerated or in a mental institution."

"Pro'bly on ice in the big house." Morrison smirked at Lindsay.

"He could have been in prison," Ryder acknowledged, "but we've had plenty of unsolved assaults over the years. Damn bad ones. The last vic's still in a psych ward. We never got her to talk."

"He could be the same guy," said Lindsay, "and he may be escalating. The murders may have begun because he felt threatened or because he was desensitized and needed more excitement. There's a lot of risk with a living victim and repetition reduces the thrill"

Ryder nodded. "That explains Susan Adams being raped, then killed and it may explain what happened to the others."

"Sexual experimentation with victims is common," said Lindsay, "but it's not his main goal. His turn-on is dominance and power."

Ryder stared at her before turning to Collins and Morrison. "Pull the files on stalking, peeping toms and sexual assault for the last five years. I'll set up tables and we'll go through them." He looked wearily at Lindsay and Wong, "It's going to take a lot of time. Let's break and meet back here in an hour."

They nodded in agreement as Ryder walked back to his office.

16

Afterthey returned, the conference room was a hub of activity. Ryder rolled in the whiteboard from his office and divided its surface into related crime types: stalking, peeping toms, rape and homicide. There was a noise at the door and Ryder pointed to a small table by the window. "Over there, Dix." The woman hurried into the room, balancing a coffee pot in one hand and a plate of donuts in the other. She started the coffee and left, returning with a stack of paper plates, cups, packets of sugar, and creamer.

"Thanks," said Ryder. "That's all we need. I know you've got a lot of work to do." His comments caught her as she was about to be seated. She fussed with the donuts for a few minutes before leaving, trying to conceal her disappointment at being dismissed.

Collins and Morrison were already sorting through boxes and computer printouts. Collins suddenly let out a loud heart-stopping sneeze. "Lord, Ryder. These files are all caked with dust. Where were they stored?"

Ryder gestured toward the door. "Dix had them down in the basement, guess she didn't think we'd use them again and didn't cover them."

"Women," said Morrison, rolling his eyes.

Collins grabbed a paper towel, dusted the tops of the files and pulled out a thick folder. "If the perp's in here, we'll find him," he said confidently. He examined its contents, returned it to its box and pulled out another one. Twenty minutes passed as they filled the board with incidents in an attempt to find a pattern.

"Whoa, look at this." Collins spread the contents of a worn and coffee-stained file on the table for the others to see. "Three years ago, a woman was raped in her hotel room." Lindsay shrugged. "So, what else?"

"She'd been walking on the beach. The reporting cop thought she'd been followed home. The perp opened the door by jamming a penknife in the lock and got in while she was in the bathtub. He held her under water until she was unconscious. When she came to, he was gone. She didn't get a good look at him."

"Sounds like a winner," said Ryder.

"Another one," bellowed Morrison, "June, the next year. Around 9 p.m., the vic was leaving the pier and heard someone walking behind her. When she was almost home, she went to a neighbor's house instead. It happened again two days later and she stopped her night walks. A coupl'a weeks passed and she called in a burglary. Nothing big was taken, but she found a window unlocked and someone had pawed through her underwear. She stayed with her boyfriend for a week, then went back home. Six weeks later, someone broke in and raped her."

Morrison smirked. "She was taking a bath when some nut burst in and pushed her under water. She didn't hear or see anything 'til he grabbed her and couldn't tell what he looked like. Here you read it."

He passed the report to Lindsay who read it aloud. "All I remember is someone grabbing me and pushing me down. I couldn't breathe and everything went black. When I woke up I was lying in the hall and he was gone.' She probably passed out from holding her breath and he thought she was dead."

Collins waved another report. "A year ago a woman was attacked in her backyard pool. A neighbor heard her screaming and saw a guy running away. He was wearing a stocking over his face."

"Here's another pool attack with the victim raped," added Ryder.

"Now he's changed his m.o.," said Lindsay, thoughtfully, as the others looked at her. "He was using water to weaken them before the assault. Now he attacks and takes them to the ocean to kill them."

"Don't see why he goes to the trouble," said Morrison. "It'd be easier to kill them on the spot." His comment was left hanging as the others continued to work with the files.

Ryder wiped his brow. "A couple of years ago we had twenty rapes in twelve months. Hell, we usually have eight to ten in a year, but when we saw the numbers increasing we formed a task force. We disbanded when the numbers went down. Most of them didn't involve water." He smiled ruefully. "The ones that did didn't set off any special alarms."

"They probably seemed coincidental," commented Lindsay.

"No such thing," said Ryder.

She raised an eyebrow. "Really?"

Ryder nodded. "There's no such thing as coincidence. There's always a pattern." He stuck a piece of gum in his mouth and chewed.

"Like bad things come in threes," offered Morrison as he pulled out the next file.

"The gap of time when the rapes went down," said Lindsay, "was probably because of the task force attention."

"During another attack, the guy escaped through a window when the victim's father walked in," said Collins.

Ryder nodded, "I remember that one. Here's the Levy case, the one I mentioned earlier."

"Dorothy Levy." said Collins, in a somber tone. "God, that was brutal. Her house was on my beat and I was the first one there. I'd had a bad feeling all day, then we got the call." He was quiet for several moments as the evening repeated itself in his mind.

"God only knows what she went through. She was half-drowned. I found her naked in a puddle of water by the john. A friend came by, saw her car in the drive but nobody answered the door. She was about to leave when she heard a scream. When she couldn't get in, she ran for help. The guy next door broke the lock while his wife called 911, but by the time he got in, the perp was gone."

"Must have been hell to go through," said Ryder.

"She was one traumatized lady," agreed Collins. "He meant to off her." His face was drawn as he looked to Lindsay expectantly.

She nodded. "He's our guy. I can feel it."

"We haven't exactly got him fingered," said Morrison. "The vic never talked or gave a description."

"I want to meet with her," said Lindsay. "Where is she now?"

Ryder frowned. "Ridgedale Retreat, a mental hospital southwest of here. Her doctor said she'd let us know when she could be questioned. We used to check every few weeks, but hell, after six months passed, we dropped it."

Lindsay arched an eyebrow.

"Ridgedale Retreat," he repeated before she could ask, "about a two-hour ride."

"I'll go tomorrow," she said.

They worked until all the files were examined and studied the results on the board where a pattern emerged. During the past three years, there were increasing numbers of stalkings and increasing numbers of rapes. Some reported break-ins and missing personal items. The numbers decreased when the drownings began. As the numbers of the first crimes increased, there were shorter intervals between them, as was now the case with the homicides.

"He's going to strike again soon," warned Lindsay.

They looked at each other with a sense of growing urgency. Ryder looked at his watch. "It's getting late. Be back here tomorrow at nine." The others left him staring dejectedly at the board.

17

The morning run was humid and hot. As he passed Ebenezer Baptist Church, he heard organ music and singing. His stomach tightened and his mood abruptly changed. Clinching his fists, he felt his shoulders constrict as his breathing became hard and labored. Seething with anger he tore along the path in the woods to a large flowing creek, pushing his way through the brush until he reached it. With a swift intake of breath, he pulled off his shoes and socks, tossed them aside and waded into the water. Swimming rapidly back and forth along the shore, he exchanged his rage for exhaustion. Finally drowning the fire within him, he crawled onto the bank. After he rested, he put his socks and shoes back on, stumbled back into the woods and slowly walked home where he showered and changed, fell onto his bed and slept. It was dark by the time he awoke. Returning to the woods, he walked to the vacant cottage on the adjoining property. A quarter of a mile away, the house was hidden from the road by tall clumps of myrtle. The yard was neatly groomed, the grass mowed and tended by a yardman who cared for the house during the summer.

Using a small flashlight, he checked the driveway for tire marks and examined the front and back entrances. With a snort of contempt, he removed the absent owner's key from a pot beneath the kitchen window. He opened the laundry room door, slipped inside and went into the living room where he sat by the big bay window, as usual watching the driveway, in easy reach of the telephone. He removed a pen and pad from his pants pocket, flipped to a blank page, reached for the phone and punched in a series of numbers. Every few minutes, he paused to write and punch in a number again. When he finished, he replaced the receiver and examined what he'd written. He reached for the phone again, entered another set of numbers and then placed a piece of cloth over his mouth to muffle his words.

"Ginny?" he said in a bashful voice. "This is Carl. Thanks for calling."

18

Lindsay scheduled an eleven o'clock appointment at Ridgedale Retreat the next morning with Dr. Martha Skalato, who reluctantly agreed on condition there'd be no contact with Dorothy Levy. "I'm not trying to be uncooperative," said the doctor. "although it may seem that way. I have to protect my patient."

Lindsay rose early to meet Patty and run their usual five miles on the beach, before starting out. "So how's the decorating going?" Lindsay asked as they picked up pace.

"Smooth as cream. In fact that's the color Rhonda Johnson's selected. That condo's gonna be so full of cream you can churn it, thick buttery cream with lime green accents, including the carpet."

Lindsay grimaced.

"It's not really as bad as it sounds. I talked her out of adding a touch of lavender and brilliant orange. Seems she's been reading some avante garde magazines. Lime and orange are the new waves of haute décor."

They ran for several minutes in silence, each forming mental pictures of the Johnsons' new home. Finally, Patty spoke, "Gawd, Lindsay. If it hadn't been for me, no telling what that woman would've done. At least by the time it's finished, it'll have some class."

Lindsay nodded. If class was what she wanted, the woman would get it. Patty Crandall's house was a perfect example. Its aristocratic style was a tribute to old money and its antiques could be traced to the Civil War. "The Wa-wa of the Northern Aggression," as Patty called it, distorting the words with her accent.

Beauregard Crandall had found his soul-mate in Patricia Melinda Moore. The two were as southern as anyone Lindsay had met. The land on which she lived was once part of theirs, part of the remains of Crandall Plantation, divided at the death of Beau's father.

Lindsay noticed Patty looking longingly at a rest area. "Need to take a break?"

Patty nodded. "Yeah, I've already got toilet separation anxiety."

Lindsay waited at the base of the dunes, taking the opportunity to bend and stretch, while Patty sought the relief of the public bathroom. The shell-speckled beach lay before her, sand mixed with sea-swept piles of ocean discards. She loved to examine the shells, each with its unique beauty, different in pattern and color. She was looking at the barnacled remains of a broken conch when Patty returned.

"Pretty, huh?"

Lindsay nodded her head in agreement and tossed back the shell. They resumed their conversation as they backtracked. After a few minutes, they stopped talking and pushed faster, then slowed to a jog as they neared home.

"See you tomorrow?" asked Patty.

"I'll be here," said Lindsay, picking up speed toward her patio.

Afterwards, she fixed cinnamon toast and coffee, grabbed her notes from the previous day and read while she ate. After a quick shower, she drove to Ryder's office, told him about her upcoming meeting with Dr. Skalato and asked if he wanted to go.

"You go on," said Ryder. "We've still got files to look through. Give me a call when you finish."

There was little traffic as she left Brunswick. Highway 17 stretched before her like a long flat ribbon. Realizing she was clenching the steering wheel, she forced herself to loosen her grip. Her neck and shoulders were tight and tense. She turned on her car radio, switched through channels and stopped at the sound of a talk show.

"This is Nathan Klineman, your host with the most, the most venom, the most vengeance. We'll get 'em, folks. Just let us know what's happened to you."

A meek-mannered man stammered onto the airways, complaining about an elected official.

"Our senator," said the host, sarcastically. "We have to call him that because of his position. I should say the senator. He's surely not mine. What an arrogant son-of-a, sorry folks, good thing I caught that, but you get my drift. What a sorry human being. Just a minute, the phone's ringing off the hook. Good for us, good for our sponsors. We have some angry callers, folks.

I think we've touched a nerve. Ha, if you want an opinion, I'll give you one. Let's take another call."

As the caller began to speak he interrupted her. "Come on now, are you defending that guy?"

"I just think you should have respect…," said a young African-American woman.

Before she could continue, he cut her off. "Respect? The man's fair game. If he wants to be treated with dignity, he should deserve it. That's the trouble with you females, you think you should treat e-v-e-r-y-body with respect. I can hear it now. We can't execute terrorists, it wouldn't be ree-spect-ful."

Lindsay changed the channel, cutting off his mocking, abrasive voice. She settled on the familiar sounds of Beethoven and was momentarily soothed as she drove toward Ridgedale. "A living victim," she mused, "could hold the key to unlocking the case."

Dr. Skalato had been non-committal and evasive, saying she couldn't discuss a patient over the telephone. Maybe the woman had responded to treatment. Lindsay felt a surge of hope, or maybe the doctor was just referring to confidentiality. If she could just talk to Dorothy… She gazed at the speedometer. Oops, eighty-five. She eased up on the accelerator just before passing a trooper parked by the side of a bridge.

It was 10:55 when she turned into the narrow unpaved drive leading to the hospital. The road was almost hidden by a forest of loblolly pine and as the car bumped against the uneven driveway she slowed to a crawl. Rounding a bend, she was surprised at the size of the complex before her. A wide, flat-roofed building dominated the landscape. Two long wings branched outward from either side. The structure was surrounded by a long circular drive, dotted by clusters of wood-frame cabins. A stocky black man in a white uniform met her as she got out of her car.

"Dr. Lindsay?" he asked, his large brown eyes squinting against the sun.

"Yes." She flashed her identification.

"Hardy Truitt." He extended his palm. "Dr. Skalato is expecting you."

She followed him into a large waiting area comfortably decorated with plump-pillowed sofas and tables piled high with magazines. A heavy matronly woman sat behind a desk, typing on a computer. She smiled and nodded as they passed. They turned into a long corridor and walked almost to its end before coming to a door marked "Evaluation." He tapped lightly before entering.

"Dr. Lindsay's here," he announced. He motioned for her to go in, stepped behind her and left.

The walls of the office were covered with posters of lovable animals and motivational messages. Medical texts and journals were stacked on a small bookcase and more were piled on the carpet. A small woman in her fifties, Dr. Skalato sat at a table covered with reports and memos. Her loose fitting flowered dress and flat-heeled shoes gave her a casual air. She pulled a strand of brown hair away from her forehead, revealing sparkling hazel eyes. "Martha Skalato," she said, extending her hand. "Sit down. We're very informal here; Makes the patients feel more at ease." She motioned Lindsay to a nearby chair.

As she sat, Lindsay gave the doctor a questioning look and Dr. Skalato's expression turned serious. "I understand your need to solve this case, but my concern is for my patient. I have never encountered anyone as traumatized as Dorothy."

"Does she remember anything?"

Dr. Skalato was silent a moment before answering. "When she came, she was terrified and unresponsive. She refused to eat or drink and we gave her food and water intravenously. Her muscles were rigid and she never looked beyond her immediate gaze. It was as if she were transfixed by images only she could see. Months passed before we made any progress."

She leaned forward and looked at Lindsay intently. "Despite their withdrawal, we find it helpful to place this type of patient in proximity to others. One evening Dorothy was placed in the group room where the more lucid patients watch TV and play cards. Some of the women were watching a movie. An orderly is supposed to screen the programs, but that night, he failed to do so. There was a scene depicting a violent sexual assault. During the rape scene, the actress playing the victim began screaming. Suddenly, Dorothy began screaming with her. She screamed without stopping for fifteen minutes."

A sad look crossed the doctor's face. "I was on call that night and got to her quickly, but I couldn't calm her. She was shaking from head to toe. Eventually, she began to cry and I held her in my arms. She clung to me so tightly I had scratches from her fingernails. I've never seen anyone so filled with fear.

"When she stopped crying, she withdrew again. The next day, I noticed eye movement and decided to have her brought to my office each morning.

Nothing changed during the first few weeks; but gradually, she opened up."

"It's been like peeling an onion, layer by layer, unveiling her personality over a period of time. As she's become less guarded, we've been able to talk, but not about the attack. She knows we'll have to deal with it someday but she isn't ready. It's something that can't be forced and I won't push her."

"Dr. Skalato, women are dying."

"My responsibility is to this woman. There may be a time when I can help you, but that time is not now."

Lindsay started to speak, but the doctor held up her hand. "Dr. Lindsay, I know your mission is critical but you must see the importance of mine. Bear with me. I'll be able to reach her. It may not be as soon as you want, but when I do, I'll call you."

"May I see her?"

"We don't customarily allow it, however I can see no harm. There's a two-way mirror in each patient's door. You may peer in if you wish." She led Lindsay from the main building into one of the sprawling wings where large double doors opened into a nurse's station. They passed through the station and entered a hall with rooms on either side. Dr. Skalato stopped beside the first room.

"As you can see, there's an outside window where Dorothy spends most of her time looking out or occasionally reading. Sometimes she sits for hours just watching and waiting. She won't talk to anyone but me, not even her family. I visit her twice a day, in the morning and afternoon."

Lindsay peered into the room where a thin woman sat in a chair by a large picture window. Her gaze seemed glued to the woods beyond. She sat still, her hands resting in her lap, blonde hair hanging limply over her shoulders.

A noise signaled a message from Dr. Skalato's beeper. "I have to go. I'll show you out." Lindsay's heart was heavy as she walked back to her car.

19

Lindsay was entering her house when her phone rang. "We've got a possible lead on the fourth victim," said Ryder. "The night commander says a woman named Sanders called in so he referred her to me. Seems when she got back from vacation, her daughter was missing. A friend told her about the body and she'll be here in an hour. If she ID's it, you'll want to meet with her. I'll call you back as soon as I know."

"I'll be here." She told Ryder about her visit with Dr. Skalato and the doctor's promise to call if there were new developments.

Ryder sighed. "Don't hold your breath. I'm sure the good doctor means well, but I doubt we'll hear from her."

Lindsay heated a left-over slice of pizza and poured a glass of iced tea. Unable to concentrate on work, she passed the time doing laundry. It was almost three when Ryder called from the morgue.

"It's her," he said grimly. "We'll meet you at my office."

As she parked in front of the station, Ryder pulled into a space beside her. Lindsay got out of her car and walked to his, where a petite gray-haired lady sat in the passenger seat.

"This is Dr. Lindsay," he said to the woman. "Mrs. Sanders has identified her daughter. She'll help anyway she can."

The woman extended her hand out the open window and Lindsay saw she was trembling. Her grip was a limp gesture of politeness. There were dark circles under her eyes and an air of defeat about her. She stayed in the car as Ryder walked around to her side and opened the door. She continued to sit for several seconds before finally placing a foot on the ground as she held onto the car to make sure she could stand. Ryder took her arm as they climbed the station's steps and led her to his office. As they sat down, she turned to Lindsay and tears trickled down her face. "Why? Why would anyone want to hurt Cindy?"

"Perhaps this isn't the best time," said Lindsay gently. "We can talk later."

She grabbed Lindsay's arm. "No, no, please stay. I'll be all right. It's just a shock, such a shock." She dabbed at her eyes with a tissue.

"When was the last time you saw your daughter?" asked Ryder.

"I left for Chicago three weeks ago. Our family's from there. Cindy, Cynthia, couldn't go because she's, was, taking classes in Savannah every Monday and Wednesday night. I wanted her to go to the local college, but her friends were in a program at Armstrong Atlantic and she wanted to be with them." She choked back a sob.

"I called her several times while I was away and left messages, but got no answer. I thought it was strange she didn't call back but sometimes she gets caught up in what she's doing and forgets to let me know where she is. That's what I thought had happened. I wasn't worried until I came home. It looked like no one had been in the house for awhile."

"When was this?' asked Ryder.

"Yesterday. I called her friends, Judy and Carmen. They said they hadn't heard from her and thought she'd gone with me." Tears continued to run down her cheeks and she dabbed at her eyes again. She choked back another sob then quickly pulled herself together. "When I talked to Dr. Karen Krider, her professor at Armstrong, she said she'd missed four classes. I knew then something was wrong."

"Who was the last person to see her?" asked Lindsay.

"The Wednesday after I left was the last time Dr. Krider saw her. She teaches Community Health. Cindy always wanted to be a nurse."

"Did she usually go home after class?" asked Ryder

"Unless she had plans with the girls. They used to go over to the island when they had the same schedule and hang out at the bars. I pleaded with her not to, but you know how young girls are. The more I fussed the more determined she became but I thought she'd be all right with Judy and Carmen. This semester, Cindy was late registering and the class she wanted was closed. Since Judy and Carmen's class meets on Tuesdays and Thursdays, they've been getting together on weekends."

"Did she have a boyfriend?" prompted Lindsay.

"Oh, she goes out now and then, but nothing serious. Actually, it's been awhile since she had a date. She's been discouraged because she's never met 'Mr. Right'. I used to laugh about it. After all, she's only twenty."

"Did you notice anything different or out of place in your home?" asked Lindsay.

"Only that it seemed empty. Everything was pretty much as I left it. The house wasn't messy but the food in the refrigerator was spoiled. Cindy'd left clothes in the washer and they were mildewed."

"We'll check it out," said Ryder, "see if there's anything we can find."

"I know this is painful," said Lindsay. "May I drive you home?"

"I drove here. I can manage."

Lindsay looked questioningly at Ryder.

"Drive her car if she'll let you and I'll follow," he said. "You can ride back with me."

They spent the rest of the day in the Sanders' home searching though the girl's things. It was time-consuming and tedious as her room was crowded with stacks of magazines, notebooks and clothes. The closet was overflowing and drawers were stuffed with odds and ends, including souvenirs from restaurants and bars. Stuffed animals were strewn across an unmade bed. The CD player was on, but its music had long since ended.

Mrs. Sanders watched silently from the doorway. "It probably doesn't mean anything, but Cindy's Saturn is not in its usual place. She always parks it on the right side of the garage and I usually park on the left. When I came in from the airport, I almost ran into it because it's parked on my side."

Ryder and Lindsay exchanged glances and followed her to the garage.

"I haven't touched it," she continued, "I thought I'd just leave it where it is and let her back it out."

Ryder put in a call for the crime scene unit. Meanwhile, he and Lindsay looked through the car's windows but could see nothing unusual. A half hour later, they watched as the car was loaded onto a tow truck for processing and followed it back to the station.

20

The next morning, the ringing of the phone startled Lindsay from sleep. It was 8:30. She rarely slept past six, but the tension of the case had drained her and Patty had cancelled their run to drive the Johnsons to the airport for their trip home.

Ryder said, "No prints in Cynthia Sanders' ride. The car's wiped clean, but it's been near the pier. The county's resurfacing the roads in the village and there are traces of tar on the tires. Why didn't the bastard just leave it on the strip?"

He answered his own question before Lindsay could reply.

"Must have been afraid somebody saw him. If the car was later identified as abandoned, it might stick in their mind."

"He knew no one would be at the Sanders' house," added Lindsay. "Cynthia probably told him her mother was gone."

"We need a break," Ryder said angrily. "It's time we got this show on the road."

That afternoon, Lindsay was working at her desk when the phone rang again.

"I never expected this," said Dr. Skalato, "but it may be the answer you need."

Lindsay held her breath as the doctor continued. "I stopped by Dorothy's room, on my afternoon rounds. We talked and I mentioned your visit. I told her you'd come to ask questions, but understood she wasn't ready. She didn't respond and I talked of other things. When I left she was preparing for her nap. An hour later, the orderly called and said she couldn't sleep and was asking for me."

Lindsay held the phone so firmly her knuckles were white.

"I hurried to her room. I found her sitting on the edge of her bed, rocking, her arms clasped around her stomach. I've seen her do this before. Patients have that reaction when they're protecting themselves from pain."

Lindsay gritted her teeth to keep from interrupting.

"At first, she didn't notice I was there so I simply sat beside her and offered my hand. Finally, she took it, gripping me so tightly I thought she would break my fingers. We sat for forty-five minutes before she said 'He's hurt someone else.' It wasn't a question, it was a statement, as if somehow she knew. I said 'Yes, he's hurt many women.' She became quiet and I was afraid I'd lost her again but, after awhile, she asked for you. 'Bring her to me,' she said. I tried to talk with her more, but she ignored me repeating over and over, 'Bring her to me.' When can you come?"

"I'll be there as fast as I can." Lindsay threw on clothes, filled a travel mug with coffee and hurried to her car.

It seemed an eternity before she turned off the highway onto the road leading to the complex. As she pulled into the first vacant space, she saw Dr. Skalato coming toward her.

"She hasn't eaten and won't leave her room. I told her you were on your way."

The halls were quiet except for muffled voices coming from a cafeteria. They passed into the adjoining wing and through the nurse's station, then paused at Dorothy's door. The woman was rocking back and forth at a furious pace, her face contorted as if in pain. They entered quietly.

"Dorothy," said Dr. Skalato softly, "this is Dr. Lindsay." She placed her arm on the woman's shoulders to gain her attention and the woman froze in position and stared at them fearfully.

"Others are being hurt," said Lindsay.

Dr. Skalato frowned.

"Are they dead?" The woman whispered.

Lindsay glanced at the doctor who nodded her head.

"Some are dead. There may be others."

The woman drew in her shoulders with a shiver. There were chill bumps on her arms. "You haven't caught him," she said matter of factly.

"No," replied Lindsay, as they sat in chairs which had been placed in front of the bed, "and he's going to keep on killing until we do."

She began to rock again, this time more slowly, a blank stare on her face and then spoke in a flat, small voice. "I had a home in Brunswick, she said. "I lived there almost a year."

88

She took a deep breath, still staring straight ahead. "I felt safe there, and then I began to feel uneasy. There were things that bothered me. One day when I came home from work, I found a magazine in a different place than I'd left it. I thought at first I'd forgotten where I put it. Another time, a stool was moved. I thought I was losing my mind, forgetting things. A few days later, when I got home from work, I found a book I'd left by my bed on the kitchen stove. I knew I hadn't left it there because I always place my book beside my pillow. I called my co-worker Arthur and…"

She paused to gather strength, took another deep breath and resumed. "Arthur said somebody must have gotten in and been playing a trick. He told me to buy new door locks and he'd install them. The next day, I stopped by Home Depot and picked up two, one for the back door and one for the front, and new window locks, too." She laughed bitterly.

"You must have been very afraid," said Lindsay.

"I wasn't afraid; I was mad. A group of boys in the neighborhood are always pulling pranks and I assumed they were to blame."

Her next words came out in a rush, as if she were trying to get rid of them. "When I came home, the bathtub was full of water. I knew I hadn't left it that way, but figured the boys had been in again. I'd had a hard day and a friend was coming for supper. I was angry and tired and decided to rest to calm my nerves before she came. Since it was early January, the sun had already gone down and when I lay down I fell asleep. I was awakened by a noise, but at first, I thought I was dreaming."

She stopped, closed her eyes, and then haltingly continued. "My bedroom's the first on the right on the second floor. There is a streetlamp by the side of the house near the window at the top of the stairs and I always leave the door open so if I wake up in the night I can find my way to the bathroom."

Stopping again, she looked into Lindsay's eyes. "As I lay in bed, I heard water running in the bathroom and a shadow blocked the light." She began shaking and her eyes stared vacantly ahead. "He's coming in, walking towards me. What is that glittering? Oh, God, it's a knife. No, please, no….."
She rocked faster and faster, pressing her arms tightly against her chest. Dr. Skalato moved toward her but she gained control and then sat still, her body rigid. Lindsay began to speak, but stopped as the woman began to rock again, this time slower. "I couldn't see his face. It was dark and he was wearing a mask but he spoke and his voice seemed familiar, like I'd it heard before."
Her words trailed off as the shaking resumed, this time more violently.

"Enough." Dr. Skalato rose and moved toward her but the woman waved her away, calmed herself and continued.

"His voice was cold, unfeeling. He told me I must obey him and I must do what he said or I was going to die. He held a knife to my throat and pulled off my gown and... he hurt me." For a full minute, she couldn't go on and Dr. Skalato again started toward her.

"It hurt so bad, I thought he was killing me, that he would never stop, but when he finished, he took the knife, dragged the tip across my throat and cut off a lock of my hair." She raised her hand to her neck, touched her hair and than let her hand drop.

Lindsay saw a thin scar at the base of her throat.

"He pulled me out of bed and carried me to the bathroom. The tub was full and he made me get in and lie on my back; then he grabbed my feet and jerked me under. He held me down by my shoulders and I almost lost consciousness, but he suddenly let go and ran out. I pushed myself up and crawled out of the tub and screamed."

The doctor drew her chair closer to Dorothy.

"I thought I heard someone calling my name but he came back and stabbed me. He threw me hard against the tub and ran out again. I don't remember anymore. I think my head hit the sink." She stopped talking and her shoulders drooped as she began rocking back and forth again, this time with a slow, deliberate motion.

Dr. Skalato gestured for Lindsay to go out into the hall where she waited several minutes before the doctor joined her.

"I've given her a sedative. She'll sleep now."

"She said she recognized the voice," said Lindsay. "She…"

"Give her time. I know you're impatient for answers. But, she's very fragile. She'll be more helpful if you don't push her. To rush her would be disastrous."

"We can't wait much longer."

Dr Skalato raised an eyebrow. "If we push her now, she may never open up again. What she knows could be lost to her and your case. Do you understand?"

"I would never do anything to hurt her," said Lindsay.

"Then it's time for you to leave."

On the way back to Brunswick, Lindsay reported the results of the meeting to Ryder. Afterwards, she restlessly switched the radio from station to station trying to escape an ominous sense of foreboding. At home, attempts to work were fruitless. Finally, she logged off her computer, turned on the television and sorted through newspapers, saving articles about the drownings and trashing the rest. She'd done all she could to get help from Dorothy. Dr. Skalato was not going to allow her to see the woman again until she was certain she was ready, and in the interim, another woman could die. Ryder was as frustrated as she was but there was nothing to be gained by pushing harder. She went into the kitchen, fixed a tomato sandwich and Coke and returned to her desk. While she ate, she listened to the news, broken by intermittent teases and commercials. As she reached to turn it off, an announcer bellowed, "Find your true love."

Lindsay scowled.

"Follow your heart. Meet the man or woman of your dreams. Call True Luv, that's T-R-U-E L-U V, for your heart-to-heart connection or look us up on our website. Do it now." As if her life were not complicated enough.

Suddenly, a thought crossed her mind. Could it be? She grabbed the paper copied from Lynn's journal, picked up her cell phone, punched in the numbers, 8783588 and waited. A monotone voice presented a recorded message, "You have reached True Luv dating personals, your matchmaking wizard. To find your own special someone, male callers press one; Female callers, press two now."

Lindsay pressed two and the voice continued, "Regular callers press one. New callers, press two now. One of our customer representatives will be with you shortly."

She pressed two again and after a series of beeps, a male voice said, "Thank you for calling True Luv. This is the opportunity of your lifetime, a chance to meet the man of your dreams."

She cleared her throat.

"Don't be shy," said the man. "I'm here to help and your true love is waiting."

"How does the system work?" she stammered.

"It's simple. You place a recorded ad with a voice mailbox for only a small charge per month. You can also use our free talkline between the hours of seven and nine p.m. and our internet services. The regular voiceline runs twenty-four hours. For that there's a minimal fee, but I guarantee you, every minute is worth it.

"Signing up for the mailbox also entitles you to register and place your ads on our website. Most of our customers use both. They like placing ads on the internet and following up with the warmth of a human voice. The ads are the same for both and there is no additional charge. Many companies allow customers to email back and forth, but we found that dangerous, not because of our customers but because of the spread of viruses and problems with hackers. I'll sign you up for a trial period. We have a special discount this week and you can put it on your charge card, or we can work out payments. Which do you prefer?"

"I'll think about it," she muttered.

"Don't wait. Our offer ends Saturday. Do it today and I'll throw in an extra two weeks."

She remained silent.

"While you make your decision, I'll give you a temporary mailbox so you can browse the ads on line. Leave a message and your box number, if you hear one you like. We add new people all the time. If you don't find someone today, you will tomorrow."

"Women give their phone numbers to men they've never met?"

"It's not advised, although they may if they wish. I admit it simplifies things. Most of the women leave their voice mail numbers. That way they can screen their choices more easily. I can assign you a permanent one if you accept our offer. We take no responsibility for arranging meetings or their consequences," he continued, "and we suggest caution, but don't be afraid. We've had lots of successes, including several marriages."

"I'm interested in a woman who may have been a member," said Lindsay.

"I'm sorry. We don't give out members' personal information over the telephone. We leave that up to them." He lowered his voice. "If you're interested in that type of arrangement, you can place an ad in our Alternative Lifestyles category."

"No, that's not what I meant," she said hastily. Embarassed, she hung up and called Ryder. When he didn't answer, she left a message. Her phone rang less than five minutes later.

"I'm on the island," he said after she described her conversation. "The True Luv office is on the mainland. I'll swing by for you and we'll pay them a visit."

Lindsay hurriedly exchanged her shorts and top for a brown linen suit and tan silk blouse, pulled on hose and slipped into a pair of brown leather pumps. She was waiting by the drive when Ryder arrived. He got out of his unit and went around to Lindsay's side. At first, she thought he planned to open the door for her.

"Wait," he said in a warning tone. He filled his arms with items from the seat and floor, walked to the trunk, unlocked it, and dumped them in.

He began talking as they got into the car. "True Luv is a relatively new operation. A guy named Jack Carson started it four years ago. I haven't heard any complaints, but it's always seemed squirrelly to me."

"If Susan placed an ad, the killer may have answered," said Lindsay.

"Or vice versa. Hell, the guy may have his own ad, an easy way to finger his vics and gain their trust."

"Could he do that without being traced?"

"That's what we're going to find out." He paused and looked at her appreciatively. "Nice duds."

"Thanks."

He stuck his hand in his pocket and hesitated. "Want some?"

"What?"

"Gum, you want a piece of gum?"

He unwrapped a stick and stuck it in his mouth, as she watched and shook her head.

They rode the rest of the way in silence, crossing the causeway and making several turns through a series of narrow streets near downtown Brunswick. They finally stopped beside a forties style bungalow.

"I called ahead." Ryder rang the bell.

A thin, balding man, dressed in jeans and a wrinkled shirt immediately opened the door. "Jack Carson, come in."

Lindsay recognized the voice she'd heard on the phone. The man was not at all what she'd expected.

A concerned expression crossed Carson's face. "Surely, you don't think the ads are connected with the drownings."

Ryder and Lindsay said nothing.

"I'll help you all I can. Where do you want to start?"

"Tell us everything," instructed Ryder. "How the ads are placed, payments made, meetings set up."

Carson explained the process as he had on the phone. "We've never had any real problems, a few minor complaints."

Ryder frowned. "You pair women up with men they don't know anything about? It's a wonder we haven't got more bodies."

"Quite the contrary, Lieutenant." His tone was indignant. "Most callers use the chat line to get to know each other. It's much better than emailing a stranger on the internet and if they decide to meet, we recommend they do so in the daytime in a public place. Our clients are advised to exchange personal information only when they're comfortable with each other. As I said, we've had several marriages from the system." He beamed. "Yes indeed, we have."

"Can you place an ad anonymously?" asked Lindsay.

"We discourage it, but, yes, we have clients who send in money with no address. We process their ads because some people are shy."

"They don't even come in to sign a contract?" asked Lindsay in disbelief.

"Oh no, that can all be done over the phone. There's no reason why anyone should have to come in." He hesitated. "If you're looking for a particular person, maybe I could trace him or her but I can't guarantee it."

"How many men do you have?" asked Ryder.

"Hundreds, but they're divided according to age and category. For instance, there are eighty to a hundred in the aged twenty to thirty range. Of those, about half are looking for serious relationships. About one-fourth are in our casual dating category. Most of the others are involved in alternatives, gay, ménage 'a trois. We also have a fetish category, but not many sign up for that."

Lindsay raised an eyebrow and Ryder looked shocked. "What? I'd have expected it from a pimp, but a dating service?"

The man chuckled, "As I'm sure you know, our society's changing. Things are different from when we were growing up. There are a lot of unusual folks out there. Some are into couples' relationships. You hear it all on the system."

"So how does one get on?" asked Ryder.

"It's simple. To become a member, you purchase a block of time and record an ad. Time is subtracted when you listen to messages left for you and, if you're male, for the time you spend leaving messages for others. Time is also subtracted when you respond to callers on the live talk line except during our free talk period. Responding to male ads and talking on the live talk line are both free for females. Females only pay for running their permanent ad , the talkline, and picking up responses. It's easier than it sounds."

"Why the differences in pricing?" asked Lindsay.

"We always have plenty of males as members and during free talk time. Females tend to be more hesitant, more cautious. They like to learn the ins and outs of the system before they commit and some just want limited participation. They feel more secure because it seems less threatening."

Ryder shot him a dubious look, shifted his weight and began rubbing his leg.

"We've made it as safe as possible," Carson assured them. "No one can find out another caller's personal phone number or home address unless that person gives it to him."

"You said a person could become a member without giving their name," muttered Ryder.

"Most people pay their fee by credit card or check. Some send in cash or money orders. A person could make up a name I suppose. We don't trace calls so we rely on what we're told."

Ryder handed him a list of the victims and the man led them into a large room crammed with telephones and computers where he keyed in a command on the first terminal. "Our only match is Vicky Laker." He scanned the printout. "At least, she's the only one who had her own mailbox. She came on the system when we started four years ago."

As they turned to leave, Lindsay heard Ryder mumbling under his breath, "Listening to the ads'll be a nightmare. Do you realize the time it'll take?"

"It may not be so bad," she said. "At least they're profiled into age and category. With the exception of Vicky Laker, the victims we've identified weren't likely to have responded to anything kinky and nothing indicates any of them were gay. Ironically, if our guy's on the system, he'll give a profile of his own. Of course, he'll alter it to attract his victims."

"And if he's not on the system," grumbled Ryder, "We'll have used up a helluva lot of time we can't afford to waste."

21

The Tourist Trap, known for its seafood, was always crowded. Stacks of decorative nets and lattice-topped booths provided island flavor plus privacy, making the restaurant a perfect spot for a rendezvous. As usual, he waited and watched from a distance, concealed by a lattice partition.

How much easier it was having the women come to him. After several close calls, he'd decided entering the victim's home was too risky and the need for constant alertness was distracting. The alternative was having them come to him, which was as it should be.

Most of the women, his women, readily gave him their phone numbers, but he was selective, calling only those he deemed worthy. If they met his criteria, he asked for a date. The first meeting was a critical time of challenge and decision-making, a pivotal event determining their mutual destiny. Quick to spot his prey, he relished watching them approach. Sometimes, he suggested they wear blue but he preferred black. It was more fitting for the occasion, more funereal, more like the true color of the ocean.

At first, he never made contact, observing them from a distance, enjoying their squirming as they waited, their dejected expressions as they were leaving. When they left, he followed. After learning where they lived, he'd return to their homes at night, standing outside in the darkness, listening for sounds inside.

Gradually, he became more daring, entering while they were away, selecting an unsecured window or slipping the lock on a door. He chose those in homes shielded from view, isolated from neighboring houses.

By the time he entered their homes, he knew them, could describe their habits, their clothing, their friends. He memorized their schedules, knew when they were usually alone, when they ate and when they watched T.V. He listened and he observed.

Soon, it became a game. Once inside, he would move something sure to be noticed, and take a souvenir. He'd remove a contact lens from its case, a bottle of make-up, pieces of jewelry, and lingerie. Meticulously careful, he wore gloves, soft sole shoes and a ski mask.

Sometimes, he watched from within, practicing self-control and denial. He secreted himself in their closets, behind their sofas and under their beds. Later, he enjoyed meeting them face-to-face, sheepishly apologizing for missing their first "date," blaming it on his shyness. "You remind me of my younger sister," he would confide. "I'm just a sucker for long blonde hair."

From there, it was all too easy. The problem was what to do with them afterwards. He'd known immediately he'd use the ocean. It enabled him to reenact his birth as Brauner, over and over, each drowning a source of ecstatic pleasure.

Afterwards, he'd run out onto the road and to the beach. When there was moonlight, he bathed in its glow. Racing into the water, arms extended, he embraced the waves, connecting again with his victims.

****

At two, the woman appeared, and settled into a booth in the back as he'd requested. Too far away to hear her voice, he watched her nod her head when the waitress brought water. She sipped slowly, eagerly looking up as new diners entered. A petite woman, her skin was freckled, her hair knotted at the nape of her neck. A pair of glasses rested pertly on her nose as she scanned the menu. Fifteen minutes passed. She looked at her watch and frowned, half rose from her seat, hesitated, and sat down again.

He silently counted to ten, enjoying the remaining moments, delaying as long as he dared. Then, with a look of concern, he rushed to her booth. "Ginny? Sorry I'm late."

A fruitful afternoon followed. He questioned her about her background, her hobbies, her job, her hopes and dreams. It was almost five when he trailed her home to a summer rental on the southern end of the island. Staying a safe distance behind, he watched her park her car and walk to her porch and laughed to himself as she took the door key from under a rock. Without looking back, she went inside.

That night he returned. The windows in front were shuttered, but the ones in the back were open. He peeked into the den and the master bedroom which was brightened sporadically by flashes from a television. A phone rang.

"Hello, Oh Darlene, you won't believe this, but..." A commercial suddenly blared, drowning her words, and by the time he could hear her again she was saying goodbye.   Frustrated, he returned to his car.

He had decided to wait several days before calling her, not wanting to appear overanxious, but he was consumed by desire. He must get himself under control and not put himself at risk. He'd worked too hard to perfect his method to blow it all now.

The next day he ran before noon, and then a second time, racing along the beach as fast as he could. The incoming waves pounded the shore and licked at his feet. He savored the coolness against his skin as he ran through, over, and around the tide line. A storm was forming, churning the water, and blowing the wind against him. The surf drummed an echoing beat, as one wave ended and another was born. He fought against the stirring inside him. It wasn't time, too close to the last. Running faster and faster, he tried to drive thoughts of Ginny Delaney from his mind.

During their first meeting, he'd learned she was down for the summer, a writer working alone. "I don't know anyone on the island," she'd said shyly. "Have you met many people this way?"

"You're the first," he lied. "You sounded so nice, I rallied my courage and called you."

"I'm glad you did."

"You are?"

"I am." She'd nodded and smiled.

"Don't tell anyone about me," he pleaded. "My friends wouldn't understand."

"I promise, I won't tell a soul."

Thunder cracked and lightning split the sky. Rain came with the sting of windblown water, yet its coldness could not calm him. His thighs began to itch and burn, mimicking the feelings within him. Still, he ran onward.

22

The phone awakened Lindsay from a fretful sleep. She stole a glance at the clock before answering. It was 10:15 p.m.

"Dr. Lindsay? Martha Skalato. I hope I didn't wake you I know it's late, but Dorothy's asking for you."

It took a few seconds for Lindsay's mind to clear.

"After you left, she slept for several hours and I completed my rounds and came home. I was already in bed when an orderly called saying she demanded to see me. When I rushed to her room, she wanted to know where you were. She says she has to talk to you."

"I'll come right now."

"Oh no, please. I've given her another sedative and she's beginning to settle down. I wanted to let you know right away but she needs to rest. I insisted she wait until morning when she'll be stronger and better able to handle it."

Lindsay was on the way to Ridgedale by 7 o'clock. Again, Dr. Skalato was waiting for her. "I have misgivings about your coming back so soon. Remember, don't push her. Let her guide you."

They entered Dorothy's wing and the doctor led her quickly to the woman's room. A small Hispanic nurse left as they entered, a look of relief on her face.

Dorothy was seated on the side of her bed with her head down, eyes staring at the floor. Her hands grasped the edge of the mattress.

"Thank you for seeing me again," said Lindsay, as she and Dr. Skalato settled into the same chairs they'd sat in during their previous visit.

The woman opened her mouth as if to speak, then quickly closed it.

"Take your time," encouraged Dr. Skalato. "Take as long as you need. We'll be here."

They waited in silence until Dorothy finally sighed and looked up. "We need to get through this. I need to get through this. I'll answer any question you want to ask me. Tell me how I can help."

"The voice," began Lindsay. "You thought you recognized the voice."

"It was familiar, as if I'd heard it before." Her face contorted with pain and her body tensed, her hands still clasping the top of the mattress as she rocked slowly. "I knew he planned to kill me. I sensed it."

She sat still for a few moments. "Have you ever smelled fear? I remember smelling fear, a sick odor, heavy and sour, and ..." she paused, "it was coming from me."

"I know you didn't see his face. Can you estimate his size?" prompted Lindsay, "his height and weight?"

"He was heavy, muscular, not fat. Average height. I say that because I didn't notice how tall he was. If he had been tall or short, I would have noticed, don't you think?"

"Probably," she said gently. "Could you see his hair?"

"No, it was too dark and his mask covered his head. Oh, I'm afraid I can't remember. It's been so long ago and when we went into the bathroom, I was too frightened to notice anything. I'm so sorry. I'm not any help at all."

"You're doing fine. Anything you tell us is more than we know now. Dorothy, before you were attacked, did you answer or place an ad with True Luv?"

She blushed. "How did you know? Oh, I'm so embarrassed. I didn't think anyone...." She froze in mid-sentence.

Remembering what the doctor said, Lindsay remained quiet, giving her time.

Dorothy laughed nervously. "I answered a few."

"Did you ever meet anyone in person?"

Again a sharp laugh, "There was one man I really liked. I talked with him every Wednesday on the Chat Line. We scheduled a meeting in a restaurant, but he never came. I guess he chickened out at the last minute. I almost did. I didn't want to hurt his feelings by not showing up, then he didn't come. We never talked after that."

She clasped her hands over her mouth.

"Dorothy?"

"Oh God, Oh God."

"Dorothy?"

"That voice."

"Was it him?"

A look of terror crossed the woman's face. "It had to have been, but how? He never came. I waited and waited."

Dr. Skalato moved toward her but the woman waved her away.

Choosing her words carefully, Lindsay spoke in a soothing tone. "He could have gone to the restaurant. He could have watched from a distance and followed you home."

"How could I have been so stupid?"

"You were not stupid, you were dealing with an evil person. We can't expect ourselves to know how to deal with evil when we aren't evil ourselves."

"You think he planned it that way? You think he set up the meeting knowing I would come, that he would see me and follow me home?"

"It's possible. Listen to me, Dorothy. You are not to blame. You're not responsible. He attacked you. You mustn't forget that."

"But, what I did was careless."

"Stop," said Lindsay. "Don't blame yourself for something he did. You're a survivor, not someone to be blamed."

"I used bad judgment."

"Dorothy, your judgment has nothing to do with his guilt. Don't punish yourself for believing in him. We all make mistakes. Everybody has bad judgment sometimes. It doesn't entitle anyone to hurt us."

Lindsay looked closely at the woman, who was clearly shaken. Dared she question her more? She looked to Dr. Skalato for guidance.

"That's enough for now. Dr. Lindsay can come back." She remained in the room comforting Dorothy as Lindsay gathered her things and left.

Driving back, Lindsay felt a mixture of sadness and hope. The information was sketchy but True Luv had been used by the killer to lure Dorothy. At last, they'd found a connection. When she arrived home, she called Ryder and told him what Dorothy had said.

"Not surprising, I had a bad feeling about that place from the start."

"Me, too," she agreed. Afterwards, she made coffee and ate the last of Patty's cookies as Dorothy's words played over and over in her thoughts. She was haunted by the look of terror on the woman's face and her readiness to condemn herself for the killer's actions. A deep explosive anger built inside her, an anger she'd prayed she'd never feel again.

23

"We can have a real good time, baby doll," cooed the voice on the line. "How 'bout I meet you tonight?"

"No thanks," said Lindsay. "I've got to go now."

"Hey, wait a minute baby." She cut off the last part of his plea with the click of the phone and then straightened the papers on her desk, putting her notes in order.

After returning from Ridgedale she'd taken time to collect her thoughts and had come up with a plan. She'd explore the True Luv system, examining the website, listening to ads, narrowing the numbers by elimination. There were fifteen male callers on the chat line when she started. She'd already talked with eight. Most were friendly and open, giving no obvious cause for suspicion and from what she knew about Susan, the ones who were into phone sex would have been too frightening.

The ads were a different matter. She was basing her judgment on recorded remarks the men had prepared. Like commercial advertisers, they attempted to manipulate their listeners into responding.

Caveat Emptor.

People could be sold a bad bill of goods in relationships just as easily as they were sold poor products. In a strange twist of logic, she saw the two as the same. After a few moments of indecision, she'd decided to screen the recordings rather than go through the abbreviated ads she'd found on the internet.

Her watch said almost six and after hours of listening, her early fascination turned into frustration. She microwaved a pasta dinner and ate it while watching T.V. Skipping through channels, she stopped on a station where the announcer was interviewing the Glynn County Chief of Police. The camera caught a group of people who were demonstrating outside the police station, demanding action in finding the "Blackwater Killer." She turned off the program, took her plate to the kitchen and then returned to her desk and picked up the phone.

Within seconds, she was back on line. Selecting the twenty-five to forty year age range, she chose males wanting steady relationships, of which there were seventy-five. She listened as the men talked about themselves and the types of women they wanted. She'd profiled the killer. Now, she used the profile she'd developed of his victims. He'd be looking for a woman in her twenties or thirties with long blonde hair. Unassertive and shy, the woman would be living alone, or likely a tourist. Raised in a religious, patriarchal family, she'd have a poor self-image despite being attractive. As the evening wore on, Lindsay realized she'd made little progress. Ryder was right. It was going to take time and if the case continued to stall, the killer would strike.

24

The call came the next day. Ryder took it, then alerted the others. A writer named Ginny Delaney had failed to meet a deadline for *Coastal Travel* and the magazine's editor couldn't reach her by phone. After numerous attempts, he sent a colleague to check on her. Finding no one at home and her car in the drive, he called the landlord who called the police. They were standing outside when Lindsay and Ryder arrived.

"I'm Tony Cofer from *Coastal Travel* and this is Ginny's landlord, Jody Neal." Ignoring Ryder, Neal extended his hand to Lindsay, "I didn't know police could be so charming."

Ryder glared at the man who quickly withdrew his arm. "How long have you been trying to reach her?" he snapped, directing his attention to Cofer.

"I came this morning. When I couldn't find Ginny, I called him." He nodded toward Neal. "He said to wait, and he'd meet me here."

Lindsay and Ryder looked at the gray-shingled cottage before them.

"I was going to unlock the door," said Neal. "I thought she might be sick or hurt, but after all that's been happening, well, I decided to contact the police."

"How long has she lived here?" asked Ryder.

"She didn't actually live here," said Cofer. "She's here on a summer assignment. Our next issue features Georgia beaches."

"She rented the house about a month ago," Neal added.

Mr. Cofer nodded his head. "It's a central location and a quiet place to work. We were to meet her at the office this morning to go over a story. It's not like her to forget, especially not to call. We're located in Savannah so we're only an hour away. The boss asked me to drive down and see what happened."

"That's her car?" asked Lindsay.

"Yes," said Cofer.

They peered into a locked gray Honda, parked in front of the garage. Seeing nothing suspicious, they walked around the house, examining windows and doors, looking for signs of entry.

"Here," said Ryder, pointing to broken shrubbery outside the bedroom window. Curtains were only partially drawn, allowing a full view of the room's interior. There were indentations in the sandy soil, but the recent rain had obliterated any footprints. "The window's locked, but the ground's trampled, as if someone was standing, looking in. Looks like a peeper spent some time here."

"Could it have been an animal?" asked Neal. "I know she had a cat."

Ryder pointed to a cluster of bent branches at the base of the window sill, "Would've been a hell of a tall one." He stared at the branches and back at the ground as he reached into his pocket, withdrew a crumpled pack of gum, and held it toward them. As they shook their heads, he pulled out a piece for himself. Wadding the wrappers into a ball, he stuffed them and the remaining gum back in his pocket. For a minute, no one spoke. Ryder continued to stare at the window and ground.

When he was finished, they followed him along the side and front of the house where dense myrtle hedges covered the lower half of its exterior, reaching above the bottoms of the window sills. The shutters were open but curtains blocked their view.

After careful inspection, Ryder took the key from Jody Neal and opened the door.

"Wait here," he instructed the others as he and Lindsay walked cautiously inside.

Ryder suddenly jumped to the side and grabbed for his gun as something shot past them, through the door, and onto the lawn.

"The cat," said Lindsay, placing a restraining hand on his as he grinned ruefully.

In the kitchen, they found a bowl on the floor caked with dried remains of food and an empty water pan. Ryder peered into the laundry room, discovered a litter box and recoiled in disgust. "Phew, I knew there was a reason I don't have a pet."

They walked through the rest of the house but nothing seemed out of place. As they started to leave, Ryder noticed an answering machine on the kitchen counter with a blinking red light. He used a pencil to press the corner edge of the button for message retrieval.

"Hey girlfriend, this is Jan," said a female voice. "Just checkin' to see how you're doin'. Call me when you take a break."

There was a beep, a pause, another beep and a series of messages from the magazine, interspersed with more messages from Jan. No others followed.

Ryder let the tape come to an end, but didn't reset it, so the messages were not erased.

While they were listening, Lindsay lifted the cat's pan to the sink and added water. Reaching into a cabinet, she removed a can of cat food, opened it and put its contents in the bowl. Then, she eased past him, emptied the contents of the cat box into a clean trash bag, poured fresh litter into the box and took the bag to a can outside.

"What are you doing?" he asked.

"The poor thing is probably starved. We've got to find it and feed it."

"We'd better get that animal back," said Mr. Cofer from the doorway. "Ginny adores her. Name is Shadow." It took thirty minutes to persuade the cat to return. Lindsay finally lured her back in with the bowl of food. As they were about to leave she saw a torn piece of paper on the floor. She carefully picked it up and handed it to Ryder who read the series of numbers and raised an eyebrow. "True Luv?"

"True Luv." She nodded.

That afternoon the task force gathered with increasing urgency.

"Frost's report on Susan Adams indicates she was in the water less than two days," Ryder told them.

"There's a period of time between abduction and drowning," interjected Lindsay. "He's keeping them for awhile before he kills them. We need to find his holding area."

"Then Ginny Delaney…" Wong began.

"May still be alive," finished Ryder.

"I think I've found something," Wong added. "We don't have a lot of information about the first bodies, but we do know where they washed up. I compared them with the others and they have something in common. They were all found within a short distance of the Sound."

"Does that tell us where they were killed?" asked Collins.

"Not exactly, but, it does limit his range."

"How?" Collins looked puzzled.

"For the bodies to float inward they have to have been dumped or killed close to the beach. Any further and the current would have dragged them out."

"Like those boats that drifted up last year?" asked Collins.

"Right," the diver nodded. "They had engine trouble, remember?"

"The Coast Guard rescued the occupants by helicopter," said Collins. "In each case when they went back for the boat it was gone. Funny, how they happened within a few days of each other. Both boats washed up on the beach, one where the first victim was found."

"Not so funny," said Ryder. "That went down on Labor Day weekend. The drivers had been drinking and ran out of gas, but Wong's right, it shows a pattern of movement."

"How the hell can we expect..." Morrison began.

Lindsay cut him off, "We've got to act fast to find Ginny alive."

The others looked at her.

"By now the guy knows we're on the lookout," said Collins. "He'll probably change his dumping spot."

Lindsay shook her head. "No. His plan's worked every time. He's locked into it now. To change would be conceding power to the police. He'll do what he's always done to prove he can."

Ryder pointed to the whiteboard behind him. "Like Dr. Lindsay said, we're running out of time. I've divided the island into a grid. We're going to make a house-to-house, building-to-building search of anything looking suspicious including the southern and northern ends." He pointed at an area at the top of the grid. "It's like a jungle in those wetlands. The undergrowth is heavy and the mud is deep, but it's got to be checked. There's only one way to do it and that's by foot. Miller and Chaffin, will cover the north, Holbrook and Hunter, the south."

He looked up as Dixie Boatright stepped hesitantly through the doorway. "Yeah?"

"Pay no attention to me," she simpered. "I don't want to interrupt but here's some Coca Colas and ice. You've been in here so long, you must be thirsty."

Ryder waited impatiently as she placed a tray with cups of ice and sodas on the table, and then tiptoed out with a last longing look at her boss.

They fixed their drinks, and settled back in their seats, some glancing at their watches.

Standing was hurting Ryder's leg and he shifted his weight. "As I was saying, we'll check those wetlands and make house-to-house searches."

"Can't do that," Morrison said dismissively. "Leastways not without warrants."

Ryder's eyes narrowed. "I'm not suggesting we go inside," he said with an edge to his voice. "We can learn a lot about who's in there just by knocking. With some, there won't be a need to do that."

"Let me get this straight," argued Morrison with a smirk. "You want us to knock on the door and ask if the killer is home."

They laughed to defuse the growing tension.

"What the hell I want you to do," said Ryder slowly, "is to find places with deep-water access, particularly in secluded areas. If the house is vacant or its residents seem squirrelly, we'll put it on our list of hidey holes. No one goes by his lonesome. I'm assigning trainees to you and Collins."

Morrison rolled his eyes.

Ryder froze him with another look as he added "We want to act like we're just seeking information, officers asking questions, looking for leads. Who knows? We might actually get one. Another thing. We've got a lotta officers coming in to help, not just our guys, but from FLETC, Camden and McIntosh…other counties if we need them. Jekyll will be handled by the State Patrol. That's their domain and they know what to look for. The rest of St. Simons will be covered under Sgt. Eddie Van Buren, our day watch commander. He'll coordinate his search with the guys coming in.

Lindsay waved for his attention. "You should leak the plan to the media. Say you're doing a routine canvass so the killer won't feel threatened."

Ryder nodded. "Good idea. I'll tell the chief. We still have time before the six o'clock news." He paused. "Any questions?"

Feet shuffled and chairs squeaked but everyone was silent.

"Collins, take the developed area on the southern end. Morrison, go north. Start at Rastus Point and work your way up. Pay particular attention to houses off the main drag. If they don't look safe, back off. Some of those places are isolated. Don't approach without telling dispatch. We want to know where you are every step of the way."

Morrison rolled his eyes again. "Maybe you'd like to send Dix with me for protection." He grinned as his fellow officers howled.

Wong asked, "What about the three houseboats anchored in Bullard's Pass and the trawlers at the dock?"

"Overlook nothing," stated Ryder, still glaring at Morrison, wondering if he should replace him.

Wong nodded. "I'll check them out. They're used to seeing me around. I'll also ask the shrimpers if they've seen anything."

"We need all the help we can get," said Ryder. "This is like sifting through beach sand."

Lindsay stood. "There's one thing in our favor. He's escalating. Something's triggering him to act faster. That means there'll be less time between victims, but it also means he's losing control."

"It's time the son-of-a-bitch made a mistake," snarled Morrison.

Lindsay shot him a steely look. "Yes, but let's hope it doesn't cost Ginny her life."

25

Collins drove over the last bridge onto the island, swung a wide right and headed toward its southern tip.

"Not much going on," commented Don Jacobs. The rookie was bored and disappointed. His freckled face, unruly red hair and thinness, made him look like a teenager. He finished a chocolate-covered donut and licked his sticky fingers.

"Give it time," said Collins, pulling a roll of paper towels from under his seat. "It's early. A lot of people aren't awake. You never know what we'll encounter." He handed the towels to the officer.

The young man tore one off, wiped his hands and face, and settled back with a dejected look.

Collins raised an eyebrow. "Something bothering you Don?"

"Yeah. When our classes ended last Friday, I was hoping to get assigned to that drug stakeout on Adrian Road."

"Tediousness and terror," mumbled Collins.

"Huh?"

"Police work. Ninety percent tediousness, ten percent terror. Most days are routine. Take an investigation like this one. It boils down to footwork, asking questions, getting leads, following them up, asking more questions and getting more leads, then bingo, your ten percent of terror happens. Trouble is you never know when it'll hit."

Jacobs looked at him with interest, assessing his calm demeanor, the crispness of his uniform, his muscular body and close cropped hair. The man could take care of himself in a fight, he thought to himself.

Collins caught his gaze and, embarrassed, the young man looked away.

"The hardest thing," said Collins, his voice firm but kind, "The hardest thing is learning patience. I wish I could tell you there are shortcuts but there aren't. The best officers are steady, consistent and patient."

"Like 'The Rock'?"

"You got it, like 'The Rock'."

They approached a narrow side road where they noted three cottages overlooking the ocean, remnants of days when island living was more affordable. Spanning large lots, they were almost on the rock-strewn tide line, their weather-beaten clapboard fronts hidden by massive oaks.

Collins parked in the drive of the first house. "Wait here," he ordered. He walked quietly to the door where he listened before ringing the bell. A series of chimes echoed followed by silence. Moving around a small hedge, he walked slowly toward the back, taking no chances. At the rear of the house, he found two windows with partially open shades. Peering through the glass, he had a clear view through the kitchen and into a family room. The refrigerator door was open, revealing an empty interior. On the counter was a sign stating "Welcome Guests." He continued around the house and returned to the car. "Rental house. Empty," he told Jacobs as he settled behind the wheel.

The young man fidgeted. "How long we gotta do this?"

"Til we're done," answered Collins. He shifted the car into gear as Jacobs fiddled with the radio until he found a station playing hard rock music. Collins grimaced, reached over and turned down the volume.

The second cottage was a hundred yards away. As they approached, they saw toys strewn across the lawn and a car backing out of the drive. Two young girls strolled toward the beach with sand-pails and shovels. They drove on by. Collins turned the radio lower. "What made you decide to become a cop?"

"I dunno," said Jacobs. "Guess I was lookin' for excitement. Not much happenin' where I'm from back in Folkston. All we got there are swamps and pines. I'm already twenty-one, figured if I didn't get out soon, I'd end up like my dad spending all day in a loggin' truck. "

The third house, nestled in a thicket of overgrown scrub oak looked almost abandoned. They parked on the road by the yard.

"Wait," Collins ordered again, getting out of the car with his senses alert. His hand hovered above his gun as he walked along the weed-covered drive. A great blue heron erupted squawking from the weeds and flew into the woods. The windows of the house were curtained and the doors were locked. Layers of sand covered the back deck and gathered in drifts against the walls. There were no footprints or other signs of life. No one could have entered or left without leaving a mark.

To be sure the house was vacant, Collins climbed a stairway to a narrow balcony. Curtained glass doors led onto it and several rocking chairs leaned against the railing, their backs turned upward. He continued his search in the front of the house where a swallow flew under the eaves. Following it with his gaze, he noted a nest over the door. It'd been there awhile, delicately balanced between the screen and door facing. To open the door would knock it down. Reassured by its presence, he returned to his car.

****

Morrison's day had started with a jolt and was getting worse. His wife was in one of her moods. Ryder had assigned him a list of houses and subdivisions on the northern end. He was late getting started and now he'd have to deal with a starry-eyed new recruit. Didn't he have enough problems? Hell, what did Ryder think he was? A nanny?

"Shit," he said, driving into the station. He'd forgotten his lunch. There was no sign of the young cop, so he decided to return home. Ten minutes later, he entered the living room. Stumbling over papers and piles of laundry, he walked to the rear of the house. Thank God, the kids were back with their mother.

"Mandy?" he called. No response. He heard the low rumble of the bedroom television.

Damn, he yearned for Doris. If only they could've worked things out but with Mandy pregnant… Shit. Life had a way of gettin' even. Screw up, he gave a bitter laugh, or screw around, and you'd pay for the rest of your sorry-ass days. He looked in the bedroom and saw her sprawled on the bed asleep, her nightgown caught around her thighs, her face hidden under a pillow. It was only ten and she'd been drinking again. God only knew what it was doing to the baby. Frowning, he turned off the sound of MTV, pulled the spread over her legs and went to the kitchen. A bottle of gin sat open on the counter. For a moment, he stared at it. Oh hell, why not? He took a glass from a cabinet and filled it half full, added a dollop of tonic water from the refrigerator and gulped it down.

"Shit," he said aloud, ashamed of himself. He didn't need any more problems but at least it'd smooth the edges of an already rough day. He glared at the food-encrusted dishes stacked on the table and, feeling a growing warmth inside, knew the gin was kicking in. His tension dissipating, he fixed another drink. He swallowed it quickly and placed the glass in the sink, grabbed his lunch and turned towards the door.

He sat in his patrol car as the alcohol and heat worked against him. Even with the windows down, the temperature was unbearable. The hot humid air overwhelming him, he remained at the wheel reluctant to leave.

"This at least is mine." He gave a short sarcastic laugh. The car was his refuge, encasing him like a bell jar. He felt comfortable in it. It was the only part of his world he controlled, a haven from the unpredictable climate of home. Sometimes at night, he sat in it just to get away. He turned the key, flipped on the air conditioning and closed the windows, listening to the engine. In his mind, the car was a living thing. The rhythm of the motor was like a heartbeat, another presence when he felt alone.

He shifted into drive, and lightly pressing the accelerator, eased onto the road. His body was relaxing. Putting his wife out of his mind, he steered out of the modest subdivision and drove to St. Simons where he saluted the guard at the gate as he pulled into Huntington Point and checked in with police dispatch.

"You have a rider waiting," said the dispatcher.

Hell, he'd forgotten the rookie.

"Be there when I get there," he answered, determined to get on with his part of the search. The guard raised the arm over the entrance and Morrison drove forward. What if the guard was the killer? He laughed. The thought gave him a perverse sense of pleasure as he looked at the homes before him, picturing their occupants.

"Damn rich bastards," he sneered. He couldn't count the number of times he'd been here, dealing with their petty little crimes, flower gardens trampled, teenagers out of control, and of course, the occasional domestic. Those were rare. Not that they didn't happen. Who'd report them? Who'd hear screaming behind closed doors an acre away?

A killer under their noses? The thought had a certain appeal.

He checked his map and turned into a cul de sac. The large lots allowed wide spaces, even woods, between houses. He remembered seeing them from the river when he'd gone fishing with a friend. From the water, their docks looked like arms stretching into the marsh. He stopped by a columned colonial, got out of the car, and slammed the door. Climbing up a circular stairway, he peered through two stories of windows, their blinds pulled high.

The first floor was dominated by a large recreation room, a pool table in its center. Its long wet-bar activated his thirst and his tongue felt thick and dry. Wide front windows offered a view of the second floor living area. Several open doorways led to other rooms. As he walked downstairs, he saw a large air conditioning unit behind a clump of azaleas. Silent, its sides were covered with spider webs. Either its owner wasn't home or the damn thing must be broken. "Too hot," he thought, "Nobody could stay in there with the windows shut." The thought of the heat inside made him even thirstier.

The second house was on the interior side. A contemporary, it looked out of place among its counterparts. He wondered how its owner had sidestepped Huntington's stringent building code. Scanning the inside through a glass door, he saw no sign of life.

Workmen surrounded the third. Recently sold, he knew it was being remodeled. Only five more houses to go before his lunch break. Seeing children at play and occupants walking dogs, he rode past them quickly. This was an exercise in friggin' futility. The killer was not going to be found in Huntington.

He saluted the guard again as he left. Were Collins and the others having any luck? He started to call in but, feeling woozy, thought better of it. The rookie might still be waiting and he'd rather not deal with him. If enough time passed, maybe the kid would be assigned to someone else.

The heat was getting to him, hadn't used to, but he was getting older. Hell, he'd be forty-eight in August. Mandy was already fussing about her age at twenty-nine. Deep in thought, he almost missed a secluded drive. He slammed on the brakes and felt a sudden surge of dizziness. Beads of sweat dotted his forehead as he turned down the zigzagging path. Tall weeds brushed the bottom of his car and he cursed as low-lying limbs dragged against its roof. "Who the hell would want to live back here?"

An armadillo scurried across the road into a patch of palmettos. "Damn developers. Even the animals don't have anywhere to go." The thought made him angry. Soon, the island was going to sink from all their damn houses. As he drove, his mind drifted to the days of his youth. There were real woods then and places to go to be alone. Now, tourists were everywhere, and kids, always getting into trouble, thinking they can get away with anything. His oldest son was an example. Doris hadn't been able to control him in over a year. He dreaded thinking how the baby would turn out, with Mandy's drinking and immaturity.

A sharp scraping sound caught his attention and he stopped, motor still running, to determine its source. Through the windshield, he could see a wire stretching across the hood. One end was attached to a tree, the other to a post. He got out, jerked one of the ends free, and tossed it aside.

"Friggin' kids." He got back in the car and continued towards the end of the drive.

26

Thoughts of Ginny and her cat haunted Lindsay's morning run.

"Beau's scared for me to be on the beach now," panted Patty. "If you weren't with me, he wouldn't have let me come. Last night I was an hour late from shopping and he had the biggest hissy fit you've ever seen."

"He's looking out for you. At least you know he loves you."

"But Lindsay, it's not like I'm a ten year old. He hardly lets me out of his sight." She paused. "I'm just dyin' to ask, have ya'll got any leads yet?"

Lindsay shook her head.

"I know you can't discuss case secrets, but I was just wonderin' if there was anything you could tell me."

"I wish there was, Patty. I really do. So far we haven't made much progress."

"Well, I'll tell you one thing. It gives me the creeps, having that body found right on the beach. Do you realize how close that was to my house?"

"The body drifted there. She wasn't killed there."

"But still. Just think about it. I mean I would have never expected such a thing to happen in a million years. Not here. Not where we live."

"Nobody ever expects it. That's why so many killers get away with it..."

Patty was silent the rest of the run and Lindsay thought again about the cat. As soon as she was home, she called Cofer and Ryder and arranged for them to meet her at the rental cottage.

Despite a gruff display of protest and inconvenience, Ryder helped coax the animal into a carrier, mumbling under his breath about the sadness of it being alone. Lindsay gathered the food, cat box and litter, and put it all into her car. The animal's cries pierced her heart as she drove. It was cruel to take it to an unfamiliar place, crueler still, to leave it in the empty house. Released inside Lindsay's kitchen, it ran through the hall to her bedroom and huddled miserably under her bed, ignoring the bowls of food and water she placed before it.

Just a few more ads. Another hour would do it. She made a second attempt at comforting the cat and returned to work. When she finished, she sorted through her notes and eliminated all but ten. Another two hours passed while she punched in their numbers and listened to them again. She recorded their messages onto cassettes, praying Dr. Skalato would allow Dorothy to hear them. If Dorothy could identify her attacker's voice, he was still in the system. When she finished, she reached for the phone. It rang before she could pick it up.

"Morrison's missing," Ryder growled. "There's no trace of him or his unit."

"When did he last call in?"

"Dispatch talked with him at eleven. He usually calls in for lunch around noon, but no one's heard from him."

Lindsay looked at her watch. Almost 3 p.m.

"That's a long time."

"Damn right," interrupted Ryder. "All hell broke loose around one, an eight car pile-up on I -95. It was after two when dispatch tried to make contact and assign him a call. When she couldn't get him, she called the chief. The last time he was seen was in Huntington. The guard remembers him leaving, says he didn't look good, might have been sick. His wife hasn't talked to him either. The damndest thing's no one's seen his ride."

"Could he have left the island?"

"Nah. Leroy Sims was running radar on the causeway. He saw Collins 'round one-thirty, says he would have seen Morrison, too, if he'd passed him."

"How can I help?"

"Stay put. If nothing pops, I'll be in my office. I'll let you know what we find out."

She hung up and thought about Dorothy, then called Ridgedale. Dr. Skalato was out of town and not expected back until evening. She walked to the kitchen, got a bottle of ginger ale, returned to her desk and turned on the tapes. The last ad bothered her. She replayed it, listening attentively.

"Hi, this is Carl. Thanks for calling. Uh, I've never done this before. My mother was sick for several years and I took care of her, so I haven't dated in a while. I've, uh, been out of circulation. It's kind of embarrassing, really, but life can get lonely when you're by yourself and I need a friend. Maybe we can get together." There was a brief silence before he continued. "My dream girl is between twenty and thirty-five, of short to average height and weight, with long blonde hair. A good Christian woman would be nice, someone loving and kind who likes to have fun." Again, there was a pause.

"Hey, if you don't mind, leave your home number. It'll be quicker and not as expensive. I'm saving my money for our date. Thanks, I hope to hear from you soon."

The words sounded practiced and detached, and beneath the man's shy demeanor, she detected a hard edge. Noting the mailbox number, Lindsay wondered if he was on the chat-line. She punched in the numbers but his was not among the voices she heard. She phoned his mailbox again. A chill ran through her as she listened to the ad repeated in the same muffled baritone. Convinced it could be Dorothy's attacker, she played the message over and over. Was there something between his mouth and the receiver, something distorting the tone?

27

It was seven when Lindsay called headquarters.

"Ryder."

"Anything from Morrison?"

"Nothing. He's vanished."

"I'm sorry, I…"

"Hell, we all are. It doesn't help the situation."

"This might. I think I've found the ad."

"Through the personals?"

"The same."

"How do you know it's him?"

"You'll have to trust me. I left a message for Dr. Skalato. I want to play the tape for Dorothy."

"You think Skalato will O.K. it?"

"Yes. Dorothy wants to help and she needs the closure. I'll call Mr. Carson tomorrow and find out if there's any way to trace that mailbox."

They were silent for several seconds.

"Ryder…"

"Yeah, yeah, I know what you're thinking. If I hear anything on Morrison, I'll call."

She was getting ready for bed when the phone rang, showing Ryder's number on the caller ID. "Nothin's poppin' on Morrison," he began, before she could speak. "We've searched every inch of the island, not a trace. Wong and I are going out on the water in the morning to take a look along the shore. Just wanted to let you know."

"I'd like to go."

"What about Dorothy?"

"Dr. Skalato hasn't called."

"Be at the Starboard Marina, five-thirty."

"I'll be there." It was almost ten. She slipped out of her clothes, took a long hot bath, set her alarm for five and went to bed.

When she awoke, she felt something heavy by her leg, near the bottom of the sheets. She froze in place, trying to think what it could be. Several seconds passed before she realized it was the cat. She reached down and gently stroked it's back, before getting up.

As she walked to the kitchen, the animal sped ahead and dashed under the table. Lindsay felt sorry for the small defenseless creature. Had they not gone into the house, it would have starved. She placed a bowl of cat food on the floor, rinsed and freshened the water pan, and fixed a bowl of instant oatmeal for herself. When she was finished, she dressed in shorts and a sleeveless blouse and drove to the marina.

As she got out of the car she was conscious of someone watching her and turned to see Ryder standing next to the dock, staring at her as she approached. Wong was walking toward him.

Ryder nodded. "We're waiting on David Reed."

Lindsay looked up in surprise. "Father Reed?"

"The residents know I work with the police," explained Wong, "and everybody knows my boat. Father Reed's is smaller and won't draw attention. We'll look like we're fishing."

Despite her discomfort, she suppressed a smile. Ryder was dressed in a blue cotton shirt and bright Hawaiian trunks. He wore black canvass high-top shoes, and binoculars hung from his neck. Wong wore cut-off jeans, a T-shirt, and dock shoes.

"You look like birdwatchers," she said.

"That's the idea," said Ryder gruffly. As they waited, shadowy profiles of boats stood out against the ashen sky. One side of the dock was crowded with shrimp boats, the other with sailboats and yachts. As the minutes passed, the trawlers came to life, each engine catching, then emitting a continual diesel drone. The sound of voices and the smell of coffee drifted on the salt-laden air.

Ryder looked at his watch and began pacing restlessly back and forth. They all looked up as David Reed's van crunched through the gravel parking lot and rolled to a stop beside them. Its lift whirred and he was lowered to the ground in his chair. Turning its wheels toward the ramp, he rolled onto the wooden boardwalk and motioned for them to follow. He'd replaced his black shirt and clerical collar with a yellow pullover.

Lindsay averted her eyes as they exchanged greetings and boarded the boat. Ryder and Wong untied the ropes and the boat slipped silently from its berth. Within seconds, Reed started the motor, set it at a low purr, and guided them onto the river. The morning dark was pierced by brightness as the shrimpers' floodlights lit their decks and surrounding water.

"They're ocean cowboys," commented Wong, "and shrimp are their salt-water gold. Most of them are loners. You might say this is their last frontier." They followed the trawlers under the causeway bridge and into the channel. Riding close to the marsh, they sliced through the slow undulating tide. Ryder opened a thermos and distributed steaming cups of coffee and Wong gave out bags of sandwiches as they entered the Intracoastal Waterway approaching St. Simons.

"Shouldn't we stay closer to shore?" asked Lindsay.

"The shrimpers say a couple of sailboats are anchored between Jekyll and St. Simons," said Wong. "If we swing a wide arc, we'll see them."

Cruising past the harbor, they encountered a flock of pelicans, drifting in the swell of the boats. Blinking channel markers lit their way around the end of St. Simons. Several trawlers were already heading home, nets raised, catch dangling. Gulls and terns flew behind them, swooping for by-catch. As they neared the ocean, Lindsay saw a cluster of lights in the distance.

"What are those?"

"More trawlers," said Wong. "It's a hot spot."

"What?"

"A hot spot, where they find lots of shrimp."

"How can they know where the shrimp will be?"

He reached into his jeans pocket and withdrew a tide-table. Running his finger down it, he explained, "See how the tide builds. It lets them predict when the shrimp will be washed out of the marsh, toward the beaches. It's like pole fishing. If you have a good spot, you hit the right time. At night, it looks like a city out here."

The rising sun glowed on the water and snatches of conversation squawked from the boat's CB.

"They know each other," said Wong, nodding toward the sound of the voices. "There's camaraderie out here."

"Come on by," said a shrimper, indicating it was someone else's turn to talk.

Wong picked up the microphone, "How's it going Jake?"

"That you Danny? Don't see your boat. Where are you? Come on by."

"I'm in the little one right behind you."

"Ain't like you to be cruisin'. Anything goin' down we should know?"

"Playing tourist, but I'll keep in touch."

"Let us know if we can help."

"Will do," said Wong.

Ryder sat by Lindsay so only she could hear him, "There's not a shrimper in this area Wong hasn't helped. They'd do anything for him. Boat people are like that, got a lot of loyalty to their friends. They have a community out here and he's one of them."

Wong pointed to where the sailboats were moored, several hundred yards apart. Sunbathers lay along the bow of one. On the other, three women were fishing.

Ryder's face showed his disappointment as he muttered "Guess we can cross them off our list."

They rounded the island's end with its golf courses and expensive homes. Passing a row of beach cottages, they turned toward the pier where fishermen and crabbers lined its concrete abutments. Wong frowned at the sight of children playing in the surf, "A dangerous area," he warned, "strong riptides." He paused. "The killer knows the tide and current patterns. He takes his victims out far enough to prevent a quick wash up on shore. If you were to drown someone here, they'd sink to the bottom and wash up with the next tide. The bodies we've found have tended to drift."

"That gives him more time to get rid of evidence," Lindsay added.

"Like cars," agreed Ryder, angrily jamming a stick of gum in his mouth.

They passed Neptune Park with its picnic tables and benches. Gulls glided and dove around a group of teenagers throwing pieces of food. As they passed the lighthouse, they saw another row of houses and the King's Hotel. Further onward, condominiums competed for space with smaller homes.

They cruised beside Massengale Park, an old Coast Guard station, a rental stand with beach floats and chairs and past more cottages. Following the shore, they wove a crisscross path around sandbars, barely seen below the ocean's surface. Several people had walked out from shore and were wading in shallow water. Wong stared at them in frustration.

"They don't pay attention." He pointed to a large 'No Swimming' sign. "No matter how many signs are put up, they still go out on the sand bars.

During slack tides, people can walk out and get back O.K. but different tide patterns mixed with strong current make them a death trap. It's also a feeding ground for sharks."

Lindsay shuddered.

"We've lost as many as six people in a year," said Wong, "on the sandbars alone."

"That's why we weren't worried about the first floaters," added Ryder. "It's tragic but it's just not unusual."

"Sounds dangerous," said Lindsay.

"It is," said Wong. "The marsh has hundreds of inlets, where the tide comes in and recedes, passing through with great force. Think of the rushing power of a waterfall and consider a similar gravitational force pulling horizontally. The bottoms of these inlets change constantly with the rush and return of the tides. There are swift currents and drop-offs. The surface of the ocean can fool you."

To demonstrate, Reed angled the boat within a few feet of a sandbar, idled the engine, and dropped anchor. The rope continued to unwind, finally stopping with a jerk. "There are underwater ravines all around barrier islands. Combined with a powerful current, they're deadly. Even strong swimmers are pulled under and out to sea, when the tide is running." Resuming their speed, Reed steered them back on course. A large boat passed close and fast. As the stern hit its swells, showers of spray fell over them.

"Damn," said Ryder.

Lindsay stole a long look at Reed as he focused on steering the boat. Ryder followed her gaze and looked back at her, with a curious expression.

Passing a small cove, they saw the hulking roof of the Crandall's massive old home and the outline of Lindsay's chimney. As they moved closer to shore and entered the marshes, the water became increasingly muddy. Small creeks threaded in and around banks of waist-high grass. Cutting the engine's speed, Reed turned into a slough.

"Bullard's pass," he said, indicating a scattering of houses.

"This area ain't been built up yet," said Ryder. "You can get to it through the marsh, but it's miles from the beach by land."

The houses were partially hidden by foliage, but one caught Lindsay's attention. A two-story, it had the timeworn patina of aged wood. A walkway led from its door to a dock and nearby boathouse. It was the perfect spot for a hide-away, but so were others they'd passed. Noting a tall stand of pines, she realized they were near the road where she'd encountered the runner. "Who lives here?" she asked.

Ryder held his hand over his eyes and squinted against the glare. "That's the old Mullis house. Their son comes down now and then. Last I heard, he'd moved somewhere up north."

"There's someone there now," she said. "I saw a curtain move."

Ryder stared at the windows. "Bears looking into." They continued to watch the house until it faded from view. It was several minutes, before another appeared.

"This is the area where Morrison was last seen," said Ryder solemnly. They were approaching Huntington Point. The edge of the marsh was covered with boardwalks, leading to upscale homes.

"Folks who live here are mostly newcomers," Ryder explained, "older and retired, or transferred in by the paper mill."

They swung around the end of the island and into the river. Houses, interspersed with wetlands, were set back further from view. Reed increased their speed and the boat beat hard against the waves. He'd said little during the outing and Lindsay was relieved. Risking a sideways look, she was glad to see him concentrating on steering. The last visit to his office had unnerved her and being near him made her uneasy.

The engine slowed and she looked up in surprise. They were already approaching the marina. Reed steered the boat into place and Ryder and Wong secured it to the dock. Reed turned off the motor, opened the gate and rolled onto the ramp.

Ryder looked discouraged, "Go on home," he said to Lindsay. "We'll finish here." He hesitated, than added hopefully, "Want to catch a bite of lunch down at the pier? Wong and I are going."

"Lunch sounds good."

They met at Papa's fifteen minutes later.

"What now?" asked Lindsay, sliding into a booth.

"A helluva lot of work," answered Ryder, sitting beside her.

Wong took the seat across from them and gave Ryder a questioning look.

"We're going to search every inch of this island," said Ryder.

"If the killer disposed of the car," began Wong.

"I know what you're thinking," interrupted Ryder, "but it'd be hell dumping Morrison's ride without being seen."

"There are lots of back-roads leading to boat ramps," insisted Wong. "He could easily hide a car and a body. At night those ramps are deserted and if he didn't have far to drive…"

"It'll take forever to search the creeks and rivers around those ramps," said Ryder. "There are six on the northern end, counting private land."

"Dogs," suggested Lindsay.

"What?" said Ryder.

"Water search with dogs," agreed Wong. "They've been used in lakes in North Georgia."

"Dogs lose scent in water," argued Ryder.

"Not so," countered Lindsay, "Well, not exactly so. A person gives off scent all the time whether they're dead or alive, in the air or under water. Dogs can be trained to pick it up."

Seeing Ryder's puzzled expression, Wong said, "A person's scent is made up of molecules. The soluble molecules dissolve in water, like sugar, or salt."

"As diffusion takes place," continued Lindsay, "the lighter ones rise to the surface and evaporate. Dogs smell the scent as it spreads through the air. Light insoluble molecules also rise but float on the surface and dogs can detect them."

Ryder looked doubtful.

"The GBI has a canine unit," said Lindsay. "I worked with their trainer, Bill Emory, on a case near the Tennessee border. The dogs located a body in a pond within an hour."

"Get 'em down here," said Ryder.

28

The boat had passed too close for comfort. Damn tourists, poking their noses where they didn't belong. He was sure he'd been seen at the window. But, why shouldn't he be? It was his house and they had no business near it.

Or did they?

Why had they turned down the slough?

Hell, they couldn't have been cops, not that group of nerds. He thought of the guy in the bright Hawaiian shorts and laughed. They were probably birdwatchers looking for osprey. Well, they wouldn't find any here.

He smirked. They were damn lucky it was high tide or they wouldn't have made it out, then their problem would have been his problem, a group of fool rednecks stuck in the mud. They hadn't stopped, probably hadn't seen anything that would interest them. Chances were they wouldn't come back, but if they did... if they did, he'd have a surprise. He'd teach them a lesson about sticking their noses into other people's property, one they'd never forget.

29

As soon as she was home, Lindsay called Bill Emory from her cell phone. No answer. She left a message on his answering machine, briefly explaining the need for his dogs. Frustrated at being unable to reach him, she started to put the phone down when she saw she had two voice mail messages from Dr. Skalato. She would be in all day and could talk between patients. Lindsay called her immediately and was relieved to catch her the first time she tried.

"I pray I'm doing the right thing," said the psychiatrist. "Dorothy's anxious to hear the tape. She wants to listen to it as soon as possible. Can you come today?"

"I can leave now."

Lindsay packed the tapes and cassette player into a satchel, changed into a dress, and stuck her hair in a bun. Just as she was about to leave, the phone rang.

"Bill Emory, Lindsay, what's up?"

She summarized the case, ending with Morrison's disappearance.

"I'll contact the team. If nothing's scheduled, we'll be there in the morning."

"Thanks, Bill." She hung up, and called Ryder.

"Yeah," he snapped, impatiently.

"The dogs will be here tomorrow unless there's a conflict. I'm off to Ridgedale to play the tape for Dorothy. Dr. Skalato's given permission."

"Call me as soon as you get back."

The short trip seemed to take forever. Tense, she tuned the radio to an easy-listening station. The music only agitated her more. She passed a convenience store and looked at it longingly. Damn, she wished she had a cigarette. For a moment she considered stopping, but it had been six months since her last one. She turned off the radio and continued driving in silence.

When she arrived at Ridgedale, she was met again by Hardy Truitt who led her to the doctor's office. "Dr Skalato's with a patient. Make yourself comfortable. She'll be with you as soon as she can. May I bring you a cup of coffee?"

"Yes, thank you." She paced several times across the small room, before finally sitting to wait. Within minutes, the nurse was back and placed a steaming cup in her hands. Lindsay barely finished drinking it by the time Dr. Skalato arrived, wearing a worried frown.

"I don't feel good about this," she said.

"It's the only chance we have to ID the killer."

Dr. Skalato hesitated, then motioned for Lindsay to follow her. "Just remember…"

"I won't push her," Lindsay assured her.

Dorothy was seated in the chair by the window and turned and looked up as they entered.

"Are you sure you're ready?" asked Dr. Skalato.

"I'm as ready as I'll ever be," said Dorothy, watching intently as Lindsay set up the tape player and inserted a cassette. They listened to several ads. At the end of each, Dorothy shook her head. Lindsay removed the first tape and inserted another.

Again, the woman listened intently and shook her head. They were almost finished when the last ad came on. Dorothy suddenly stiffened.

"Do you want to hear that one again?" asked Lindsay.

She nodded and Lindsay rewound the tape and repeated the message.

"That's him," she whispered, clenching her hands and closing her eyes. "It's him. I know it is. That voice. It's muffled, but I'll never forget it as long as I live."

Lindsay switched off the tape as Dorothy folded her arms and rocked back and forth. Her face was pale and she was shaking. Dr. Skalato reached for her hand and held it until she was still. For several moments, Dorothy was motionless, tears trickling down her face.

Lindsay stared at the two women, wondering if she'd made a mistake, pushed Dorothy too hard.

The doctor removed her hand from Dorothy's grasp and put her arm around her. "Take a deep breath. That's right. Breathe deeply until you feel calm. Let your hands and arms relax. We're here with you and no one can hurt you." Dr. Skalato and Lindsay locked eyes as the woman inhaled and released a slow breath.

"Another," the doctor whispered.

"I'm all right," Dorothy said at last. "I feel better now."

After a few minutes, Lindsay rose to leave. "Thank you," she said. "I know this was hard."

"She has a lot of strength," said Dr. Skalato, patting the woman's shoulder, "and she's showed a lot of courage."

Color returned to Dorothy's face.

"Will you let me know what happens?" she whispered to Lindsay.

"As soon as we have him, I'll call."

"Will you come back?"

"If you want me to, I will."

"I'd like that. I'd like that very much."

30

Lindsay phoned Ryder to arrange a meeting with Mr. Carson before leaving Ridgedale. "Dorothy recognized his voice."

"It's been a long time since the attack. Are you sure he's the right guy?"

"Judging from her reaction, I'd say yes. The ad gave me the creeps when I first heard it, sounds like his voice is disguised."

"I'll call Carson," said Ryder, "and meet you there."

Ryder was pacing the sidewalk in front of the True Luv office when Lindsay arrived. She rang the bell and Mr. Carson opened it almost instantly. "Oh dear. I thought that was you on the sidewalk," he said looking at Ryder and wringing his hands, "I never thought it would come to this, not in my wildest dreams. I can't believe one of our clients is a murderer!"

He motioned them inside, then abruptly stopped. "You don't think we'll be sued do you?" he asked, turning to Ryder. "We couldn't have known he was a killer. It's not our fault."

Ryder's face flushed with anger.

"Women are dying," said Lindsay coldly. "A lawsuit is the least of our concerns."

"Yes, of course, it's a bad situation for all of us. I must call my partner Albert. Albert will know what to do. He'll know a lawyer." He turned and walked toward a telephone.

Ryder's eyes narrowed in anger as he carefully measured his words. "Mr. Carson," he said firmly, "we aren't worried about litigation. If you won't help us, we'll get a warrant, tear this place apart and shut your ass down."

Lindsay shook her head and touched Ryder's shoulder to calm him as he turned to head out the door.

Carson paled and grabbed Ryder's arm. "Please, give me time to pull myself together. I never expected this to happen. I'm not unwilling to help.

Oh no, I'm not unwilling at all." He looked at Ryder, then at Lindsay. "You say you have a tape? A recording of one of our ads?"

She pulled the tape player and cassette from the satchel and he guided her to a table.

Ryder started to unroll its cord and plug it in.

"It's O.K.," said Lindsay. "I stopped and picked up fresh batteries."

She punched the play button and a man's voice filled the room.

Carson nodded."I know the box number and the message, but I can't guarantee the name. The gentleman who placed the ad pays by money order and makes his recordings by phone. He calls himself Carl Medert, but it may not be his real name." He walked over to a file cabinet and removed a bright blue folder. "Carl Medert," he repeated. "Here it is. These are our records of his ads and payments,"

He opened the folder and placed its contents on the table. "He paid a month ago so he's good for the next six weeks. No contact number or address listed."

Ryder and Lindsay looked through the material from the folder as Carson walked to a computerized switchboard.

"What are you doing?" asked Ryder.

"I'm taking him off the phone line and the internet."

"No," Ryder shouted.

Carson jumped.

"Leave it," said Ryder. "It's our only connection."

"But, what if someone else calls him?"

"Leave it like it is," Ryder repeated. "We'll set up a tap and a tracer. When he calls to check his messages, we'll nab him."

"The money orders," said Lindsay. "Do you have duplicates?"

"Why, yes. We keep copies of all of the checks, charges and money orders we receive. Our accountant demands it." He walked to another file cabinet and removed a thick manila folder. After several minutes of searching, he pulled out the records, ran them through a copying machine and gave the copies to Ryder.

Ryder glanced over them. "They're from convenience stores. Only a few are from the same place and they're months apart."

"Nobody will remember him," said Lindsay.

"The phone line's our best bet," agreed Ryder. "But, I'll put Collins on these right away." He turned to Carson. "Don't change anything and don't tell anyone about this."

"Act as if everything is normal," Lindsay added.

"But, I..."

"Mr. Carson," said Ryder. "If you do or say anything that hurts this investigation, I'll haul you into jail for obstruction of justice. Do you understand?"

"I understand," he said in a voice they could hardly hear.

Within the hour, Collins was questioning the convenience store clerks. Only two remembered the money orders. None remembered who'd bought them. By evening Ryder had tapped Carl Medert's voice mailbox and arranged for incoming calls to be traced. He, Collins, and Lindsay gathered again in his office.

"What if he doesn't check his mailbox?" said Collins. "He already has a vic, so why make the call?"

"He'll call," said Lindsay. "He'll be curious about new messages; he's not going to break his routine."

"We don't even know what his routine is," objected Collins. "It could be weeks before he calls again."

"I agree," said Ryder. "I'm not going to sit and do nothing with Morrison and the Delaney girl missing.

"He'll check," said Lindsay, "and if we can't find him, he'll find us." She looked squarely at Ryder. "I have a plan."

.

31

Morning brought window-shaking claps of thunder and wild flashes of lightning. Rain poured, washing color from the sky, drabbing the water and marshes into blending shades of sepia. The canine unit arrived at headquarters by 10 o'clock but could do nothing until the storm subsided. Brought inside to avoid the heat, the dogs followed their trainers untethered. They obeyed every low-voiced command and rested by the conference room door as Lindsay and Ryder reviewed the cases.

When they finished, Bill Emory pushed a lock of gray hair from his forehead. The short stocky man looked discouraged. "I hate to tell you, but picking up scent in a salt-water creek is a crap shoot. After the rain we just had, chances are slim …"

Ryder glared at him. "You can't win the lottery if you don't buy a ticket and I never won anything I didn't bet on."

"We'll give it our best shot," said Lawson Stone. Emory's tanned six-foot assistant looked more like a lifeguard than a law enforcement agent. His sun-bleached hair reached the top of his shirt.

At noon, Dixie Boatright brought in coffee and sandwiches and water bowls for the dogs.

By mid-afternoon, the clouds were gone and steam rose as the sun beat down on the wet streets and sidewalks.

"Let's get this show rolling," said Ryder.

They were about to leave when he got a call from Wong. "Get to Dead Horse Creek as quickly as possible. It's on the eastern side of the island, near Lindsay's house." He hung up before Ryder could reply.

Lindsay and Ryder drove separately with the agents and dogs following them in a black Ford Explorer. They were there within fifteen minutes.

Wong's van was parked beside a steeply sloped ramp. Several antennae protruded from its roof and the back door was open, revealing shelves full of diving and recovery equipment. As they arrived, the diver climbed out. Lindsay followed as Ryder walked over and helped him slip into his gear. "You must have found something," said Ryder.

"Not yet," the diver answered. "A couple of people think they saw a vehicle in the creek." He nodded toward two fishermen standing at the bottom of the ramp near a Bass Boat.

"They'd just started out when their boat bumped something below the surface. When they looked down, they saw what they thought was a car."

"Where?" asked Ryder, putting his hand above his eyes to peer at the water through the glare.

Wong pointed. "Over there, but the boat knocked it so hard, it moved sideways and deeper."

The agents unloaded the dogs and joined them.

As Ryder introduced Wong, a man and a boy came up beside them.

"Buddy Davis," said the older one. "This here's my son Dan but he answers to Catfish, learned to fish 'fore he learned to walk."

He ran his hand over the teenager's head, affectionately tousling his hair.

"It scared us when we ran into it," said the boy excitedly. "You can see where it scraped our stern. You think anybody's inside?"

"That's what we're gonna find out," Ryder answered.

"At first, I thought it was a sunken boat," said the man. He turned away and spat out a stream of tobacco juice, then wiped his hand across his chin. The boy followed suit, spitting longer and harder than his father. He pulled a can of Copenhagen from his pocket, extracted a pinch between his fingers and put it inside his cheek.

"We thought we saw taillights as it was sinking," his father added.

"Was anyone else here?" asked Lindsay.

"No Ma'am. It was still drizzlin'. Mos' people don't like the rain. We go out anyway, don't we son? Helps churn up the fish."

"How long has it been since you saw the car?" asked Wong.

"Let me think a minute. We got here about two-thirty, would'a gone right out but I had to work on the motor. It was idlin' too low and kept stallin'." He scratched his head and looked at his watch. "I'd say prob'ly 'bout 2 o'clock. It took us a few more minutes to get back in and look at the damage. Catfish waited while I drove to Quik Trip and called 911. Been back a half hour."

"The tide'll start out soon," said Wong. "We haven't got much time."

The boy edged closer to the dogs.

Bill Emory pointed to the one nearest to him. "This is Daisy. The other one's Ben. They're going to help."

The boys' eyes widened with interest. He started to ask a question, but Ryder cut him off. "I don't see how the dogs can be much help if the car is drifting."

"The water's still now," said Wong. "Without the current running, it'll stay in the creek and if it sank, it's on the bottom."

Ryder looked at the expanse of water before them. It was as wide as a river.

"We'll start where they last saw it," said Wong. He nodded toward the fishermen. "They'll take me out. If it's there, we won't need the dogs."

He snapped a tool belt around his waist and got in the boat. The boy pushed them off and his father started the motor. Within seconds, they were in the middle of the creek Wong put on his mask, leaned backwards from the side of the boat and disappeared. It was a full five minutes before he resurfaced and climbed back in. He shook his head as they started back to the ramp.

"I don't see how dogs can help." repeated Ryder. "If the car keeps moving, they won't smell anything."

"Give them a chance," said Emory. "If the water's stirred up, more bubbles surface. You brought something with Morrison's scent?"

Ryder went to his unit, opened the trunk and took out a T-shirt. He gave it to the agent, who handed it to Stone.

"I got it from his wife," said Ryder. His voice sounded thick.

The muscular agent bent down and held it in front of the dogs. They sniffed it for several seconds, then waited. "Go," he commanded.

No one spoke as the dogs ran up and down the ramp before inspecting the bank, pausing now and then to smell the air.

Wong looked at his watch. Ten minutes had passed.

Ryder let out a sigh of defeat as the dogs headed back.

"Put them in the boat," said Emory.

Wong nodded and looked toward the fisherman.

"Whatever ya need," the man answered.

"Take us to the mouth of the creek," instructed Stone. We'll work slowly back and forth in a grid." The agents led the dogs to Davis' boat where they all climbed in. The engine caught as Emory pushed them off. When they were about thirty feet away, he set the motor on idle and the dogs began barking excitedly and pawed the boat's bottom.

Wong, who'd waited at the ramp, put on his mask and flippers again. He walked into the creek until it was deep enough to swim and eased under the surface. A trail of bubbles followed his movements as the water where he'd been became still.

Ryder paced back and forth on the ramp, pausing now and then to look for Wong. Catfish offered him his can of tobacco, but he shook his head. Instead, he reached for his gum, crammed several sticks in his mouth and began chewing hard.

They watched as Wong's bubbles slowly reappeared and moved toward them and he emerged from the water. "I found it, but I can't see inside. There's debris all over the creek bed. The car's not stable and the tide's turning. If the current catches it, we'll lose it. Call Sidney Barnes. Tell him to bring his tow truck. If I can hook a cable to the axle, he might be able to pull it out."

They waited twenty minutes for the wrecker. The driver backed the truck midway down the sloping incline. There was a sharp noise as he turned on the winch, releasing a thick cable with a heavy metal hook. Wong picked up the hook and carried it into the water.

Ten minutes passed. Ryder and Lindsay exchanged anxious glances.

"There he is," shouted the boy.

Lindsay uttered a sigh of relief as Wong rose to the surface, held up his thumb and swam back to shore.

"O.K., Sid." He said to the driver. A clanking of cable signaled the reversing of the winch, followed by an ongoing loud grinding sound. The others waited anxiously as the cable tightened and the tide began to ebb. As the creek level slowly lowered, swirls and ripples formed and disappeared.

"Look," shouted the boy. He pointed as the car's metal roof broke the surface. Its red and blue lights reflected in the sun as if they were flashing.

"I hooked the cable under the trunk, but I couldn't get into the car."

"Morrison?" pressed Ryder.

Wong shrugged. "No visibility. The windows are partially open, but I couldn't see in."

He lowered his voice. "I'm sorry Ryder. You know if he's in there …."
He left the sentence unfinished and walked to the tow truck. "We just did have enough length," he told the driver.

The truck jerked backward, and the line became taut. "The tide's got it," the driver yelled. The truck shuddered and slid a few inches backward. "Damn thing's going to pull us in." He reached into his pocket for his phone.

"Clyde Russell's coming off the causeway" he said when he finished talking. "He's on his way back from the pier. Ya'll got something we can put behind these tires?"

Ryder and Collins pulled pieces of driftwood from the mud and wedged them behind the rear wheels. By the time they finished, the second driver arrived. He parked at the top of the landing and secured the cable from his truck to Barnes', locking it in place.

Again, the winch began to grind. The water level had lowered to the top of the unit's windows and the car inched slowly nearer, then suddenly dropped from sight.

The first truck tilted against the weight, its front wheels off the ground, but it didn't move, held in place by the second wrecker's cable. Barnes turned off the winch, then started it again.

Minutes passed, then, the car reappeared a few yards away. It came closer and closer, dragged upward, outward and backwards onto the ramp, its rear end suspended. Water poured from beneath its doors.

Ryder motioned the others back, as he and Lindsay approached the vehicle.

"Want me to lower it?" asked Barnes.

Lindsay nodded and the man gradually released the cable so that the car was no longer raised.

"Empty," said Ryder. He sighed with relief.

Wong joined them. "The front windows aren't down far enough for a body to drift out. I checked as well as I could along the creek bottom. If he were there, I'd have found him. The car couldn't have been in more than six hours, so the tide wouldn't have moved him."

As they peered inside, they saw keys in the ignition, the transmission in neutral, and Morrison's clipboard attached to the dash. Ryder looked at the rear seat and stiffened. The cushion was out of line, as if pushed forward.

Quickly recovering, he went to his unit, took out a pair of latex gloves, and went back to the car. Carefully, touching the edge of the handle, he opened the driver's door. Water gushed out as he reached in and pulled the trunk lever. Its top popped open, then slowly rose, as Ryder walked to the rear and Lindsay gasped. Morrison's bloated body lay on its back, his feet wedged tightly against the back seat.

"Damn, Damn,…" Ryder stared at the corpse, then averted his eyes.

For a moment no one spoke. Lindsay reached out her hand and touched Ryder's arm.

"I'll call the crime techs," he said, his voice hoarse.

32

He would have to make a decision about the woman. Had the policeman's car been found? If he could have dumped it sooner, it'd be in the sound by now, but the island was covered with cops with a hot vendetta. Good thing the storm had come. They'd cleared out like rabbits, giving him the chance he'd needed to get rid of it. Maybe he should leave, take care of the woman and let things cool off.

No!

If he could just calm down, put it all in perspective.

He paced.

There was nothing to fear and no reason for them to suspect him. Eventually, another cop would come but he'd just act natural and maybe offer to help. Ha, wouldn't that be a joke?

They had no reason to come into his home and they couldn't if they didn't have a warrant. He'd never agree to a search. He'd just say he was a writer who liked having his privacy. Yeah, that's what he'd say. Like Ginny Delaney. He was a writer who'd come down to check on the house and decided to stay.

The house. Well, here's to the memories. He laughed bitterly. He had memories, all right. His hands clenched and his chest tightened as he paced faster. He stopped and took a deep breath. He must stay rational.

A noise came from the next room and he walked to the door and listened. The woman was becoming conscious. Time for another dose. He'd found the medicine in his mother's closet. It was old, but, hell, it worked. A couple of pills and Ginny Delaney was out like a light.

Damn, he hated keeping her but he didn't dare get rid of her yet. He'd have to wait until things cooled down. Saturday would be July 4th. The cops would have more then they could handle and the water would be covered with boats. Independence Day. How ironic. It would be the day he was free of this bitch. He grabbed the medicine from a table and threw open the door.

The woman was lying on her back on a cot in a corner by the closet. She looked up as he entered and whimpered. When would she stop that damn whining? He smirked in disgust. Again the keening sound. He balled his fist, but caught himself in time. Blood meant evidence and he was too smart to have blood in the house. He looked at her with contempt, his hate-filled eyes riveted on her face. She'd been so damn confident when they'd met, flirtatious and sure of herself. She thought she was a hotshot writer. He snorted. Look at her now. She was weak like the rest. Only this one was harder to handle.

He inspected the cords binding her wrists and ankles. Wide leather belts fastened her to the bed. A scarf, tied around her mouth, allowed only muffled cries and that incessant whining.

He removed the gag, held up her head by her hair and forced the pills between her teeth. "Swallow," he commanded. He took a glass of water from a nearby table and pressed it hard against her lips. "Swallow."

She obeyed. Her head fell back as he released her and he replaced the scarf, tying it tighter. Seeing her lying so helpless, he felt even more contempt. As her eyes pleaded with his, he spit in her face.

The room reeked of urine and fear and the memories from his childhood rushed back. Pushing them from his mind, he returned to his room. He couldn't be still. He was energized, his blood coursing through his veins like electric current. He changed into running clothes, locked the door behind him as always and headed through the woods. At the road, a ray of sunlight raked his eyes. He blinked hard, turned to the right and ran as fast as he could southward through the shade of the oaks.

33

Sidney Barnes transported Morrison's car to police headquarters where Frost painstakingly examined the body before moving it to the lab. Gathering the dogs and their gear, Bill Emory and his partner left and Wong went home to clean up, while Lindsay and Ryder remained at Dead Horse Creek. Bonded by sorrow and anger, they searched the ramp and adjoining area. Several officers joined them. Finally losing interest, the fisherman and his son headed into the channel to fish, leaving their truck and trailer behind.

"Morrison's car must have come through here," mumbled Ryder. He pointed to a dirt road leading into the woods. It was a service road in the old days, before the parking lot was built."

"Where does it go?' asked Lindsay.

"North, through a gate to Frederica Road. It's hardly ever used. Most people use the main entrance."

"Is it usually locked?"

"Nope, nothing to protect. It's closed to stop the kids from Huntington coming in at night, but they aren't going to drive through the woods, don't want to scratch their BMWs."

Collins, trailed by two rookies, walked over to them. "Everything's been covered," he said. "Not a trace."

Ryder nodded to the cut through the trees. "Over there. He drove through the woods so he wouldn't be seen. The tracks are all screwed up so he must have come during the storm."

The officers walked to the road.

"Don't overlook anything," ordered Ryder.

"Think he left this way?" Collins asked.

"Not likely," said Ryder. "Too much chance of leaving a footprint. Besides, no one would notice him in the rain. He probably went out the main road."

Lindsay followed his gaze to the end of the parking lot. If there'd been tracks, they were covered by now.

After another hour of searching, Ryder stopped. "I've got to get out of here." He checked his cell phone for messages, got in his car and left. After a few more minutes, Lindsay, too, decided to leave.

Opening the door to her house, she saw movement. The cat. She'd almost forgotten it. As she watched, it ran down the hall into her room and under her bed. She started to make a sandwich, but wasn't hungry. Instead, she brewed a pot of coffee. Its comforting familiar smell filled the room. As soon as she sat down to drink it, the phone rang.

"You were right," said Ryder. "The perp called, checked his voice mail."

She put down her cup and listened.

"We traced it to a gas station south of Brunswick, just off I-95. By the time we got there, he was gone. A bunch of kids were already yakkin' on the line."

Lindsay sighed.

"We're checking it for prints, but there's not much chance there'll be any."

"I'm sure he used gloves," she agreed.

"Good bet. He'd had four calls to his mailbox, local women, sounded young. Van Buren's men are handling it, gonna make sure nobody makes a date."

They disconnected and Lindsay finished her coffee and carried the cup to the sink. For a minute, she stared out the window. She knew what she had to do. She opened a drawer and removed two rubber jar grips. Fifteen minutes later, she was at the pay phone by the pier. She punched in a series of numbers and waited. At the signal, she placed the rubber grips over the mouthpiece and cleared her throat.

"Hello," she said in a deeper than normal tone. "This is Pam."

34

That night Lindsay was so mentally and physically exhausted, she fell asleep as soon as she got into bed. Patty had begged off their run so she'd not set the alarm. When she awakened, the room was bathed in morning light. How long had she slept?

Shadow was hiding under the table as she entered the kitchen. She fixed her a bowl of food, poured water into her pan, made fresh coffee, showered and dressed to run. As she opened the door, heat flooded in. Closing it quickly, she retreated to the kitchen, strapped a water bottle on her waist and walked to the dunes.

Running onto the beach, she veered southward. Sunbathers read while children played in the sand. A crowd gathered as two men dragged a seine net through the water. She'd entered another dimension, a world of smiles and squeals of laughter, superimposed over reality. Terns watched her from a distance and, as she got closer, took flight. She climbed the stairs to the first boardwalk, jogged to the road and ran northward along a row of wax myrtles. Her shoes were sticky against the pavement and traces of hot melted asphalt covered her soles. At the intersection, she crossed to a shady lane where massive oaks blocked the sun. Her clothes were clinging, as humidity blended with sweat. Pausing, she drank several large swallows of water before pressing on.

A figure in the distance ran steadily toward her. It was the runner she'd passed the previous week. He recognized her as he approached, his head jerking slightly as his body stiffened. She raised her hand in greeting but his eyes looked dead ahead. Was he purposefully avoiding contact? She ran on, not looking back, feeling strangely alone and vulnerable, although there were houses on either side.

A loud horn startled her. Absorbed in thought, she had wandered to the center of the road. The motorist gunned his motor in protest as he passed.

She continued until the road forked, then cut back to the beach. Finding an overturned boat, she sat on its bottom, her skin stinging from the heat of its sun-baked surface. Looking at the waves splashing and receding, her thoughts drifted to the killer. Each time he'd emerged he'd disappeared just out of their view.

As she watched a ghost crab scurry away from her across the sand and pause, half in and half out of its hole, her mind flashed to the past. Three years ago, her partner and lover, Jim Scott, was killed walking into an ambush. A "set-up," her commander said. They were entering an abandoned house, with Scott first in line and Lindsay covering him.

Hearing a noise, she yelled "Stop."

Spotting the killer and wanting to protect her, he'd waved her back and walked into a hail of bullets. She'd never forget his hand clutching hers as she knelt by his side, the gurgling as he strangled on blood and the nightmares that followed.

"Post-traumatic stress," her doctor had called it. Scott's death had triggered a return to the time years ago when her husband had died.

The day had been rainy and cold. After work, she'd cooked dinner, built a fire, and waited, but he never arrived. His precinct captain appeared at their apartment at midnight and drove her to the morgue where she'd had one last glimpse of the man who'd changed her life.

Paul was twenty years older. After his family was killed in a wreck, he'd devoted himself to his work. Five years later, he and Lindsay had met. They'd been together only two years when… She took a deep breath, trying to calm the emotional surge overwhelming her.

Her husband had been tortured and stabbed by a serial killer. "The Blade," as he was called, eluded police for months before being caught. Dragging on for years, the case was repeatedly appealed. When his execution finally came, it did nothing to ease her torment.

Paul had saved her from a life of pain, playing the role of both husband and father as they fell in love. A descendant of generations of devout Catholics, he'd persuaded her to convert to his faith. The last time she'd been in church was for his funeral.

Alternating between anger and despair, she used the money from his pension to enter college, earning doctorates in Psychology and Criminal Justice. Offered a position on campus, she turned it down, preferring the trial by fire of a cop. Life without Paul was unbearable and her job had become an obsession. Each time she saved a victim, it was as if she were saving him.

She blinked back tears, tried to pull herself together and wandered along the edge of the tide line where she scooped a handful of water and splashed it onto her face. Finally in control, she walked slowly home. Other than a call from Ryder for another meeting, there were no messages, yet.

35

The task force was seated around a table in the conference room near Ryder's office.

"No one saw the car," said Ryder. "There were police all over the island and nobody saw it." He pounded his fist on the table. "How can that be?"

"Let's face it," said Frank Duggan, "Morrison broke the rules. He knew better than to go out alone."

Collins shot a resentful look in his direction. Duggan was good at his job, but he was an opportunist who lost no time in volunteering to be Morrison's replacement. He returned Collins' stare.

"Cut the crap," snapped Ryder. "We got enough problems without having to deal with personalities. If it's anybody's fault, it's mine. Morrison wasn't himself; we all knew that. I should have taken him off the case."

"Don't blame yourself," muttered Collins. "It won't help him now."

"Save your anger for the killer," advised Lindsay.

Ryder coughed and started again, "According to Frost, Morrison was hit hard from behind."

"It cracked his skull, but didn't kill him," added Lindsay. "Must have knocked him out."

"He was alive when he was put in the trunk," Ryder continued. "The back seat was kicked forward but not enough for him to escape."

"Damn hard way to die," said Collins, his eyes bleak.

"The rain was a perfect camouflage," interjected Wong, "It poured for hours."

"Low visibility and no one on the streets," agreed Ryder.

"If the current had caught the car, it would have floated into the sound," said Wong. "We'd never have found it."

"So what's our next step?" asked Duggan.

Ryder flinched at the word 'our'. "We're continuing the search with two-men teams. Nobody goes anywhere, not even to piss, without their partner."

"You know whether or not Morrison was at a house?" asked Duggan.

"No. He could have been killed at a house, in the woods, or beside the road," Ryder said edgily. "We just don't know." He stopped and took a deep breath. "What we do know is the killer has a place to hold his vics. There were weeds on the car that didn't come from the service road but the only prints were Morrison's, in the trunk."

"The only prints?" pressed Duggan.

Ryder was becoming increasingly annoyed. "The only prints were Morrison's," he repeated. "The rest had been wiped clean. That's all we have, except a long thin scrape on the hood. The car got caught on something, but it could have happened in the water."

They started to leave.

"Oh, yeah," said Ryder. "One more thing. People are getting paranoid and the press is eggin' 'em on. Chief White's called a meeting tonight in the island library. He wants a panel for a crime prevention program."

As they were going out, he touched Lindsay's shoulder. "I'd like you to be there."

"No problem," she answered.

"We need to talk about what we're going to say," he added. "Let's head over to Papa's for lunch."

The small café was already full, but they decided to wait, finally spotting an available booth near the far back corner.

"Ryder," said a man, giving him an affectionate slap on the shoulder as he walked past.

The man looked Lindsay up and down and gave Ryder a smile of approval. "Bout time you concentrated on something 'sides policin'. How are ya ma'am? I'm Codger Kinsey, one of Ryder's ol' fishin' buddies." The man beamed at the two of them as Ryder turned red.

"Catherine Lindsay," she offered, seeing Ryder was too tongue-tied to introduce her.

"Gotta be goin'. Glad I had a chance to see ya". He winked and nodded knowingly at Ryder as he strode away.

"I, uh, I'm sorry, I…" Ryder stammered.

She stifled a laugh when she saw his pained look. "It's O.K. Ryder. I took it as a compliment."

He brightened and looked at her intently. "I can see how he could make such a mistake. I mean, you're so beautiful any guy would be…" He realized what he was saying, grabbed the menu as if it were a lifesaver and fell silent.

This time it was Lindsay who stared. Who was this man seated before her? Was he interested in her? She remembered his gruffness at the meeting, then thought of his gentleness and concern for the cat. Perhaps there was more to the handsome lieutenant than she'd first thought.

36

The library where the meeting was to be held adjoined the island's Chamber of Commerce and community theatre. All three were housed in an old brick building in the village by Neptune Park. Lindsay drove into its circular driveway which was bordered on one side by parking spaces, the other by live oaks. All of the spaces were taken so she eased back out onto the street and pulled into a parking slot two blocks away; then walked along the broken sidewalk leading to the building. She looked at her watch in dismay. Ten minutes late. The meeting had already started.

Inside, the library was almost empty. A female police officer quickly walked up beside her. "Dr. Catherine Lindsay? Officer Bobbie Faye Grimes. Lt. Ryder asked me to watch for you. The crowd's so big, we moved into the theatre." They quickly walked across the building's courtyard.

"Dr. Lindsay," bellowed Ryder as they entered. He motioned her to a raised platform at the rear of the room where a panel was seated behind a long table.

She walked towards them, her face flushed with embarrassment.

"We were just talking about the recent drownings," he said. "I'm sure you'll have something to add."

She was barely settled when he thrust a microphone toward her. The platform gave her a wide view of the audience. Elderly men and women filled the front seats. Those remaining held people of all ages, including a group of teens. Women outnumbered men, two to one. There was a soft murmur of voices as they waited for her to speak. She managed a reassuring smile.

"I don't want to alarm you anymore than you already are, but, you must be cautious," she said. As she talked, more people trickled in. A man entered and leaned against the door-frame at the back of the room. A cap was pulled low over his forehead and she couldn't see his face, but he seemed familiar.

There was an arrogant air about him as he stood with his arms folded against his chest.

She waited for the latecomers to sit down before continuing. "The first thing you should do is acknowledge your lifestyle. Pretend you're observing yourself. Look at how you live. Ask yourself questions about your safety. Where and when are you vulnerable? If you were an attacker, where, when and how would you strike?" Everyone was silent as they focused on her words.

"Sometimes, people think of reasons to blame a victim. They think victims bring crime on themselves by being careless or using bad judgement. That way of thinking gives people a false sense of security. It allows them to feel they can avoid being hurt, that crimes aren't random. In some cases, this is true, but even a careful person can be attacked. You reduce your risk if you plan ahead."

A young woman placed a pitcher of ice water and glasses on the table. Nodding her thanks, Lindsay poured a drink and sipped. "If you know your weakest areas, you can strengthen them."

"How?" asked a voice from the second row.

"If you're a woman living alone, put a male message on your answering machine. Have timers turn on lights and talk radio programs when you're not home. Be ready if someone breaks in when you're there. Try to get out of the house or take your cell phone and go to a safe-room. It should have locks and a solid door."

A woman raised her hand. "We've got an alarm system. Is that enough?"

"An alarm is a deterrent but a determined burglar can disconnect the wires." She scanned the group before her. Some of the women were talking among themselves. "Any more questions?"

"Please continue," said a man in the front. "We'll ask questions when you finish."

The audience became quiet and looked at her intently. "Keep doors to your home well lit and don't let strangers in, no matter how friendly they are. If someone needs your phone, place the call for him. Psychopaths don't look like devils. In fact, they can be charming. One of the most vicious rapists I've known wore a three-piece suit and kept a knife, rope and tape in his briefcase."

"I installed peepholes and door chains on our doors," a man volunteered.

"A good idea," said Lindsay, "but don't rely on door chains. They can be easily broken. Install dead bolts and keep keys away from windows."

"What if somebody's prowling outside?" asked a teenage girl.

"Phone the police," interjected Ryder. "That's our job. If you're alone, call out as if someone's with you. Keep lights on in several rooms so it looks like more people are home."

"Never go into your house if it's been entered," added Lindsay, "even if you think the intruder is gone. Let the police go in first."

"Thanks a lot," said Ryder, with a wry grin. The audience laughed and began to relax.

"What's the best type of weapon?" asked an elderly woman. "I don't know how to use a gun."

"The best thing's whatever's handy," answered Lindsay. "Not many people have guns with them all the time. Defend yourself with anything you can. I've known cases where people used lamps, even their shoes."

"I can see how," said a man, eyeing his wife's stiletto heels.

A few people chuckled. As they became more at ease, they asked more questions and the session lasted into the night.

When it was over, Lindsay looked for the man at the door, but he was gone.

"Walk you to your car?" said Ryder.

"O.K." They strolled onto the sidewalk and towards the Porsche. The heat was gone and a breeze cooled the night.

"Wanna walk by the water?" asked Ryder.

Lindsay hesitated, then nodded. Changing direction, they followed a path leading to the beach and onto a walkway. Ryder plopped down on a concrete bench and motioned for Lindsay to join him. He placed his arm on the bench's back, his fingers brushing against her neck. The moon cast a silver beam across the waves and Lindsay saw sparkles.   "What's that?"

Ryder strained to see.

"There, where it's shining and the tide's coming in." She pointed to the shoreline.

"Oh," said Ryder, relaxing again. "That's bioluminescence."

"Bio what?"

"Bioluminescence. It comes from tiny sea creatures that glow in the dark."

"I never heard of such a thing."

"Stick with me," he said, lightheartedly patting her back. "You'll learn a lot."

She became aware of his arm still resting against her back as they listened to the waves.

"Lindsay," he began in a low tone, then changing his mind, looked away.

"Did you say something?"

"Uh, no," he shifted weight and looked at the water. "I, Lindsay, I---."

A loud noise burst from the pier as a crowd cheered for a fisherman who almost landed a shark. The laughter changed to jeers as the line snapped and the man fell backward and the shark escaped.

"I've been doin' some shark research," said Ryder, seeming to change the subject. "The number of attacks is on the rise."

Lindsay turned to him with interest.

"They say it's 'cause so many swimmers are in their feedin' zones."

She looked back at the pier. "Sure are a lot caught here."

"Yeah there are." He followed her gaze. "The sharp drop-off attracts other fish, and…"

"Surely nobody's dumb enough to swim there."

"Not here, but they do by the sandbars. Lotta drop-offs and fish there, too. As I was saying, drop-offs attract fish. Current and whitecaps make it hard for sharks to see. Anyway, the sharks go for the fish and end up biting humans. In Australia, it got so bad, they've got nets offshore from some of the beaches blocking swimming areas."

She shuddered. "I'll confine my swimming to a pool."

"You like to swim?" asked Ryder hopefully. "I've got a friend who has a pool in his back yard. All I have to do is tell him we're coming. We could go when things settle down and probably have it all to ourselves."

Surprised by the invitation, she searched for words. "It's getting late," she said quickly, looking at her watch and rising to leave.

There was a line of traffic when they got to the Porsche. She unlocked it with her remote and he opened the door. "See ya tomorrow," he said as she eased into the driver's seat. She turned on the engine, but Ryder still held the half open door.

"Anything wrong?" she asked.

He shook his head. "Maybe we could…."

"What?'

"Maybe sometime you and I could…"

"Could?"

He hesitated. "Just be careful," he said as he closed the door and walked away.

He stopped and looked back after she pulled onto the road, watching her taillights and the stream of cars behind her.

37

Stupid bitch. He was following her car and she'd never noticed. Big crime prevention expert. Ha.

And that message. Did she think he wouldn't recognize her voice? It'd taken awhile to put it together, but after tonight...

What was she trying to do? Set herself up as bait? He could handle that. He'd take the bait and she'd reel in something bigger than her wildest dreams, bigger than those sharks they caught at the pier and a hell of a lot more dangerous.

She'd seen him over and over and never known it, when they were running and now at that theatre cop show. What a joke. They didn't know who they were dealing with but he'd fix that. He'd let them know. He let out a deep gutteral laugh. They'd found the cop. That meant they'd scored one against him, but he'd get even and they hadn't found Susan Adams' Toyota. It should be deep in the sound by now. He'd give himself a pat on the back for that.

The woman had wanted to take her own automobile. Agreeing to meet him at Dead Horse Creek, she'd parked on the ramp to watch the sunrise as he'd instructed. After he drove in behind her, he'd pushed back the gate so it looked like the park was still closed. He'd lured her to the back of his van, held her down until he bound and gagged her, then driven behind her car. Lining up their bumpers, he'd placed a folded cardboard box between them so they wouldn't touch. He pushed the car slowly until it jumped out of gear and rolled into the water. It sank in the outgoing tide. Granted, he'd been lucky. It was early on a weekday and no one was at the ramp. But luck, he decided, could be created. He'd learned how and that was his forte´.

Getting rid of Susan and her car was easy. Not like the damn cop and his, but this one would be easy, too. He cut his lights and continued behind her until she drove into her garage. He stopped a short distance away and watched as the garage door eased down.

So, this was where she lived. He felt a thrill of anticipation. How convenient, wooded and close to the beach, not far from his house. It was almost too easy but he mustn't think of her now. The time wasn't right. He had other business at hand.

His thoughts turned to Ginny. With the attention drawn by the murdered cop, he'd postponed their outing. But, he would create his luck and at the first opportunity… Hotshot writer, huh. Maybe he'd keep her awhile.

38

Lindsay rose at dawn. She and Patty ran long and hard, a push of ten strenuous miles. After returning home, she checked True Luv. The message was there.

She called Ryder. "He got two more calls," he said before she could explain. "Duggan traced the number and will warn the woman."

"I left long slow messages", she said. "I'm hoping they'll keep him on the line."

"What the hell? Why didn't you clear this with me?"

"I disguised my voice," she said defensively. "The first time I just talked. After I hung up, I had Mr. Carson set up a mailbox. I called back and left the number."

Ryder remained quiet, and she went on, "When I checked my box, I taped his call. Listen and I'll play it."

He waited while she rewound the tape, placed the phone by the recorder and turned it on. "This is Carl," said a muffled voice. "Thank you for answering my ad. You sound nice and I'd like to meet you. In fact, I can hardly wait. How 'bout today? The Tourist Trap at two? Can you make it? I'll be checking my mailbox. I hope you can come. Oh,… Pam, wear something I can recognize. Wear something black." She turned off the cassette.

"Lindsay…" Ryder said in a warning tone.

"I have to go through with this. We're running out of time."

"All right," he said reluctantly. "Answer as if you'll be there."

"There's no as if."

"You can't be going!"

"If I don't go he'll be suspicious. Since we can't find him, we'll make him come to us."

"This is crazy. He probably saw you at the meeting last night."

"He won't recognize me from a distance. I'll make sure of it. If he gets close enough to see who I am, we'll have him."

"No."

"Either you help me or I'll go by myself."

"Damn it," he said angrily. "We'll be there."

Consumed by nervous energy, she devoted the next few hours to catching up on work for FLETC. She forced herself to stay on task as the minutes dragged, but periodically checked her voice mailbox.

At last there was another message. Carl was anxious to meet her, would be wearing a black windbreaker with gray stripes on the shoulders.

After going through the clothes in her closet twice, she drove to the Island Dress Shop where she bought a low-necked gauzy black sundress, a push-up bra and strappy stiletto sandals. Finding a display of wigs, she selected a long blonde one with spiral curls and bangs. She chose sunglasses with wide-plastic frames and joined the growing line of people near the cashier. Despite the slow moving checkout, she was home by 1 p.m.

She changed into the new outfit, applied a heavy layer of make-up and bright red lipstick and put on the wig and then surveyed herself in the mirror. Something was missing. Plundering through her jewelry box, she settled on a silver chain necklace and matching hoop earrings. She added a bangle bracelet and looked at the total effect. It would have to do.

It took less then ten minutes to drive to the village, where she parked near the pier. By the time she entered the restaurant, it was almost two. The hostess assured her no one had come fitting her 'friend's' description, then seated her as requested, at a booth in the back.

Lindsay looked at the other diners. One gave a subtle nod and she sighed in relief. Ryder's people were in place. Now, all she had to do was wait.

"You wanna go ahead and order, honey?" asked a plump brunette waitress. "Looks like your date's takin' his time."

Two glasses of lemonade later, he'd still not arrived. The lunch crowd left and the only ones remaining were Lindsay and scattered diners she was sure were cops.

A woman walked over and sat in the chair across from her. "Dr. Lindsay, we're going to pack it up. We've been here since noon. We watched everyone who came in and we don't think he's coming. Follow me and I'll take you to your car."

Lindsay left a tip on the table, paid for her drinks and walked with the female officer to an unmarked car. They rode around the pier and down a couple of side streets to be certain no one was following before she let Lindsay out at her Porsche.

To be sure she wasn't being tailed, Lindsay drove to Brunswick, repeatedly checking her rearview mirror. Satisfied, she decided to face Ryder.

Dixie Boatright gaped at her as she passed by her desk, started to speak, stopped and shook her head. "Well, I'll be..."

Ryder looked up from his work and stared. His jaw dropped. "Lindsay?"

She blushed and pulled off the wig.

"Can't fault you for tryin," he grinned.

39

He'd watched the bitch come out of her drive. Staying a few car lengths behind, he tailed her all the way to the village where he parked near the restaurant and watched her go in. He knew it was full of police, waiting for him.

He got out of his car and walked to the pier where he sat on a bench, pretending to read. She was in the restaurant over an hour before she came out, walking with a second bitch who had to be a cop too. He smiled to himself and laughed. This was better than television. He'd created his own damn cop show, only the people were real.

Back home, he couldn't get her out of his mind. Dumb broad. Did she think she could trick him? A noise came from the next room, but his thoughts were on the woman who'd been at the restaurant, the one he knew was working with police. This was not good, thinking of the other, when this one was unfinished.

He became conscious of his hands, his fingers active, thumbs and forefingers rubbing against each other, his arms tense at his sides. He stood beside the window in his room and moved the curtains slightly and looked out. A heron was circling the creek.

Dizzying memories flashed like revolving lights. As a child, he'd stood by this same window time after time. He'd waited for his father's release of the boat from its lift, reassured by the metallic noise of the hoist as it descended into the water. Within seconds, his father would appear beside it, heaving fishing gear and supplies into its hull. He'd step in and vanish into the depths of the cabin, then reappear, climb into the captain's seat and start the motor. Only after the engine caught, could he, Timmie, relax.

Listening, he held his breath as he had then, but instead of the noise of the inboard, there were only sounds of suffering from the next room. Damn, he wished she would stop. In another hour, he'd give her more pills. He continued his gaze out the window. Something moved near the corner of the house and his muscles tightened, but it was only a rabbit, looking for food.

He'd had a rabbit once, had taught it to come from the woods and eat carrots from his hand. He'd felt its whiskers tickle the tips of his fingers and in time, could have trained it, but, his father… He clenched his fist and blocked the vision from his mind, then thought of his mother. She, too, would watch his father's boat disappear. As soon as it vanished from view she'd scream for Timmie to come to her, her voice as piercing as a peacock's cry.

Filled with dread, he'd descend the stairs, the anger toward his father replaced by despair as the day's rituals began.

She'd be waiting on the landing, her open robe revealing a stained transparent gown. Drooping, pendulous breasts hung to the top of her bulging abdomen. Drawing him to her, she'd press his face against her damp pasty skin and run her ragged nails through his hair. He remembered her rancid breath enveloping him as she clung to him, holding him tighter and tighter until he felt his energy draining as if she were sapping his strength.

"Now," she would say, relinquishing him at last. As if on cue, they would walk to the kitchen, where she patted the back of his chair. Seated, he would eat his breakfast, aware of the sound of the whiskey bottle clinking as she held it to her glass. She'd add water and ice and sip as she cleared the remains of his father's meal.

Caught in the memory, he thought of the day he was ten. "This is your day, sugar," she'd said, placing a plate of toast and grits before him, her words already slurred. He'd cringed at the thought. Excused from school, he knew he'd be alone with her until his father returned when, because of his birthday, he'd be the object of his father's attention.

"Happy Birthday," she'd sung. "Happy Birthday to Timmie." She'd covered him with wet sloppy kisses. When she finally pulled away, he'd been unable to choke down his food.

They spent the day together on the living room couch, watching T.V., his mother falling asleep, waking to the blare of commercials, refilling her glass, and dozing again.

At dusk, when his father came home, he helped him unload the usual cargo of heavy brown boxes. His father referred to them as supplies and Timmie pretended he didn't know they were filled with drugs.

An hour later, a man arrived in a large blue van and took all of the boxes away. As he left, his father went into the boathouse and brought out another box, which he placed at Timmie's feet.

"Your birthday present will be a good guard dog," he said gruffly. Inside the box, was a Rottweiler puppy.

Timmie and the dog became inseparable. He recalled the puppy's smell as it licked his face, the softness of its tummy against his chest. Then came the day the puppy chewed out the corner of one of his father's boxes, scattering its contents across the dock and into the water. The next day Timmie found its body by the side of the creek, its head bashed in by a hammer.

The sound of the woman's whimpering broke through his thoughts. Clenching his fist, he headed for her room.

40

Remembering her promise to visit Dorothy, Lindsay arranged a morning meeting. On impulse, she stopped on the way to purchase a bouquet and a couple of magazines.

"You'll be amazed," said Dr. Skalato, as they walked together to Dorothy's room. The woman was sitting in a chair by the window wearing a yellow flowered dress and bright pink lipstick. Her hair had been curled and cut into a fashionable bob. She smiled as they entered.

"Thanks," she said cheerfully as Lindsay handed her the magazines. An orderly took the flowers and then returned with them in a vase.

"She's beautiful, isn't she?" the doctor said proudly.

"Dr. Skalato says I can leave in a few days," said Dorothy. "My sister is coming Friday. She's going to move into an apartment with me until I can find a job." They talked for over an hour before Lindsay left. She drove back through Brunswick and decided to report to Ryder on Dorothy's progress.

"He's not here," said Dixie Boatright in a triumphant tone.

Lindsay scribbled a note and slid it in the inbox by his office before leaving. As she opened her car door, she heard her name. She turned to see David Reed's van pulling up beside her. "Lindsay---," he repeated her name and then seemed at a loss for words.

"Yes?"

"I'm sorry about…"

"It's forgotten,' she said, turning back to her car.

"I'd really like to talk to you. How about something to eat? My treat. It's almost noon."

She hesitated.

"There's a nice restaurant around the corner."

"That's not necessary."

"I was rude. I'd like to set things right."

Lindsay nodded and closed the car and locked it. She walked around the van, climbed into the passenger's seat and they rode to a small café not far from the police station.

"I'm sorry for the way I acted in my office," he said. "I hope you're not still angry at me."

"It's forgotten," she repeated.

"It's not forgotten. I know that. Will you give me a chance to redeem myself?"

Struck by the sincerity of his plea, she nodded her head and smiled. "Now you sound like a priest. You're forgiven. I grant you your redemption."

He looked relieved.

Despite her initial misgivings, her discomfort was abating and she felt at ease.

"Did you know Ginny Delaney?" she inquired.

"No, Wong told me she was missing when he called about using my boat." He fell silent.

"Am I under suspicion again?" An edge had come into his tone.

"No, I didn't mean to imply that at all."

"I'm sorry," he stammered. "Here I go again. It was a reasonable question. I intended this to be a pleasant lunch and I'm already ruining it."

Seeing his forlorn look, Lindsay reached over and touched his arm. "Truce?"

"Truce," he said as he took her hand and squeezed it.

Several minutes passed as he lowered his chair, locked the van, and they entered the restaurant. Although it was nearly full, the hostess walked them briskly to a table where a tall black man took their order. They chatted about books and weather until he returned with their drinks and a short while later brought their food. By the time they started to eat, the tension between them was gone.

A woman walked past, stopped, looked at Reed and raised an eyebrow. "Nice to see you, Father," she said with a mischievous smile.

As Reed returned the smile, Lindsay gave him a questioning look.

"Mrs. Abken," He grinned. "She's a member of my congregation, been after me to get out."

"Get out?"

Reed's face flushed. "I mean go out," he stammered, "go out with someone. She's always trying to pair me up with the women in our church."

"All of them?" Lindsay laughed.

"Well no, not all of them," he blushed again. "Just the ones she approves of." He fell silent as the woman again walked past, smiling in their direction.

"Do you think she approves of me?" asked Lindsay in a serious tone.

"Why yes, I'm sure she does." He caught the twinkle in Lindsay's eye and they both laughed.

"Being a single priest does have its benefits," he said.

"Oh?"

He patted his stomach. "I get lots of leftovers and desserts. Mrs. Abken's apple pie is out of this world."

When they finished, he drove Lindsay to her car. "I enjoyed being with you," he said shyly. "May I see you again?"

She thought of the evening ahead and the loneliness of waiting for something to break on the case. "Come over tonight," she blurted. "I'll make spaghetti." As soon as the words were out of her mouth, she regretted them. What was she thinking? Why was she inviting him into her home?

"Can I get in?"

"What?"

"Will I be able to get into your house? Are there any stairs?"

It took her a moment to comprehend what he meant. "Oh, no. My house is built on a slab. You won't have any trouble getting in. Is six o'clock O.K.?"

"Six is fine."

He waved goodbye and drove away as she was getting into her car.

She sensed someone was watching and looked up. Ryder was standing at the door of the station. He quickly turned and walked inside. She stared at the doorway, hesitated, then shrugged and started the Porsche. She stopped by the grocery store to buy pasta, tomato sauce and fresh spices. Impulsively, she added a bottle of Walnut Crest Merlot.

She finally pulled into her driveway at four, raised the garage door and parked inside. The priest would be able to drive almost to her porch. She pushed the button on her remote and the garage door came down making its usual grating sound and then stopped before continuing to close with a thud She thought of Frost and his oil can. The house could use some maintenance.

She went inside, put the groceries on the kitchen counter and walked to the living room. Even it needed work. One of the blinds was bent and it wouldn't be a bad idea to get an extra chair. She gathered her files and neatly stacked them, then quickly dusted and vacuumed and rushed back into the kitchen. Only after the spaghetti sauce began to simmer, did she rest.

An hour passed before she realized she hadn't seen Shadow. Searching the house, she found her far under the bed against the wall. That was odd. The cat had become so friendly. She gave up trying to coax her out and turned on water to take a bath.

A wave of uneasiness came over her as she stepped into the tub and rested her neck against its sloping back. She took a deep breath and tried to relax, closed her eyes and lay still. She awoke at the sound of a loud click. What could it have been? How long had she been in the tub? She must have fallen asleep. The water was no longer warm and she felt chilled. Reaching for a towel, she stepped out onto the rug as she heard the noise again. The cat, she thought with relief. It must have come out from under the bed.

She pulled on a robe, walked into her room and raised the bed ruffle. Shadow was still huddled in the furthest back corner. She arched her back as Lindsay peered under the mattress. Puzzled, Lindsay walked to the front of the house and into the kitchen.

The spaghetti was no longer simmering, its burner turned off. "I'm almost positive I left it on," she muttered. "Maybe I turned it off when I went to bathe." Setting the burner on low, she returned to her bedroom to dress.

She chose a v-neck red cotton sweater and jeans, then put on makeup and a few dabs of perfume. Pulling her hair up and into a twist, she secured it with a large barrette. Feeling better, she put out linen placemats, wine glasses and flatware before going into the yard, where she picked zinnias and fern to arrange in the center of the table. After preparing a salad and pouring the wine, she put on soft music and waited.

41

He'd only been home an hour when he heard the sound of something tripping the cord across the drive. This time, he'd used clear fishing line, attaching it to the sentry box only a short distance above the ground, where it couldn't be seen but would be easily caught by an approaching vehicle. It was simple, but effective. The trick was attaching the line to a switch connected to the wiring and alarm in his house. He walked to the panel box in the downstairs hall and turned the system off. Moving to the kitchen, he found a tiny opening at the side of the curtain from which he could see outside.

A police car stopped at the end of the drive and two officers got out. One cop walked cautiously toward the house as the other leaned against the fender and watched.

He'd been expecting them. Each day when he returned from using his van, he'd pulled it into the garage. He'd then painstakingly brushed the tire tracks from the long wooded drive and scattered small branches and pine straw at intervals. The yard looked neglected and untended. Grass was ankle high and he'd left several decaying yellow newspapers on the step by the door.

Last night, he'd locked the boathouse with the cruiser inside before scattering dry leaves across the walk and on the steps leading to the porch. The overgrown lawn added to the effect. The place looked deserted.

He had to concede the cops were thorough. One made his way cautiously to the back and checked the boathouse door. He strained to see inside, but it was impossible. Its window was covered with a layer of dirt and grease.

Hearing a noise, he soundlessly pulled off his shoes and ascended the stairs in his sock feet. The damn woman was awake. He entered the room where she lay and gave her a threatening look. Instantly, she became quiet. As he went back down, he heard the police car turn around and leave. He'd created his luck, by being prepared, and cops were dumb. The newspapers had announced they would be checking every house on the island, looking for the "Blackwater Killer," looking for him. Hell, they might as well have sent him a letter announcing their visit.

"Blackwater Killer." Who'd come up with that? He had to hand it to the media. They could be dramatic. Well, if drama was what they wanted, he'd give it to them. This was his show and he was damn sure directing it.

42

David Reed arrived at six-fifteen. With Lindsay's assistance he was able to roll the chair through the doorway and into her living room. She was thankful the house was flat, allowing free movement.

"Ah," he said, as she offered the wine. "A nice touch."

As they settled into conversation, he wheeled his chair over to her bookcase, examining the titles of the volumes inside, including some new bestsellers.

She flushed. "Those pop-psych books you detest."

He sighed. "You have a lot of them. How to manipulate yourself and others, same songs, different tunes."

"Manipulate?"

"External controls are always manipulative. They work through behavior modification instead of spiritual development."

"Is that wrong?"

"Think about it. We apply advertising techniques to manipulating ourselves and others. These books are just a substitute for improving character. We feel better when we read them, but nothing really changes. Everybody wants a quick fix. That's what's wrong with our country today."

"You're blaming my books for our nation's problems?"

"I'm not blaming any one thing. It's just something to think about. People have been conditioned to instant gratification, having what they want without waiting. They get ahead by using others like objects or things, like your serial killer. And, it's not just individuals. They're only microcosms of nations. What difference do you see in a bully who kills for a kid's leather jacket and a country killing for the rights to another nation's oil?"

She started to speak, but he continued, "What difference is there in parents neglecting their children to acquire things and a country neglecting its values while acquiring most of the world's resources? People have become conditioned to value things rather than human beings and to use humans as things, like your killer."

"Oh come on, we've had serial killers since before Jack the Ripper."

"Yes, but, they were an aberration. Now we're seeing more. They mirror our society, compartmentalizing and exploiting their victims just as some businesses exploit their customers. Cigarette manufacturers are an example." He sipped his wine and returned to examining the books.

"You think cigarette manufacturers are as bad as serial killers?" she asked incredulously.

"You don't?" he countered. "Their stock holders are like dealers fronting money for crack. With serial killers there may be less suffering."

"One is legal, the other's not," argued Lindsay. "I have a mutual fund with a little tobacco stock. I don't consider that a crime."

"That's the problem, Lindsay, everyone just has or does a little something bad. No one's held accountable."

"With that way of thinking you probably hold me responsible for our nation's wars."

His face darkened. "War is just another form of serial killing," he said in a low voice. "Sometimes it's necessary. Most times, it's not. You rarely see those promoting wars fighting them. They say they fight because they're patriotic, then, may even cut back on helping returning troops."

They were both quiet. He picked up another book and looked at its cover. "Reading these self-help books is like taking drugs. That's why so many of them sell." He swirled his remaining wine. "Like alcohol, they make problems seem to go away. Then, like bumps in the night, they come back to haunt you." He swallowed the wine and Lindsay refilled his glass. As he continued to scan through the books, she went into the kitchen and returned with their supper. As he rolled his chair towards the table, she looked at him in dismay. There was no way his chair could slide beneath its edge. "It's O.K. just hand me a tray and I'll prop it on my armrests."

She went back to the kitchen and brought out the top of a metal T.V. table. He balanced it on the arms of his chair and placed his plate and the glass on top of it.

Their talk turned to the case, and the fear now gripping the island. "The Chamber of Commerce is putting pressure on the Chief," said Lindsay.

"I'm not surprised. Tourism is down and business is suffering. They've already lost sales with the shark scare. The Fourth of July is next weekend. This should be the peak of the season." He turned his head sharply as there was a movement in the hall.

Lindsay followed his gaze. "That's Shadow." She explained how she and Ryder had found the cat. "I'm just keeping her for her owner."

"You think Ginny Delaney's alive?"

"I don't believe the killer will vary his pattern. He'll keep her alive until he thinks it's safe to take her out and drown her, to complete his ritual, and, to prove to us he can."

"He may have already killed her."

"I think we'd have known it by now. He knows Morrison's been found and the island's under surveillance. He'll wait until he thinks he's safe."

"If she's conscious," said Reed, "maybe she can talk him out of it, form a bond."

"He'd never allow it. He can't risk personalizing her. Remember what you said about compartmentalizing. Once he's decided she's a victim, he'll keep her that way." After they finished, she cleared the table and brought in coffee and ice cream.

He was at the bookcase again. "Your boyfriend?" he said, picking up a picture of a young man in a police uniform.

She hesitated. "He was my husband."

"What happened...?" he began.

She ignored his questioning look and cut him off.

"Would you like dessert?" Before he could answer, she placed the coffee and ice cream beside him and held out another frame.

"My brother," she said.

"Where is he now?"

"He died in the Gulf War."

He looked stricken. "Lindsay, all I've said. I'm so sorry."

"His last letter came from Bahrain, after his death."

He held the picture as she went on. "I tried to talk him out of joining, but he said it was his way of proving he was a man. He was barely eighteen when he enlisted." She sipped her coffee, her face full of pain.

"I was drafted," he said, bitterness in his tone.

"At least you got back alive. I know you're still angry, but you've somehow managed to adjust. You're O.K."

"No," he whispered softly. "I'm not O.K. I can't walk and never will again. One can never adjust to that. I've learned to live with it because there's no other choice. The only other options are death, death of the spirit or death of the body, the coward's way out. I tried each way and failed miserably at both." He took a deep breath. "Your brother wanted to prove he was a man. I question my manhood every day, physically, and emotionally. The emptiness doesn't go away." His sadness tore at her heart.

The phone rang. She ignored it but the ringing began again and she finally picked it up. "Dr. Lindsay, this Dr. Skalato. Dorothy's been attacked."

"What? Is she all right?"

"We don't know. She was unconscious when the orderly found her. I'm at the emergency room now." She stopped, as if gathering strength to go on. "Most of the patients were watching television but Dorothy was in her room reading. About nine, the orderly went to her room to look in on her. As he opened the door, a man ran out. Dorothy was on the floor unconscious. She'd been strangled."

"Where are you?"

"Southeast Georgia Regional Medical Center."

"I'll be right there."

She hung up the phone, explained the situation to David Reed, then punched in the numbers to Ryder's cell phone and told him about the call.

"I'll contact the crime techs and head to Ridgedale," he said. "I'll call you when I get back."

She looked at Reed. "I have to go to the hospital."

"Let me drive you. My van's blocking your garage and you'll get there faster."

Her thoughts consumed by fear for Dorothy, Lindsay felt a surge of anger as they sped across the causeway and turned right onto Highway 17. They turned left at Parkview Drive, went another five blocks and drove into the emergency entrance.

"You go ahead," he said. "I'll catch up."

She stepped out of the van and rushed into the emergency room.

"Thank God you're here." Dr. Skalato reached for Lindsay's arm and led her through a hall lined with patients. They turned into a treatment room partitioned by curtains where she pulled one of them open. Dorothy's frail body looked almost lifeless as she lay against the large bed pillow. An I.V. pumped fluid into her arm as she breathed from an oxygen mask and her only movement was the rise and fall of her chest. A nurse stood beside her.

"The orderly couldn't revive her," said Dr. Skalato, "so he started CPR. The paramedics took over and put her on oxygen. Poor, poor Dorothy. She's been through so much and now this. Why? Why would anyone want to hurt her?"

She turned to Lindsay, a horrified look on her face. "You don't think it could have been the same person?"

Lindsay was silent.

Dr.Skalato frowned. "I don't understand. We've been so careful with our records and you were her first visitor in months. How could he have known where she was?"

"I don't know," Lindsay answered weakly.

A man with a stethoscope came up behind them and walked to the bed. "I'm Doctor Edwards," he said. "She's had a rough time, but she's coming out of shock. We think she's going to make it."

The woman uttered a small cry.

"Dorothy?" Dr. Skalato leaned over her.

Her eyelids fluttered as she focused on the figures beside her. In a shaky voice, she whispered, "Dr. Lindsay ...it was him."

43

Dr. Edwards insisted they leave so Dorothy could rest and Lindsay and Dr. Skalato walked to the waiting room where they found David Reed.

"She's conscious," said Lindsay, before introducing them. "Do you want to spend the night with me, Dr. Skalato, so you will be close to her and can see her in the morning?"

"Thanks, but I've got to get back. I'm still on call. Dr. Edwards said he'd let me know if she needs me. I'll come as soon as I finish my morning rounds." After she left, Lindsay and Reed returned to the van and drove back to the island.

"Are you going to be all right?" asked Reed as they pulled into her drive. He started to roll his chair onto the lift.

"It's late. You don't have to stay. It's Dorothy I'm worried about."

"Do you mind?"

"Mind?"

"If I stay a little while? It's been a hard night. I don't want to leave you alone."

"You're always trying to help people aren't you?"

"Sometimes, I get lonely. It's a way of helping myself. "

"But, it's your decision to be alone. You decided to become a priest. You could have married and had chil… I'm sorry, I wasn't thinking." She blushed.

"Episcopal priests are allowed to marry," he said, staring at her, "and my legs are the only parts of me that don't work."

Lindsay gave him a wry smile.

"That was the first thing I had to prove after the war," he said. "I had my disability check and there were plenty of women to take it. Whores and alcohol, quick fixes, filling the empty spaces, then leaving them gaping again."

She looked shocked. "What changed you?"

He hesitated. "The story will be better told inside."

They went into Lindsay's house where she made a pot of decaffeinated coffee and they settled in the living room.

"The story?" she prompted.

He looked at her uncertainly.

She nodded and he began, "After the war, after I got out of the hospital, a group of guys started hanging out and drinking with me in my apartment. One night they brought in a girl. She'd been with them all evening and they thought they'd do me a favor and share her. She was only thirteen and I was too drunk to notice. I woke up the next morning with a child in bed beside me. She was a runaway, with the typical story so many have. Her stepfather had raped her, molested her since she was seven. Ironic, isn't it? Most prostitutes have been sexually abused as children." He looked downward, ashamed to meet her eyes.

"I never touched her again, not in that way. She had nowhere to go and I let her stay with me. Eventually, we contacted her family, told them she wouldn't press charges against her stepfather if they made me her guardian. They were glad to get rid of her. I paid her to do chores and enrolled her in school. After a few months, she was like a daughter and I became the father she never had."

"Where is she now?"

"She's in social work, working in a program for female offenders, trying to help girls like herself."

"She could have gone in the other direction," said Lindsay.

"There's a thin boundary between good and evil," agreed Reed. "That which turns one into a social worker can turn another into a sociopath."

"We're certainly not born evil." She sighed. "Nor are we forced to become that way. Why is it some people...?" her voice trailed off.

"It begins with a series of increasingly wrong choices," said Reed. "Eventually, they poison us. Just as low doses of venom build tolerance to snakebite, immoral decisions desensitize us to larger and larger immoral acts."

He sipped his coffee. "When I took Katie in, I thought I was saving her but she was my salvation. She taught me to heal my pain by reaching out to others. We don't heal alone."

Lindsay stared into space and a tear trickled down her cheek.

"I didn't mean to upset you. Are you all right?" he asked, puzzled and uncertain how to react.

"I was a Katie," she said.

He moved his chair close to her side, reached out and pulled her against him.

She rested her head on his chest as he gently stroked her hair and held her tighter.

"What saved you, Lindsay?"

"Our parents were killed in an automobile crash and my grandmother took us in. When she died, I was put in a foster home. At first my brother was with me, but after awhile the family moved and we were given back to family services. He was taken in by another family and I was put in a group home. There was a group of men and women who were supposed to stay in the group home with us at night. They alternated watching us and sneaking out. When the women were gone," she stopped, caught her breath and then went on, "When the women were gone, the men came into our rooms. They said if we ever told, they would kill us and we believed them."

"Late one night, I ran away. There was no place to go but the streets. At first I slept in a park. That was where a pimp named Prince found me. He was looking for one of his girls and came across me. He said if I'd work for him, he'd give me food. I could have a place to live and he'd protect me. I was with him for a month. I gave him my money and he watched over me but I had to do whatever he wanted."

"One day I got hooked up with a bad john who beat me and Prince didn't come. When I tried to defend myself, he fractured my skull and broke my arm. The next day, I woke up in a hospital. I was only fifteen, so I was put in juvenile detention. The problems there were the same. At night, one of the guards came into our rooms, but there was no running away."

"Finally, I was released, but, since I was still a minor, I went back into foster care. This time, the family wanted to help me, but I was too confused to know it. I ran away again and worked with a group of hookers in the inner city.

"I was working the streets one evening when I heard a woman scream. When I went to see what was wrong, I saw a man robbing and beating her, like the john had beaten me. I became so angry; I hit him as hard as I could and knocked him down. I grabbed the woman's hand and we ran until we were safe.

"She was a call girl, who lived a nearby hotel. There's a difference, you know."

Reed nodded.

"She didn't have to work the streets. She said since I'd helped her, she owed me, said she'd take me in and teach me the ropes." Lindsay reached for her glass and drained the last of her wine.

"I moved in with her and she began what she called my 'education.' She taught me how to speak, how to walk and how to dress. When we were finished, she said I had 'class.' She said 'class' would earn me more money and I'd be safer. That was how I met my husband."

"He was a john?"

Lindsay laughed.

"No, no, he wasn't a john. I met him when he almost arrested me." She was quiet for a few minutes, as he continued to stroke her hair.

"I've never told anyone," she said, choking back tears. "My husband was the only one who knew."

"It's going to be all right Lindsay," said Reed. He kissed the top of her head as he continued to hold her. "Your past is past."

44

Someone pounded on the door, startling Lindsay, who awoke, still in the arms of the priest. It was 6 a.m. Embarrassed, she stood and smoothed her clothes before she went to open the door.

Ryder brushed by her, looking as if he hadn't slept. He stalked into the living room where he glared at David Reed. "You're here a little early aren't you? Or should I say a little late?"

Reed looked at him curiously.

Lindsay lifted an eyebrow. "Is that why you're here? You were concerned about David Reed?"

"No," he said, flustered. "We've got one woman missing, another in the hospital, and you didn't answer your phone. I came because I was worried about you."

"I didn't hear the phone," she stammered, "and I left my cell phone in my purse." She looked at her answering machine.

"You won't find a message," said Ryder. "The outside wires are cut. I checked when I came."

As if needing proof, she picked up the phone on her desk. Dead.

"Who…?" She suddenly realized what he was saying. "Ryder, you think the killer knows where I live?"

"He knew about Dorothy. You're the only person who has visited her in months."

She looked at him in dismay. "You think he followed me to her?"

He eyed the files on her desk, "Either that or he broke into your house."

Her hair stood up on the back of her neck.

He pointed to the files. "Are these the copies from the station?"

"Yes, I was putting them on my computer."

Ryder jammed a stick of gum in his mouth and frowned. He thumbed through the files, pulled out the one with Dorothy's name and then returned it to the box.

"How can we protect Lindsay?" asked Reed.

"I've put the house under surveillance but it looks like she's already being taken care of."

Lindsay gave him a puzzled look. She thought of yesterday. She'd come in with a large bag of groceries, but surely, she'd locked the garage. "I heard a noise yesterday afternoon but I thought it was the cat." As she told him about the clicking and the burner turned off, a panic-stricken look came over her. "You think it was him? Oh dear God, if he knows where I live, he could have found the information about Dorothy. Oh, God, what have I done?"

Ryder walked through the hall and inspected each room, testing the locks on the windows. He hesitated when he came to her bed and stared at its neatly tucked covers. Exhaling a sigh of relief, he returned to the living room. Mumbling into his shoulder radio, he turned to leave. "Jacobs and Munson are on the way. I'm meeting with Duggan and Collins. We'll be in my office at nine."

"I'll be there," said Lindsay.

He glanced at Reed, "I'm sure you won't mind staying until the officers arrive," he said gruffly, then turned abruptly and walked out the door.

45

"We're back to point zero," said Ryder, his eyes red from lack of sleep.

Collins, Duggan and Lindsay sat squeezed into Ryder's office, while Wong stood at the door. Lindsay took several moments to focus on what Ryder was saying.

"Time's running out," continued Ryder, "that is, if Ginny Delaney's alive. The orderly who surprised Dorothy's attacker doesn't know what the perp looked like, said the man was wearing a mask and knocked him down as he ran out the door. He didn't go after him because he saw Dorothy on the floor. We've got nothing, zilch, nada, not even a print."

He ran a hand through his hair and rubbed at a coffee stain on his shirt. "Dorothy was reading when he barged in and grabbed her." He cleared his throat. "I think he followed Dr. Lindsay home from the library, or from the Tourist Trap, got into her house, saw Dorothy's file and recognized the name. Hell, it even had her room number."

Lindsay looked down at the floor.

"When Dr. Lindsay went back to Ridgedale, he tailed her again. Piece 'o' cake. All he had to do was wait until dark when there weren't many staff. It was easy to slip into Dorothy's room without anyone seeing."

"What about tire tracks?" asked Wong.

Ryder replied, "By the time we got there, twenty cars must have been though the drive. We did a grid search of the grounds, found a patch of grass where he might have parked, otherwise, nothing."

"How is Dorothy?" asked Collins.

"I stopped by the hospital on the way," said Lindsay. "She's being released today."

"We've got a guard outside her room," said Ryder. "He'll go with her to

Ridgedale and stay with her until they decide where to move her. I don't want her there. She's our only witness and the scumbag knows it."

"And Lindsay?" asked Wong.

"Her house is under watch. We've got men at the front and back."

"That's strange," said Wong. "I passed by on the way but didn't see anyone."

"You won't," snapped Ryder. "We aren't after publicity."

"We're hoping he'll come back," said Lindsay, "won't realize we know he's been there."

"This time," said Ryder, "we'll be ready." They talked a few more minutes, before he ended the meeting.

Lindsay was the last to leave. She started to speak, but Ryder interrupted. "I'll check on you later, that is if you ain't too busy."

As she started down the hall, she heard a noise and turned to see Dixie Boatright rush into Ryder's office and close the door behind her.

Lindsay walked to the street, unlocked her Porsche, settled into the seat and turned on the engine. The car's fan blew hot air on her face. She hurriedly lowered the windows, backed out of the parking space and turned toward the island. Upset by Ryder's demeanor, she realized she was speeding as she started onto the causeway. At ten-fifteen, there was a fair amount of traffic on the road. It was unlikely the killer was following, but the thought of him behind her chilled her soul.

An Acme Cleaning van was pulled into the driveway of a rental cottage near her home. She glanced at it, betting an undercover officer was in it. She scanned the yard as she entered her house, but saw no one. Locking the door behind her, she tested the knob and walked to her desk. Her answering machine was blinking.

There was a message to call David Reed followed by five hang-ups. She was convinced they'd come from the killer.

She pressed *69. The phone rang and rang.

She tried again.

"Yeah, hello," answered a male voice.

"I'm returning a call."

"Not from here, lady. You're calling a pay phone."

She called David Reed and assured him she was all right. As she put the telephone down, she looked at her clock. It was time for the mail.

She walked to the street, retrieved a handful of envelopes from the box and went back inside. As she tore into the first envelope, she noticed it didn't have a stamp. Inside was an index card, its message printed in large block letters,

"GREETINGS DR. LINDSAY, THIS IS THE BEGINNING OF A SERIOUS RELATIONSHIP. DON'T BOTHER TO CALL. I'LL SEE YOU SOON."

46

"What the hell do ya mean, you don't know who put it there?" Ryder's face was dark with fury, as he stood in Lindsay's kitchen, staring at the envelope and message on the table.

"Like I told you," said Don Jacobs, "a lot of people come down that road. I mean it's not just people in cars; there are a lot of walkers and runners, too. I didn't expect anybody to…"

Ryder opened his mouth to speak and then thought better of it.

"If he'd turned into the yard, I would've seen him." Jacob's voice trailed off, and he hung his head, shifting his weight from one foot to the other.

"From now on," said Ryder, "I want you to look at every friggin person who comes by. Log in the time and their description."

"Sir, what about the cars?"

"The cars?"

"Do you want me to try to get their license numbers?"

"Believe me son, if I thought you could get the number of every damn ride zooming by on Frederica Road, I'd say do it. No, I don't want you to try to get every license, only if they look suspicious or stop."

He gave Lindsay an exasperated look.

The rookie glanced from Ryder to Lindsay and back again.

Ryder said, "Look kid, if this is too much for you, I'll get somebody else to handle it."

"I can handle it."

Using a pair of tweezers, Ryder slipped the envelope and card into an evidence bag and led the young cop out the door.

Watching from the window, Lindsay saw the crime tech by the mailbox shake his head. As they had expected, there were no prints. Before she could turn away, Ryder came back.

"Start packing."

"Packing?"

"You heard me. He knows where you live. Dammit, he's been in your house. Hell, he's even letting you know he's been here." He paused. "You can stay with me."

"He's not scaring me out of my house," snapped Lindsay. "That's what he wants. Besides, he may see us leave and follow us there."

Ryder protested, "But…"

"It would just be one more place to have to cover. You don't have enough personnel as it is with the July 4th weekend coming." Lindsay stared at him stubbornly.

"Lindsay," he said in a warning tone.

"I've already caused enough problems, Ryder. Let's use this to our advantage."

"You're making yourself a target again."

"Exactly, I made Dorothy a target. Now it's my turn."

"It makes no sense to get yourself killed because of guilt. You won't be any help to her dead."

"It's not a matter of guilt. It's opportunity. I'll be the bait and he'll bite. If we work together, we can set him up."

"Damn it, don't you think he'll know? We can't be everywhere. He'll watch, and he'll wait and the first time, and don't kid yourself, there will be a time, when somebody's guard's down, he'll strike."

"Listen to me, Ryder. If he thinks he can get to me, it will distract him. He won't focus on Ginny. It may be our last chance to keep her alive. It's a way to get him."

"No!"

"Am I breaking the law?"

He was silent.

"You can work with me or against me."

"Have it your way," he scowled and started out the door. "I'll be back with my things."

"You'll what?"

"I'll be back with my things," he repeated. "You stay. I stay."

He stalked to his Ford and spun the car out of the drive, its wheels squealing on the pavement.

47

Hunger pangs reminded Lindsay she hadn't eaten. She fixed a snack of crackers and cheddar and carried it into the living room where she sat back in the leather armchair and thought of Patty. She'd have to warn her. She lived too close and might unknowingly get involved. Reluctantly, she called and told her what happened. The press would release most of it anyway.

"Gawd Lindsay, what are we going to do?"

"*We* aren't going to do anything. You're going to stay put and away from me until this is over. I've got plenty of protection and there's no use your being in danger."

"You could sneak over here and stay in one of the guest rooms. You'd be safer. I just know you would. Beau and I will both feel better if we know you're O.K. I'll have him grill some steaks, get Molly to bake a cake..."

It took awhile to calm Patty's fears and assure her Lindsay would be safe at home. Peering out the window, Lindsay caught a glimpse of Jacobs talking to another rookie. A few seconds later the phone rang. Sure it would be Patty again, she was surprised to hear from Ryder so soon.

"Lindsay, I'm sorry I was angry. I want to make it up to you. We've both been under a lot of pressure. I, uh, I'm going to get you out of the house awhile, take you to a nice restaurant for dinner. It'll be good for both of us, get our minds off this case. I'll be there at six." He hung up the phone before she could respond.

What was it with Southerners? Did they think everything could be resolved with food?

She was at her computer until five, networking with other criminologists, reading through journal articles and briefings, trying to more fully understand the killer and his patterns. There must be some way to predict his behavior. Emotionally and physically exhausted, she settled back into her chair and sat for several minutes. Her neck hurt and her shoulders were tense. She looked at her watch. Ryder would be here soon. Reluctantly, she put up her work, walked into the bathroom, turned on the tub faucets, poured in several capfuls of bath oil and climbed in. Propping a plastic pillow against the back of the tub, she nestled her head against it and dozed, only to waken with a start. What was it she heard? Must be Jacobs or one of the others, or could it be Ryder? Listening intently, she heard a muffled bump, than the air conditioner started. She peered through the blinds and seeing no sign of him or the others, toweled dry, put on her robe, and walked methodically through the house. To her relief, both doors were secure. The case was getting to her. The attack on Dorothy had left her mentally drained and her nerves on edge. An evening away from the house might be good.

She let the water out of the tub, set her hair on hot rollers and opened the door to her closet. Thumbing through the hangers, she selected an emerald green sundress with spaghetti straps and matching high-heeled sandals. Lightly applying makeup, she brushed her curls into waves down and around her shoulders. Giving a nod of approval to the mirror, she grabbed her purse as she heard a knock.

Ryder burst in as soon as she opened the door. In one hand he carried a small cloth suitcase. In the other hand, he carried a bouquet of daisies. "Collins dropped me off so nobody'd see my ride…" he began, then stopped and stared at her, his mouth hanging open. "Lindsay!"

"How lovely," she said, taking the flowers from his hand. She grabbed a vase from the hall table, filled it with water and arranged them in it. "I'll put them in the living room." She placed them on a table by the sofa and stood to admire them. "What a nice thing to do."

"Just thought you could use some cheerin' up." He was still holding his bag and staring, his deep brown eyes studying her reaction.

"Ryder…"

"No use to say anything, I'm staying. It's a done deal. Either that or you're moving to a motel. Or, if you just don't want me in here, I'll sleep outside."

"O.K. Ryder, you win. Make yourself at home. Guest room's first door on the right."

He took his suitcase and dropped it on the guestroom bed, came back into the living room and looked at his watch. "We gotta go. I made reservations for seven."

Reservations? Where could Ryder be taking her?

"What's wrong?" he asked self-consciously.

Now she was staring. This was not the Ryder she knew. His hair was combed and trimmed, his clothes crisp and new, and his light blue shirt was tucked smoothly into his pants.

"Why Ryder, you look…" She groped for words. "You look so, so presentable."

Bad word choice, she thought immediately. "And handsome," she finally blurted.

He beamed like a kid who'd pleased his teacher. "We'll have to take your car since I don't have mine."

Touched, she made her way to the garage where she threw him the keys. "Ryder, if this is a date, you better drive."

He started to get in, stopped, walked to the passenger door and grabbed the handle. Lindsay noticed he was watching as she tucked her bare legs inside. He cranked the engine and the car was filled with classical music. A look of discomfort crossed his face.

"You can switch to 99.9," she suggested.

Instantly the music was replaced with sixties' rock and roll. Ryder put the car in reverse and swung out of the drive, then tapped his fingers to the music as he drove. Within a few miles, he turned onto a dirt road leading to the Frederica River on the other side of the island. Stopping at a small restaurant by a tidal creek, he parked by a concrete walkway leading onto a large wooden deck with a floating dock. Several small pleasure boats were tied to its posts. A sign announced "Welcome to Marshwinds." The hostess motioned them to a driftwood table beneath a wide white awning and then left as a waitress appeared.

Ryder pulled out a chair for Lindsay. "You'll have a great view of the water," he said proudly.

The waitress took their drink orders and handed them menus as a motorboat stopped at the dock. A young couple disembarked and went inside.

"I never knew this existed," said Lindsay.

"We locals keep a few things secret. It's hard to get into good restaurants in the summer. This one doesn't advertise and it's off the beaten path. It's nice for residents wanting quiet, away from crowds. It's pricey, but we come year round."

She studied her menu, and then looked questioningly at him as the waitress approached.

"I'm going to have steak with a baked potato and salad." He looked at the waitress, "and make sure it's rare."

"Make that two but I'll take mine medium well."

The waitress nodded satisfaction at their selection and took away the menus.

Lindsay looked out at the water, then turned back to see Ryder staring at her intently.

He quickly averted his eyes. They sat in silence, each trying to think of something to say.

"I enjoy being with you," he blurted.

"This place is wonderful," she said, "and you're wonderful too, for sharing it with me." She sipped her drink and then rested her hand on the table. Ryder reached over and put his hand over hers without speaking. There was an awkward silence until, finally, she frowned, gave a reassuring squeeze and pulled away.

"You were happy and now you're sad," said Ryder dejectedly. "I screwed it all up."

"It's not you," she answered in a low voice.

He gave her a questioning look and sighed. "I knew it was a long shot. Hell, it's like playin' football against Southern Cal. You're pro'bly gonna lose but you still gotta try."

"What are you talking about?"

"You, Lindsay. You're outta my league. No reason for you to feel bad. It's me that's the problem."

Lindsay smiled. "Ryder, were you making a pass at me?" Her expression turned serious. "Ryder, you're not a problem. There's a lot you don't know about me, a lot you wouldn't like. You think you know me, but you don't. You're just judging by what you see."

"Just judging by the facts ma'am," he joked. Then, he spoke in a serious tone, "What I see looks great." He leaned towards her and lowered his voice. "I know everything I need to know. We're not gonna do a show and tell, 'cause I'd be the first one to fail it. Who or what a person was doesn't matter Lindsay; it's who they are. I learned that from AA. Besides, I know you're streetwise, caught on to that right away. It's not something you get from a book. You learn that the hard way."

He sighed. "Guess what I'm tryin to say is I'd just like a chance."

Before she could reply, the waitress came back to refresh their drinks and a band began to play.

"Want to dance?" asked Lindsay, glad for the interruption.

"I'm rusty, but if you'll wait for a slow one…"

As if on cue, the tempo changed to the soft sounds of "I Needed You."

They left their seats and joined a small group of couples on the dance floor. He pulled her tightly toward him, guiding them in a two-step, barely moving from where they first started.

She was conscious of his body pressing against her as they moved together. His shoulders were muscular and his arms felt strong and safe. As the song came to an end, he tilted her chin and kissed her forehead. People began to leave the dance floor and they followed, Ryder's arm around her waist as they found their table.

A fish jumped nearby, startling her.

"Yagim," he said in a deep exaggerated tone.

"Yagim?" she repeated.

"The word means sea monster, a spirit that turns over boats so it can eat their occupants. It's a creature in Northwestern Indian mythology. Yugim causes horrible storms, dangerous seas, and sometimes destroys whole tribes. As good as you look, he may be heading our way."

She laughed, then frowned.

"What's wrong?" he asked.

"I was thinking about the case. I'm afraid one monster is enough."

She reached out and touched his hand. "It's nice having a break and being with you." Before Ryder could respond, the waitress delivered their food.

The meal was excellent. Afterwards, they sipped iced latte and watched a boat in the distance, making its way along the edge of the river. The band took a break and Lindsay asked "There sure is a lot of water traffic. Do a lot of cargo ships pass through Brunswick?"

"Hundreds a year," he answered. "Most carry cars. Brunswick's one of the largest distributing points in America, and being on the intracoastal waterway, you have a lot of boat tourists as well." They talked on, watching the sunset, followed by the ethereal gray cast of the moon. People came and went, their boat lights approaching and fading in the night.

"It's like watching a black and white movie," she commented.

"And I have the heroine all to myself."

"Are you a villain or a good guy?"

"You'll have to find out," he said as the band played another slow dance and he pulled her to her feet.

It was midnight when they parked in her driveway. They'd only been inside the house a few seconds, when Ryder's cell phone rang. After a short discussion, he turned to Lindsay. "Jacobs. Nothing popped while we were out."

Lindsay stood in the kitchen doorway. "You might as well make your self at home. Cup of decaf? Glass of wine?"

"Coke?"

"Coke it is." She turned back into the kitchen and returned with a glass of Coca Cola for him and glass of wine for herself. They sat silently sipping their drinks.

Lindsay stifled a yawn. "Time for me to turn in."

As she passed his chair, he reached out and took her hand. "Thanks for the evening." He rose from the chair, followed her down the hall and stopped at the guest room door, pausing to watch as she walked into her bedroom.

She closed the door and sat on her bed, listening to the sounds coming from his room. When it was quiet, she opened the drawer in her nightstand and took out her husband's badge, now tarnished with age. She held it to her chest, then holding back tears, replaced it and slid the drawer closed.

48

Lindsay awakened to the smell of brewing coffee and burning toast. Putting on her robe, she walked into the kitchen in time to see Ryder bending over the stove door, pulling out a pan of charred bread.

She climbed onto a stool by the counter as she watched him toss the black remains into the trashcan and pull fresh slices from a bag on the breakfast table. After covering the tops with thick slabs of butter, he returned the pan to the oven.

"Guess the heat was too high," he said apologetically.

He poured steaming black coffee into mugs, placing one before her.

She took a swallow and gasped.

"Too strong? Sorry, I'm not used to doing it in an automatic."

"How do you do it?"

"You know, the usual way. I put a cup of grounds in a pot, add four cups water, boil it, then drain."

Lindsay went to the refrigerator, pulled out a carton of milk and poured a large portion into her cup. Turning to Ryder, she sniffed the air.

Hastily, he went for the toast. "Got it in time."

He divided it onto plates and they sat down to eat.

No words were spoken during the remainder of the meal. When they finished, Lindsay went to her room, returning shortly, dressed to run.

Ryder frowned. "You can't be going out."

"I'm not going to be a prisoner. There's plenty of traffic on the main road. I need to run and you need some rest." She eyed him critically. "You look like hell warmed over."

"I had a hard time sleeping." He self-consciously touched the stubble on his chin.

"I just bought that mattress," she said with concern.

"It wasn't the mattress, Lindsay. I was thinking of you."

She blushed, took a quick sip of her coffee and downed her toast.

As she left for her run, he saw the bulge of her Glock under the edge of her shirt and breathed a sigh of relief.

She was back within the hour, heard the phone as she entered and caught it on the second ring. There was silence at the end of the line. Checking the caller ID, she recognized the pay phone number.

Ryder keyed the number into the computer and had the location in minutes, a convenience store on Highway 17. He dispatched a unit but by the time they got there the caller was gone. Still connected, the abandoned receiver was hanging by its cord. Again, there were no prints and no one had noticed its user.

Arranging an around the clock trace on her phone, Ryder assigned another set of officers to man it. Two hours later, it rang again.

"It's the hospital," said Ryder, looking at the ID.

Lindsay hurried to answer it.

"This is Dr. Skalato. Dr. Edwards came by to check on Dorothy. He says she's going to be fine."

"We'll still need to keep her under guard," said Lindsay.

"Lt. Ryder's already taken care of that. She's going to stay at my house until the person who attacked her is caught. It will be a good change for her and she'll be company for me. She wants to see you," she added.

"It's my fault she's…"

Dr. Skalato interrupted, "She knew you would say that. In fact, she's very concerned about you. She wanted me to remind you of something you said to her, something about not blaming yourself for the evil of others. Do you remember?"

"Yes." She paused. "I remember."

"Think of that now and don't worry, she's in good hands."

"When can I see her?"

"Once we get settled, we want you to come."

Relieved, Lindsay, hung up the phone and repeated the conversation to Ryder.

There was a knock at the door and he answered it. "It's Collins. I'll be gone an hour," he said with a warning look. "but there are two new guys posted outside."

Lindsay went in the kitchen and cleared the remains of breakfast, then showered and returned to her work. It was noon when Ryder returned, wearing a fresh shirt and khaki pants. He had shaved and combed his hair and smelled of cologne. "No more calls?"

"No more calls."

"Something smells good." He walked into the kitchen and lifted the lid of a simmering pot of beef stew.

"That's for tonight."

"Tonight?"

"David Reed's coming over. Of course you're welcome to join us. I made a peanut butter and jelly sandwich for your lunch. It's on the counter."

There was a clang as he hastily replaced the lid.

"I'm not hungry." He picked up the morning paper, mumbling as he walked back to his room.

"I can't hear you."

"I said since you have plans, I won't be needed here. You can call me when Reed leaves."

"Do you really think all of this is necessary, Ryder? There are policemen outside. The house is secure. I have double barrel dead bolts on the doors, window locks, and an alarm system. If he manages to get through all of that, I'll hit 911 on my cellular and greet him with my Glock."

"Call me when Reed leaves," repeated Ryder, gruffly.

During the interval between Ryder's departure and Reed's arrival, the phone rang again. By the time she reached for it, the ringing had stopped. She shuddered, wondering if the timing of the call was a coincidence. Could the killer have seen Ryder leave? The doorbell stopped her thoughts. Retrieving her gun from the bedroom, she cautiously walked to the front and looked through the peephole. Seeing David Reed, she put the weapon in the drawer of a nearby table and opened the door.

"I passed Ryder as I was coming over, anything new?" She told him about the continuing calls and related the news about Dorothy.

They went into the living room where she poured Cabernet Sauvignon into a glass for each of them. They sat quietly sipping their wine until Reed spoke. "How was your night with Ryder?"

"Uneventful. I don't need an inside guard," she said resentfully.

"Maybe that's not the reason he's staying."

Lindsay blushed.

"You're welcome to stay with me. I have an extra bedroom," he hastily added.

"That would put you in danger."

Reed's expression showed a momentary flash of anger. "I can handle a gun."

"It has nothing to do with your marksmanship," she assured him. "I've already made one person a target and I'm comfortable here." She refilled their glasses and they spent the rest of the evening eating, drinking, and talking.

"We've killed that bottle," said Reed, "No pun intended."

He got ready to leave.

"You'll be staying awhile longer," said Lindsay. "You can't drive unless you're sober."

"I have no argument with that."

She brought in their usual coffee and placed a cup before him.

A flash of light reflected from the hall mirror. Lindsay walked to the kitchen window.

"It's Ryder."

They waited as Collins let him out, but he didn't come in.

"He's going to stay out there until I leave," said Reed

"We might as well invite him to join us," said Lindsay. She opened the door and waved. Ryder turned his head as if he hadn't seen her and started walking down the path to the beach. Finally she went outside and caught up with him.

"I'm fine until ya'll finish up," he mumbled.

After several attempts to dissuade him, Lindsay gave up and started back.

"O.K," he said, and followed her. Instead of joining them in the living room, he placed a box on the kitchen table. "Go on with what you're doing, I'll work on these reports."

"We've got some more stew and a bottle of wine, and there's beer in the frig."

"I don't drink," he reminded her icily.

"There's Coca Cola and root beer. Oh, and there's ice cream."

"I brought my own food," he said, withdrawing a Mountain Dew and a sandwich from a lunch-box.

She bit back a comment, turned and returned to the living room where she talked with David Reed for another hour.

"It's late, Lindsay," Reed said finally. "I need to go. I'll call you tomorrow."

She nodded, walking with him to the door, where she waited until he had backed his van out of the drive.

Ryder was settled in a chair, watching television and munching on a Snickers bar when she returned. "Brought one for you," he said, friendliness now in his voice. He pulled the candy from his shirt pocket.

"No thanks," she said, "I'm going to bed," She turned toward the bedroom, but not in time to miss his crestfallen look.

The next morning she got up early enough to fix breakfast. "This is ridiculous," she said to Ryder as he walked into the kitchen. "He's not going to risk getting caught just to cause problems for me."

"You don't want me here? Maybe you'd rather have David Reed."

"He's just a friend, Ryder,"

"He's my friend too, but that doesn't mean I gotta stay up half the night with him."

Lindsay was about to protest when he held up his hand. "Sorry, I was out of line." He gave a wry smile. "Guess I was feelin' jealous. I had hoped after the other night... but if you don't want me here..."

"It's not a matter of not wanting you here Ryder. You're welcome to stay, but it's not going to accomplish anything. If I'm going to be bait, I've got to be alone. Besides, it's Dorothy he's really after."

"I wouldn't be so sure."

She took both of his hands in hers. "Ryder, as far as you and I are concerned, the timings all wrong. Maybe someday..."

Ryder brightened, "You're saying there's hope."

"The killer's not coming near me with you here," she said, quietly changing the subject.

"That's the point."

She sighed. "The best chance for us to save Ginny is to lure him to me. Damn it, Ryder, he's so close. Can't you see we're drawing him in?"

He hesitated. "All right," he said walking back into the living room, "but, Jacobs and Munson'll stay on duty and I'll have a unit nearby. You'll keep the gun on you?"

"And the cell phone."

He looked at her with skepticism. "I..." he began again, then went to the bedroom to pack. He gathered his things and walked out the door as Patty came up the walk.

"Just wanted to see you in person," she said. "I had to know you're all right." She looked at Ryder's suitcase and gave Lindsay a questioning glance.

"I'm well protected I assure you," she said, with a frustrated look.

Patty handed her a plate. "Molly and I've been making pies for the church bazaar. We baked one for you. With all of your 'protection,' you may need it. It'll give you something to serve."

"Aren't you going to come in?"

"No, Beau's waiting to take me to town." She looked toward the road and he waved from the car. "I'll call you when I get home."

After Patty left, she vacuumed and dusted, releasing pent-up energy and making sure everything was in order. When she was finished, she collected her mail, answered correspondence, and looked again at her files. Briefly resting, she went out on her deck where she saw Jacobs standing by a tree, met his gaze and nodded. She swept away leaves, twigs and pine straw, rearranged chairs and moved flowerpots while he watched. Still adrenalized, she started on the yard. She checked under the windows, but there were no footprints. Satisfied and armed with her pistol and cell phone, she secured the lock on the back door, and slipped onto the path to the beach.

The light was fading and she sat at the base of a dune to watch the sun go down. The tide ebbed and for a few brief minutes, she felt peace. Her thoughts turned to the victims and their families, then to Reed and Ryder and backward in time to Paul. "Why?" she asked softly. "Why Paul?"

Their lives had been intertwined, interwoven by their experiences, events that drew them together, their memories, their bond. He had become full of hope and it had spread to her. He'd shown her life could be beautiful...and then? She choked back tears and stared at the outgoing tide, feeling guilty as she thought of Ryder. He was not the first man she'd been attracted to since Paul's death. There'd been Jim, who also was dead. Jim, who'd been her drinking buddy as well as her partner, her friend as well as her lover.

What was it Ryder had said? "It's not who you were; it's who you are." But, her past was still a part of her, had formed the person she had come to be. Ryder's interest scared her. Was she ready to form an attachment to another man? If she did, would he, too, be taken from her? She knew with Ryder, if she gave in, it wouldn't be a one-night stand. There would be no turning back.

49

He shouldn't have left the letter. Now they knew he'd found where she lived. On the other hand, it made the game more enjoyable and no one had seen him. The cop near the house had been ogling a female jogger.

He would have loved to have seen the broad's face when she opened the envelope.

Clenching and unclenching his fists, he fought against a wave of nausea. The pungent odor of urine and fear was seeping from the woman's room into the rest of the house.

If he could only be free of her. Would it be worth it to kill her now, get rid of the stench? No, his mind shouted. He must stick to his original plan.

The smell. He tried to block it out of his mind, but the penetrating acrid air surrounded him. That same air had enveloped him as a child, waves of it, stirred by the wind from the windows as he lay in bed, afraid to move. His skin chilled by the wet sheets beneath him, he had been terrified, listening, always listening.

His body jerked involuntarily as he remembered the slapping and yelling; the noise of his mother's body falling and furniture overturned. An intolerable silence would follow as he lay frozen in place, waiting for the sound of his father's footsteps coming for him.

He touched his genitals, reassuring himself of his wholeness, his lack of physical damage, cringing at the thought of his father's threats and the coarseness of his hands as he touched him down there.

For a moment, he thought he heard his mother's mewling, but it was not her. It was the woman again, the whining whore. He breathed deeply to calm himself and then walked methodically to the room where she lay, steeling himself against the stench.

He unbound her, pulled her upright and ripped the sheets from the bed.

Pinning her hands behind her, he led her into the shower and tore away her clothes. He turned on the water and he handed her soap.

She hesitated and he took a menacing step forward. Frantically, she began to clean herself. He grabbed her by the hair and dumped shampoo into her sweaty, tangled locks; then turned the water hotter and hotter and he watched her skin redden as she choked back screams.

Her eyes widened in horror as he turned the water to cold and she realized he, too, was now naked. Staring at her, he began to harden and swell. His mind swimming, he turned off the water and pushed himself against her.

When it was over he left her cowering in the corner of the stall. He opened the bathroom cabinet and pulled out a bucket, rags and cleanser, then filled the bucket with soapy water and dragged her back to the room. He observed her every move as she scrubbed the top of the mattress. When she finished, he pulled fresh bedclothes from a drawer and watched as she fitted them onto the soaking cot.

Pointing for her to sit, he bound her hands and feet and left her there. Within minutes, he returned with a piece of bread and a glass of water. He untied her hands and held out the food. After she'd eaten, he gave her the pills and forced her to drink, then retied her hands and strapped her back on the bed.

"Please," she said, as he began to cover her mouth.

He smirked and retied the scarf.

50

Lindsay walked back through the shadowy path to her yard, aware she shouldn't have stayed after dark. She looked for Jacobs and Munson, but decided they must be in front. Feeling a breeze, she thought of rain. Her senses acute, she passed the edges of old flowerbeds now covered in decaying pine straw. She really must do something about the lawn.

Fallen branches were strewn over the grass, which was long overdue for mowing. A mimosa tree drooped over the edge of her deck, its branches covered with fern-like leaves, its wisps of pink and white flowers bathed in shades of gray.

She jumped as a squirrel darted into the shrubbery beside her. Light spilled from her windows onto azaleas and oleanders, casting dappled patterns which changed like a kaleidoscope in the breeze. What was that noise? Was there something between the trees? A screech owl shrieked as it flew from a pine. Relieved, she climbed onto the deck and unlocked her door. Still apprehensive, she checked every room and closet, her Glock held close to her side. Finally satisfied, she fixed a simple supper of fruit and crackers, made a glass of iced tea and settled on the sofa to watch the news. The anchor was interviewing a guest about a senator. A favored presidential hopeful, his popularity dropped abruptly when it was learned he was having an affair.

The newsman pressed relentlessly as his guest discussed the politician's divorce, showed pictures of the man's children and discussed his history of depression. The anchor ended by describing how the man may have felt at his mother's death and when he was molested as a child.

How odd, that an idol, once fallen, was seen as something to be destroyed. She guessed Reed would blame that on the corporate mindset, would claim the motive was media profit and it probably was. Again, the parallel with serial killers. Whatever one wanted to destroy had become fair game.

Lindsay looked out to see trees bending in the wind and the moon hidden by clouds. She was about to change channels when she saw a crawl at the base of the picture warning of thunderstorms, lightning, and hail. The Porsche was still in the drive.

Rain was already drizzling as she raced through her kitchen and into the garage, pressed the button to raise its door, and dashed to her car. She pulled in and parked, again pressing the button, for the door to come down. There was a thump as it momentarily hesitated before closing.

Passing the laundry room, she grabbed a load of clothes from the dryer, taking them into the kitchen to fold. She stripped the linens from the guest room bed, then returned to the garage and dropped them into the washer. Still feeling uneasy, she checked the rooms again. The lights went out as thunder crashed and lightning lit the house. There were a series of clicks as the current came back and the air conditioning restarted.

Still wary, she decided to take a shower, taking her gun into the bathroom and locking the door behind her. Ryder would come if she called, but after all, she had asked him to leave. She shook her head as if shaking the thought from her mind. There was no need to worry him. Cops were watching the house. She had nothing to fear.

Finishing quickly, she went to her bedroom, closed the door and pushed in the lock. She put on an extra large T-shirt and climbed into bed. Shadow jumped up behind her and curled up at her feet. She lay still and alert, the Glock and cell phone under her pillow. An hour passed before she fell into a restless sleep.

Suddenly she awakened, every fiber of her body alert. She was sure she'd heard a noise. The glow from her alarm clock was gone. Was the power off again? Holding her gun in one hand, she reached for her watch. The illuminated dial said 2 a.m. She opened the drawer of her bedside table, pulled out a flashlight and shined it over the room. She was breathing a sigh of relief as her breath caught in her throat. The bedroom door was open.

Momentarily rooted in place, she forced herself out of bed, ran and locked it. Using all of her strength, she managed to jam her dresser against it. Stepping back, she heard a thud on the other side.

She picked up the telephone from the table, but found it dead. Retrieving her cell phone, she quickly punched 911.

"County Police."

"This is Dr. Lindsay. Call Lt. Ryder. Someone's in my house."

There was a pause. "Address?"

She impatiently related her house number and street.

A full minute passed before the dispatcher responded.

"Lt. Ryder's on his way."

Lindsay held the phone tightly against her ear. "Ma'am, are you still there?"

"Yes."

"Ma'am, I need you to stay on the line."

Again, there was a pause. "What room are you in?"

Before she could answer, there was a sound at the bedroom door. She could hear the lock release and the noise of the chest scraping the floor as it slowly moved forward. She groped for the flashlight. Unable to find it, she strained to see in the dark.

"I'll shoot," she warned, tightly clutching her gun. She fired and the noise stopped. Did she hit him? Was he in her room? For a few seconds there was silence, then he was on her. The gun fell from her hand as she struggled against him and they fell to the floor. He pinned her arms with his knees and her legs with his feet. Finally, unable to move, she lay still. His hands moved over her chest, lingered at her breasts and reached for her throat.

He pressed tighter and tighter. Unable to breathe, she began to lose consciousness. As she tried to push up, he leaned onto her chest. Her lungs felt as if they would burst and the pain was unbearable. Her body felt limp, then numb.

She heard a noise in the distance and someone calling her name. Then, as quickly as he'd come, he was gone, running back through the hall.

Using the bed for support, she pulled herself to her feet as she gasped for breath.

"Lindsay, Lindsay are you all right?"

"In here," she answered in a croaking voice.

Ryder pushed through the doorway, shining his flashlight back and forth until he found her. "Thank God, Lindsay, Thank God."

In an instant he was at her side, holding her to him.

"I'm O.K.," she stammered weakly, "but he's getting away."

"Where's Jacobs?"

"Jacobs?" she said hoarsely.

"Jacobs and Munson. Where are they?"

"I haven't seen..."

"Shit." He turned abruptly and ran out of the room.

She fumbled in the dark for jeans and a shirt. As she hurriedly put them on, she heard sirens, the squealing of tires and loud voices. She cautiously made her way through the darkened hall to the front door. Cops were gathered in the yard, talking excitedly. She saw Ryder walking slowly toward them. He spoke in low tones and the men grew silent.

"Ryder," she called, hastening to join them.

"They're dead," he said flatly.

"What?"

"Jacobs was hit from behind. Munson was strangled."

It took a moment for his words to sink in.

"They're dead?" she repeated.

"Been awhile," said Ryder. "They checked in an hour ago. I tried to reach them after dispatch called. They never answered."

"I've caused this."

"No, Lindsay. You didn't cause it. They almost caused your death. They should have been alert. That was their job." He put his arm around her shoulders. "I think Jacobs had fallen asleep.

"The bodies were dragged out of sight, near the beach," he continued. "The M.E.'s on his way." Lindsay followed him to where the other policemen stood, staring at the remains of their colleagues.

Fifteen minutes later, Frost appeared. Lindsay watched the cops stringing tape around the yard as the crime techs set up flood lamps.

"Where is your breaker box?" asked Ryder.

"The kitchen closet," she answered. They walked back inside where Ryder turned on the power and they went through each room flipping on lights. "Shadow," said Lindsay, as two female crime techs started work in the entranceway.

They searched the house, but she was nowhere to be found. They went into the yard and she called the cat's name. Just as they'd given up, they heard a faint cry. The cat had climbed into the mimosa and was lying on its lowest branch.

As Lindsay talked to it, Ryder came from behind and snatched it. He held it against his chest as they went back in the house.

"She's shaking," said Lindsay. Taking the animal from Ryder, she cradled it in her arms and began rubbing its back. For a few minutes, it was still, then, with a cry, jumped down and raced to the bedroom.

"Back under the bed, where she feels safe."

By dawn, the bodies had been taken away. Several cops were walking a grid in Lindsay's yard, searching for clues but so far, they'd found nothing. Seated with Ryder at the kitchen table, she tried to recall everything that had happened.

"The doors and windows were locked. I rechecked them before I went to bed. I don't know how he got in."

Two more crime techs joined them and following Ryder's orders began checking inside the house.

"Start with when I left," he said to Lindsay. "I want to know everything you did between then and now."

His expression was pained as she methodically retraced her housework, her work in the yard and her walk on the beach.

"It doesn't make sense. There's something you've forgotten."

Just then, Collins appeared in the doorway. "Crime scene's found traces of mud on the floor of the garage on the passenger side of your ride."

"When Lindsay?" said Ryder. "When did you open the garage?"

She looked at him, appalled.

"The weatherman said it was going to hail, so, when it started to rain, I brought in the car."

"He must have come in with you. Did you lock the door from the garage to the house?"

"No," she said dejectedly. "I was in and out of the laundry room washing clothes."

"That would have given him time to get inside. He probably hid until you went to bed and turned off the power when you were asleep.

"Your bedroom door can be opened with a credit card," he added.

Lindsay took a deep breath, "I can't believe he was here all that time."

"One thing that puzzles me," said Ryder, "is why he waited, why he didn't go after you when he first had the chance."

"I was wearing my gun," said Lindsay. "He must have seen it and waited until I went to bed, but why didn't he kill me then?"

"Something must have distracted him. It could have been Shadow."

As if on cue, the animal appeared from the living room, turned, and walked through the hall toward the end of the house.

Ryder stared at the cat, "She probably saved your life."

"There's not enough mud to get a footprint," said one of the techs, as the two came in from the garage. "And from what we can't find on the doors, I'd say he was wearing gloves." They finished their work and began to pack up as two officers came in from outside.

"Not a trace," one of them reported. "We figure he was on foot. The units coming off the road didn't see anything." As they left, Ryder gave her a piercing look. "Your place or mine?" he said firmly.

The thought of staying at Ryder's made her uncomfortable.

"You don't have to get your face all scrunched. I can take a hint. Collins will stay here with you until I get back."

51

Out of breath, he ran into his house, slamming and locking the door behind him.

Damn bitch. He'd almost had her.

The first time he'd slipped in through the garage, he'd only turned off the stove while she'd been in the tub. Oh, the temptation was there, but he'd maintained his cool. He'd wanted to pick his time and he wasn't ready.

He liked that, picking his time and place, like he owned them. Well, timing it right had paid off. Dorothy's file was right out in the open. If it hadn't been for the orderly, she'd be dead. She would be sooner or later. Like he'd said, it was just timing.

Tonight, the friggin' police whore'd almost been his. She'd gone to sleep with him in the house, without a clue he was there. She thought she was so smart, just like the rest of the dumb broads he'd known. Worse, she thought she was a crime prevention expert. Now that was a laugh, a friggin' crime enabler was more like it.

He'd disconnected her alarm when he cut the outside phone line. The two cops on duty never saw him. They'd been an easy take down. Hell, one of them was asleep. It had been a breeze to get inside the garage again, crouching beside the car, kneeling behind it as the door went down; and then, the bitch did her laundry. He'd gone in when her back was turned and hidden in the hall closet. The stupid woman had even taken a shower. He'd started after her then, but she'd locked the door and come out too quickly. If he'd stayed in her room…but, she'd have seen him. There were few places to hide and he'd not wanted to ruin his surprise. Once she'd gone to bed, he'd turned off the electricity, waited, then opened her door.

That damn cat. It was the scratching that had thrown him, then the thing racing by. How the hell could he have known there was an animal in the house?

The cops must have suspected he'd be there. Cops don't usually come that fast. Dorothy's attack must have them alert.

He felt sticky and wet. His clothes were damp from the rain and sweat. He took them off, angrily threw them onto the kitchen floor and then waited at the base of the stairs. There was no sound. Creeping to the woman's room, he looked in the doorway. She was asleep. The drugs were doing their thing. Tomorrow he'd be rid of her. It was the Fourth of July and the bitch would go out with a bang. Hell, there'd even be fireworks. He could picture the look on the woman's face as she realized what he was going to do. She would beg and plead with her eyes, then she would shake. They all did. So melodramatic, but so fitting. It was a scene he wouldn't miss, each detail as he'd planned it.

Detail.

He was an expert detail man. He was producing this show; could add any detail he wanted. He could even add special effects. If she was a drama queen, he'd make her a star.

52

By the time Ryder returned it was almost seven a.m. As he came in, he glanced at the kitchen counter.

"Hungry?" she asked. "I'll fix some breakfast."

"It's really no trouble," she said as he started to protest. She pulled a carton of eggs and package of bacon from the refrigerator, placed bread in the toaster and poured coffee into cups. Within minutes, they were seated at the kitchen table. "Now this is a breakfast," he said appreciatively.

"Would you like some more?"

He hesitated and patted his stomach. "Just coffee."

"Today's the day," she said solemnly. "July 4th."

"You seem damn sure."

"With so many boaters watching the fireworks, he'll take her out. He'll think he won't be noticed in the crowd." They finished eating and went to town to meet with the others. Wong and Duggan were in the conference room by Ryder's office when they arrived. Collins came in behind them.

"What now?" asked Duggan.

"The main thing's being prepared," answered Ryder. "If Dr. Lindsay's right, this is the night."

All eyes turned to Lindsay. "He won't admit it, but he's screwed up," she said. "Yesterday was an example. He's getting anxious and less organized but he'll be determined to go through with his plan."

"The pressure's on," said Ryder. "Every cop in the area's after him and he can't get rid of his vic."

"Almost getting caught's unnerved him," added Lindsay. "He's edgy and that makes him more dangerous."

"I thought he was a control freak," said Duggan.

"He is," she said, "and at this stage, that's in our favor."

A dubious expression crossed Duggan's face.

"He's like an addict," she explained. "The more he loses control, the more he'll fight to regain it and the more he'll lose it again."

"You think the Delaney woman's still living?" asked Wong.

"Every minute he has her lessens her chances but I believe she's alive."

"He's got no reason to keep her," Duggan objected. "By now she'd be a nuisance. If you ask me, tonight's a waste of time."

"He's not going to change his m.o.," said Lindsay. "That'd be admitting he's lost control."

"Jeez, what a nut case," said Duggan. "How in hell's he have time for all this? Doesn't the guy ever work?"

"Probably not," said Lindsay.

"Coastal living takes big bucks," said Ryder. "How does he survive?"

"He could have gotten money any number of ways," said Lindsay. "He may have inherited it."

"Makes no sense," said Duggan. "I thought guys like this were drifters or came from the projects. I can see some scumbag like that doin' somebody in."

"You think being poor makes a person become a criminal?" asked Collins defensively.

"No, but I can see a guy mad 'cause he never had nothin' or whose parents abused him."

"Violence and abuse occur across all social classes," said Lindsay.

"I know what you're saying," said Collins, "but look at the stats. Most crime's committed by poor minorities."

"Not many serial killers are minorities. Besides, crimes committed by the rich often go unpunished."

"Like what," said Duggan, his interest piqued.

Lindsay thought for a second. "Domestic violence. The poor live in crowded neighborhoods where it's harder to hide and more likely reported. They seek help in emergency rooms and become statistics. Those who can afford it are treated by family doctors who often don't tell."

"Sounds like the courts," said Collins. "Big money buys you a big lawyer who buys you off."

"So what does this have to do with the case?" Ryder demanded.

"I'm just making a point," said Lindsay. "We can't I D the killer according to whether he's rich or poor. We don't know why or if he isn't working."

"Enough Sociology 101," said Ryder. "Get back to the case."

"This is not as far away from the case as you think," said Lindsay. "The killer may have been abused, but he's probably not poor and his personality is a paradox. Lack of control of his life causes his obsession with controlling others."

Duggan frowned. "Just another sicko we gotta figure out."

"True," said Lindsay. "He's like a puzzle whose pieces never fit and he's constantly trying to rearrange them. That's what he does in his fantasies and rituals. But, his relief is only temporary. Just when he thinks he's got it together, it all falls apart."

"Sounds like Humpty Dumpty," said Duggan. "All the psychs in the world can't put a shitbag like that back together."

No," agreed Lindsay. "The pieces to his puzzle will never be found."

"Hell, if we can't piece the puzzle together, why are we talking about this?" asked Ryder.

She took a deep breath. "If we can understand him, we can see patterns in his behavior, maybe save Ginny. Her best chance is for us to make sense of the pieces we have. Knowing which ones are missing lets us guess what he'll do. "

"I'm not sure I understand," said Wong.

"Criminal profilers become puzzle-masters. They figure out which pieces are missing and see the killer's choice of victims as a match. If they can make sense of what's missing, they can predict what the killer will do."

"How?" said Ryder, now interested.

"Back to domestic violence," said Lindsay. "Batterers often choose formerly abused children as their wives. The women, feeling unloved and used to abuse, may choose them in turn. During dating, the woman mistakes possessiveness for affection and toughness as protection."

"Surely people can tell the difference in someone who's normal and a wife beater," said Duggan, dismissively.

"Not always," said Lindsay. "Who's to say what's normal? And, in the case of victim and predator, there's another factor involved."

"Go on," encouraged Ryder.

"Think of families, "said Lindsay. "Children repeat patterns they learn from their parents, even bad ones."

"I've always wondered about that," said Wong. "Most of the people arrested for child abuse were abused."

Lindsay nodded, "Bear with me and I'll give you an anaolgy. Most people who have parents or guardians can't change them, just like some people who have a pair of shoes they can't exchange. They may be secondhand and not fit, or pinch and misshape their feet, but they may not be able to get another pair."

"I know I wouldn't keep wearing 'em," said Duggan.

"You would if you didn't have a choice," said Collins.

Lindsay nodded impatiently. "By the time they can afford another pair, the damage is done. The right size would be uncomfortable. The same thing happens in human relationships. People become used to them no matter how hurtful they are. They may not know they have a choice or they're afraid of change. They play out the patterns, even wrong ones, because they're the only patterns they know."

"At which point some damn liberal steps in sayin' a crime's not the criminal's fault," snapped Duggan.

"We've all got a choice," said Ryder. "There are plenty of kids who've been abused who don't become criminals. I know that for a fact."

"You're right. But, seeing the patterns emerge shows cause and effect. It tells us where the pieces come from, and how they fit."

"So how's this going to help Ginny Delaney?" Ryder demanded.

"The killer's puzzle becomes our guide," said Lindsay. "That's what psychological profiling is about. For instance, we know he despises women while he obsessively longs for them. He'll treat his victim abusively to control her, but he won't kill her yet because it's not his plan. He'll take Ginny on the water tonight, under the full moon where he can see her. He'll repeat what he did to the others unless we stop him."

Ryder took out a piece of gum and offered the pack to the others who shook their heads.

"He's had her too long," said Lindsay. "Keeping her was not his intention and he'll be angry, less careful, blaming her, blaming us, anyone but himself and he'll want to prove he can finish his ritual." She turned to Wong. "We have to pinpoint the area he's taken the others as closely as we can and establish a time-frame. He'll go to the same place tonight."

The diver thought a minute. "There are three possible sites on the northern end where the tide ranges up to eight feet. He won't get out of the creeks when it's low, so he'll go after midnight when the level is high."

Wong pulled a pad from his pocket, began scribbling, and then looked at the others.

"Smuggler's Creek. He has to come out of Smuggler's Creek. That's the only place on the northern end where there won't be a crowd."

"That creek's not near a ramp," objected Duggan.

"No," Wong agreed, "but there are plenty of private docks and access to open water." He held up a map, then walked to the conference room and spread it on the table. The others followed.

"Right here." He made a circle with his finger on a spot south of Hampton as they bent over the map to see where he was pointing. "If he's coming from anywhere in this area he'll have to go through the creek. We'll need to set up watch here." Wong placed his finger back on the map and drew an imaginary line.

"All the way to Neptune Park?" asked Duggan in disbelief. "That's a hell of a lotta water and every boat in the county'll be out there. What's he going to do? Attach a sign to the side of his craft, so we'll know it's him?"

Wong ignored the remark.

"The other boats will give him perfect cover," agreed Collins.

"For us too," said Wong, "especially if we use Reed's boat again."

Ryder flushed and worked his jaw against his gum. "I'm sure we can find another boat," he said, "No use in bothering him again."

Wong gave him a puzzled look. "It will be a lot easier to go with him than find another one this late."

"All right," agreed Ryder reluctantly. "Call him. Make sure he can do it."

"So what kind of boat will we be looking for?" asked Duggan. "Anybody gotta clue?"

"The boat will be small enough to maneuver in and out of the deeper creeks, but it will have a cabin," said Lindsay. "He won't chance having her out in the open."

Wong nodded his head, "I'd say we're looking for something ranging from twenty to thirty feet."

"I still don't see how we're going to tell the difference between him and the tourists," said Duggan. "All the squirrel's got to do is blend with the crowd, dump her and rabbit."

Lindsay nodded. "Duggan's right. He'll try to blend in, but he won't get close to the crowd. He'll stay at a distance."

Duggan laughed. "He'll be lucky if he's not run over. Last year, the Coast Guard had twenty calls for BUI."

Lindsay raised an eyebrow.

"Drunks," explained Ryder, "Boating under the influence."

"If it's the Fourth," chuckled Duggan, impressed with his own humor, "they have to have a fifth." When they ignored his comment, he continued. "Shit, I don't think you have a chance in hell of catching him under those conditions."

"Well, we're sure as hell going to try," said Ryder, becoming irritated. "We've got a plan."

"I've been talking with some of the shrimpers," said Wong, "guys I know I can trust. They usually take their families out anyway so they aren't likely to draw attention. If they anchor at three-hundred yard intervals, they can keep watch on the whole area."

"If we can't describe the boat, how the hell will they know which one it is?" asked Duggan.

"Good point," agreed Ryder grudgingly.

"Remember," said Wong. "It'll have to be in the range of twenty to thirty feet."

"That's three-fourths of the boats out there," said Duggan.

Wong went on, "We also know it'll have a cabin."

"And he'll stay away from the other boats," now it was Lindsay interrupting, "and won't stick around."

"Right," said Wong. "He'll come out of the creek, then go beyond the breakers and further out to sea." Again, he drew his finger across the map. "Can we get night vision binoculars?" he asked.

"We can borrow them from FLETC," said Lindsay.

"O.K.," said Wong, "if we can get the night vision binoculars, we can establish a perimeter here." He tapped at a place not far from the mouth of the creek. "We can have a spotter on each boat, watching for anyone coming in or out." He looked at Ryder. "We'll have to be in constant radio contact."

"Might as well use a megaphone," said Duggan.

Wong frowned, "There are several rarely used frequencies. Granted, he could scan them all but..."

"That's unlikely," said Lindsay. "He'll have enough to deal with controlling the boat."

"And the vic," added Collins.

"We'll use cell phones," said Ryder, "They're clearer and quicker."

"What about the Coast Guard?" asked Duggan. "Are they going to be in on it?"

Ryder frowned. "They'll be busy, but, yeah, they'll be there. When we're ready to nail him, they'll be ready."

"It'll be dark at nine," said Collins. "Fireworks begin at ten."

Ryder looked at his watch. "It's already noon," he said. "Go home and get a nap. Dr. Lindsay and I will pick up the supplies and binoculars. We'll meet at Starboard Marina at eight."

53

Huddled against the corner, he shook with terror. The screaming had subsided. All that remained were his mother's whimpering cries and he knew he would be next.

His father's heavy footsteps grew closer. Every nerve of his body seemed alive as he listened to his approach. Closer and closer he came.

He watched and waited, unable to move, his body going limp as the doorknob turned.

Suddenly, he was jerked away from the wall and thrown against his bed. He tried desperately to escape as tears flowed down his cheeks.

"So I have a little girl here do I? Is that what you are? A girl? Sniffling and crying like your mama?" His father's words were loud and slurred with whisky. Spittle flew from his mouth and onto Timmie's face.

He tried to turn away, but his father's slap caught him on the side of his head, knocking him down on the mattress.

"You want to act like a girl? I'll show you what girls are for."

He was abruptly twisted onto his stomach as his father ripped away the bottom of his pajamas. Then all he knew was searing pain.

The whimpering cries continued.

He awoke with a start, memories flooding through him, intermingling with reality.

The woman. She was whining again.

He got out of bed and went into her room, his anger rising like vomit.

She looked up as he entered, then, terrified, looked away.

He tightened the scarf across her mouth. He raised his hand and the threat was sufficient. After a muffled choking sound, she was silent.

54

Shadow was in the kitchen and this time didn't run when Lindsay entered. The cat waited patiently, watching as her food bowl was filled and eagerly tasting its contents.

The animal was so small and vulnerable. Lindsay realized with a pang she was becoming attached to her and was glad for the quiet companionship.

Reed had offered to pick her up, but Ryder insisted she ride with him, and knowing they were sleep deprived, insisted on rest. She could hear him near the deck, checking the outside of the house. He'd already been inside checking the windows. Hearing a light tap at the front door, she pulled back the curtain and saw a young officer talking with him. She walked to the door, opened it and stepped outside.

"This is Officer Bleakley, Ed Bleakley," said Ryder. "He and Officer Tanner will be keeping watch. That's in addition to our unit on the road." Lindsay shook the officer's hand as Ryder continued, "He'll stay inside, in case we've made a mistake about tonight and our scumbag gets ideas."

"The sofa folds out," Lindsay began.

Ryder's eyes narrowed. "He's not going to sleep. Like I said, he's going to keep watch."

She offered the officer drinks and snacks and showed him the leftovers in the frig.

"Thank you ma'am." His accent was thick enough to cut.

Ryder trudged into the guest room and collapsed onto the bed with a thud.

Lindsay smiled at Bleakley. "I guess I'll do the same." The cat followed, scooting in beside her as she entered her room.

Lindsay pulled off her clothes, put on a robe, and ran the water in the tub, pouring in several capfuls of Lavender oil. When it was full, she climbed in, adjusted the pillow behind her head as usual and felt the tension leaving her body. With two cops in the house, she wasn't worried. After she finished bathing she dressed in a soft nylon gown, went to her room and closed the door. Minutes after climbing into bed, she fell asleep.

"Lindsay, you in there?" She leapt from the bed and flung open the door.

He stared at her see-through gown and his face turned red.

"I didn't mean to scare you," he stammered. "I didn't realize you were already asleep."

"It's O.K. Ryder. What is it?" She led him into her room, pulled on a robe and motioned for him to sit on the edge of the bed beside her.

"I was going to go over the plans for tonight, I ..." He fell silent then gently took her into his arms and kissed her. Caught off guard, she found herself responding.

"I need you," he said hoarsely. He looked into her eyes and began hungrily kissing her again, moving his hand down her shoulder and over her breast.

"Ryder," she whispered. He kissed her neck, moved downward and kissed each of her hardening nipples. He paused to take off his clothes and came back to her, again starting by kissing her mouth and moving further and further downward. He held her to the bed and straddled her, gently parting her thighs with his knees.

She pressed her lips firmly together to keep from moaning as he explored her, tentatively probing with his fingers and tongue. When he finally entered her, she gasped, and began moving her body rapidly in unison with his. When their passion was spent, he collapsed on top of her and they lay still. Several minutes passed before he covered her face with tender kisses and turned onto his side, his arm encircling her.

"Ryder..." she began.

He pressed a finger to her lips. "Later," he said softly. "We have a lot to talk about." They slept for an hour before he left the room, quietly shutting the door behind him.

Four hours later, they were preparing to meet the others at the marina.

"You don't have to go Lindsay. It might be safer for you to stay put."

"I'm going," answered Lindsay as they walked out the door. "Ryder, this is part of my job."

He started to open the door of his car for her but Lindsay shook her head. "No," she said. "This is business. This time I'm on my own." They sat for a minute as he pulled open a new pack of gum and held it out.

"No thanks," she said as he stuffed a piece in his mouth. From then on they rode in silence, preoccupied with thoughts of what had been and what lay ahead.

The others were already on the boat when they arrived. Wong helped Lindsay on board while Ryder untied the ropes then sat beside her. Reed gave Lindsay a searching look before easing the boat away from the dock, weaving in and out of waterway traffic.

A motorboat sped past, its large wake rocking the nearby boats while a deep bass beat of rap music carried across the waves. Three young men on its deck waved bottles of beer.

"An accident waiting to happen," said Ryder.

"Lots of accidents waiting to happen," said Duggan as another boat sped by.

They cruised around the tip of St. Simons and went farther outward to make better time. Lindsay spotted several sailboats in the distance and the silhouettes of trawlers among the gathering vessels.

Reed jerked the boat sharply, narrowly missing a boy riding a jet ski as they held onto the railing behind their seats for balance.

Gazing toward the beach, they saw hundreds of families vying for position on the sand as the incoming tide drove them farther and farther back against the dunes. For twenty minutes, they moved northward, finally maneuvering into position a hundred yards behind the nearest shrimp boat. Despite the distance, they could hear voices and laughter from the other boats across the water. Reed dropped anchor while Ryder and Duggan tested the reception on their cell phones.

As they waited, the sky turned into a haze of orange and aquamarine. Collins opened a cooler and handed out cold bottles of an off-brand cola. Ryder took a swallow and made a face. "Yuck, I'll wait until this is over and have the real thing." He handed it back and reached for his thermos of water.

Reed passed out ham sandwiches and packages of potato chips as darkness enveloped them. Sky and ocean seemed one as stars and boat lights blended in the night. The moon looked like a fluorescent beachball streaming light across the waves.

Suddenly, there were several booming sounds, followed by crackles and the sky was showered with colors. Over and over the noise was repeated, interspersed with whishing sounds and whistles. After a final frenzy of booms, the sky was lit in patterns of red, white, and blue. For a few minutes, there was silence; then engines started as people realized the spectacle was over.

Wong picked up his cell phone and talked in low tones. "They'll stay with us," he said to Ryder, nodding towards a cluster of trawlers. "They'll be here as long as we need them."

Ryder leaned back, settling deeper into his seat. "Might as well relax, it's going to be a long night."

Feeling as if someone was watching her, Lindsay looked up into Ryder's eyes. She gave him a reassuring smile, then through the dimness of the boat-light, saw a questioning look, followed by a smile of approval on the face of David Reed.

55

Everything was ready. There was just enough time to navigate through the creek before the crowd of boats dispersed. Looking out of his window, he saw the cruiser straining at its ropes, ready and waiting. He put on a pair of black nylon running pants, a black pullover shirt, and shoes and stepped into the room where the woman was sleeping. She moaned as he unbuckled the straps holding her to the bed and unbound her ankles. Grabbing her by the arm, he pulled her to her feet.

She wavered and then gradually gained her balance as he put his arm around her waist and led her toward the stairs. As they passed the bath, she made a motion to enter. Damn bitch. He dragged her onward as she resisted, frantically making motions for him to stop. If he didn't let her go she'd wet on the floor or in the boat. Cursing, he pushed her inside, placing his foot on the threshold to prevent her from pushing the door shut.

"Hurry," he commanded.

There was a muffled sound from inside.

He stood a minute more, then tired of waiting, he turned to go in.

Suddenly she lunged, striking his temple with the edge of a can of shaving cream.

With one swift shove he pushed her hard against the wall and grabbed her arms which she had somehow worked free. The rope dangled loosely from her left wrist.

"Bitch," he growled. Swinging her around, he gathered the ends of the cords and tied her arms tightly behind her back. He stuffed a handkerchief in her mouth and gagged her with the scarf, stifling her cries. As she struggled for breath, he felt her beside him, her chest heaving. He pressed himself against her. No! He mustn't. Not now. There wasn't time. He moved away, gripping her arm and pulling her towards the stairs where he dragged her downward and out the door and onto the dock.

56

The boat rocked sharply under Duggan's weight as he walked to the cooler for another sandwich. Lindsay talked softly with David Reed as the others kept watch. The trawlers had remained after the fireworks ended, along with a few of the larger yachts. Voices and music carried on the wind. Lindsay jumped as a fish hit the side of the boat.

"Mullet," said Reed. "They're attracted to the light."

Duggan started to close the cooler, then looked at the others. "Anybody want another sandwich? Beats just sitting."

When nobody replied, he unwrapped his sandwich and stared moodily at the water. "Seems to me if he was coming he'd be here by now."

"Give him time. It's not even midnight," said Lindsay, stretching.

They waited, breaking the silence with occasional conversation. There was a beep, and Wong reached for his phone. The others waited expectantly. "About 2 o'clock on the ocean side," he said, pointing northeast. They could barely make out movement in the distance. Gradually, they heard the sound of a boat making its way around the last trawler and veering toward them.

"Let's go," said Duggan.

"Not so fast," warned Ryder. "We don't want to attract attention, and it may not be him." Just as he completed the sentence, the boat turned again and headed toward shore.

"Shit," said Duggan. "This is like fishin' in a damn bathtub. Nothing's gonna bite."

"Give him time," Lindsay repeated. The cop's impatience was getting on her nerves.

They settled back in their seats, listening to the waves slapping the boat as the tide gained momentum.

Another beep.

Wong listened for several seconds and then turned to the others. "This is it. A small cabin cruiser is coming out from the point and bearing towards us. Cap' Taylor said he was hauling ass 'til he saw the *Sea Queen*. He cut the motor like he was out for an evening ride. After he passed the *Queen*, he picked up speed. Cap wants to know if he can help."

"Tell him to hold off," said Ryder. "We'll let him know if we need him."

"Take down time," snapped Duggan. "I been sittin' on ready."

Reed cranked the engine, turned off the light, and they sped into darkness.

57

As the twenty-four-foot cruiser plowed through the waves, he pointed his flashlight into the cabin where she lay still, her body wedged between two large cushions on the floor, her hands still bound behind her back. He lowered the boat's speed to an idle. Hearing a motor in the distance, he watched the lights of the nearest trawler grow smaller. Still, the noise continued. Probably a bunch of drunks out for a joy ride. At least they'd keep the cops occupied.

He drove for another ten minutes, then cut the engine and let the boat drift. Adrenaline raced through him as he pictured what was ahead, acting it out in his mind.

Despite the cloth stuffed in her mouth, he could hear the woman's stifled sobs.

She knew.

He savored the thought.

Restarting the engine, he let it run in case the bitch managed to scream. He stepped down beside her, shining the light on her face as he drew her towards him and to her feet, half-dragging, half-carrying her to the deck. She shook with terror as he held her against him. Reaching behind her, he removed the scarf and handkerchief, placing his hand on her mouth as a warning before untying her wrists. After cutting the rope binding her ankles, he lifted her into his arms and climbed out and onto the deck. Kneeling slowly, he lowered her into the water. He grasped her shoulders, turned her toward him, and pushed her downward.

58

Ryder signaled Reed to cut the motor to a hum as they moved closer to the idling boat. "We have to make it to his boat before he spots us."

Reed swung a wide arc, easing into position diagonally in front of the cruiser's cabin where they would be less likely to be seen. The larger boat's outline loomed ominously against the pale moonlit sky as they struggled to see in the dark.

Reed turned off the ignition. As the boat began to drift, he pulled a paddle from the floor of the boat and handed it to Wong who swung it soundlessly through the waves until they were almost at the other craft's stern.

Lindsay pointed to the silhouette of a man leaning overboard. Reed immediately fired the engine and they surged forward so fast they almost crashed. He cut the motor as Wong dropped into the water, Lindsay grabbed the side of the cruiser and Ryder, Duggan, and Collins charged on board. There was a scuffle and a loud cry as a figure leapt from the deck onto the cruiser's bow.

Collins quickly followed, catching him by the knees, trying to wrestle him down. As the man wriggled free, Collins lost his footing and plummeted into the sea.

As the figure tried to regain his balance, Ryder grabbed him from behind. For a moment they paused as if caught in midair, then crashed on and into the windshield, the man's head cracking the glass. Again, they were momentarily still, then as Ryder slowly got to his feet the man slid from the deck and slipped beneath the waves.

Duggan shined his flashlight in the water. "Where'd he go?" He played the light over the boat and illuminated a puddle of blood trailing over its edge.

"Gone to join his victims," muttered Ryder. "Couldn't have been more fitting."

"Hey, give me a hand," yelled Collins, gripping the boat's rail as he struggled to climb from the water. Ryder reached down and helped pull him in, then snatched the light from Duggan and shined it across the ocean's surface. They heard a gurgling sound and turned to see Wong swimming toward the boat as he held a woman partially out of the water. Ryder and Duggan pulled her on board and Wong followed.

"She's alive," exclaimed Lindsay as the choking woman began spewing out sea water. Finally able to breathe, she collapsed, too weak to hold herself upright.

"Ginny?" asked Ryder.

"Yes," the woman said weakly.

Lindsay rushed to kneel by her side. "You're going to be all right," she said trying to comfort her.

Reed threw Collins a rope to join the two boats as Lindsay started to stand, holding onto the rail for support. Suddenly, something grabbed her hand, pulling her sideways, and toward the water.

"No," she screamed, struggling to break away.

Reed released the brake on his wheelchair and the chair lunged forward, pinning her in. Unable to release her hand, she watched in terror as a man rose from the water, bracing his feet against the boat as he attempted to pull her towards him.

Ryder sprung from the darkness, grabbed the discarded paddle and swung as hard as he could towards the man's head, making contact with a crack as the paddle split.

The man held on for an instant and then eased his grip as he dropped back into the water. There was a splash, then the water was still and Lindsay was in Ryder's arms.

Epilogue

It had been three days since Ginny Delaney's rescue. Ryder, Reed, and Lindsay had been invited to the Crandall's home for a discussion of the Blackwater Killer Case.

"Good meal," said Ryder, looking toward Patty. "Damn good meal."

She gave her husband an approving wink. "We have to give Beau credit for the steaks. He fixed them on his new grill. Anyone want another piece of Molly's key lime pie? There's plenty left."

Reed shook his head. "Not me, I'm too full."

Patty rang a small bell and her housekeeper appeared from the kitchen and began clearing the table.

"I may never need to eat again," said Lindsay, putting down her fork on her empty dessert plate. "If I could cook like you, I'd open a restaurant."

"We've been told that before," said Patty. "If you'll come back for Beau's barbecue, you'll know why."

Beauregard Crandall looked lovingly at his wife, pleased at her praise. "Enough," he said. He looked questioningly at Ryder. "It's time for you to tell us about the case."

"My curiosity's killing me," added Patty.

Lindsay and Ryder looked at each other and Lindsay nodded.

He started with Ginny Delaney.

Blindfolded when the killer had taken her, she'd been unable to describe where he lived. They'd located the address through the cruiser's registration. Licensed in the name of Timothy W. Mullis, the boat contained fibers and hair matching the earlier drowning victims.

In the old Mullis home, the police found several boxes of the killer's souvenirs. Jewelry and articles of clothing were traced to the murdered women and to those filing police reports. They also found a stash of money.

For years, islanders had passed down tales of drug shipments on the northern end of the island. Although it was never proven, Timmie's father was thought to be involved, as was his wife. The drugs had supposedly stopped with their deaths in a boating accident.

Ginny's description of the killer was given to a police artist who made a composite sketch. When it was released to the media, several more women came forward and reported assault. Although the killer's body had never been found, the issue was moot. Shops were packed with tourists and the island was back to normal.

Dorothy Levy had been the key. Knowing she'd helped save lives helped her recovery and with the killer no longer a threat, she'd regained her sense of security. She'd accepted a job at Ridgedale as Dr. Skalato's assistant.

Lindsay had helped in the search of the killer's house, uncovering hiding places and putting together pieces of his past.

"The family had a reputation for drug smuggling," said Reed. "But that's all I'd ever heard."

"That and running a ring of prostitution," added Ryder. "We could never pin anything on them, though God knows we tried."

"How long has it been since the Mullises died?" asked Lindsay

"I'd say about eight years. The son reported them missing after a storm. We figured the boat got swamped and they went under. The Coast Guard looked for several days but didn't find them, guess he'd made sure of that."

Patty shivered. "There's one thing I don't understand. How could he have been here that long without anyone knowing?"

"He didn't call attention to himself and he had everything he needed," said Lindsay, "a place to stay, plenty of money, and the endless stream of tourists helped him remain anonymous."

"What about the money angle?" asked Beau. "Wouldn't somebody question such a big bank account?"

"Drug dealers don't use banks," said Ryder. "If it was as big an operation as we think, his father had plenty of cash. He probably hid it all over the place." He stood and looked at his hosts. "I think I'll call it a night. I've got more paperwork to do in the morning." He glanced toward Lindsay.

She who feigned a yawn and said, "I think I'll head out too."

Patty arched an eyebrow, gave Beau a knowing look and then turned to Reed. "Stay awhile," she urged. "Beau said he wants to ask you about that fishing hole you found near Christmas Creek." As she and Reed talked, Beau escorted Lindsay and Ryder to the door.

Since Lindsay had walked, Ryder offered her a ride home.

"Would you like to come in?" she asked, as they stopped in her drive.

"You better believe it," said Ryder, already opening his door.

Lindsay led him into the kitchen, put on a pot of coffee and picked up a cat toy from the floor. "Won't be needing this anymore," she said sadly. "She's back with Ginny, now."

"You liked that cat, didn't you?"

"I have to admit, it's lonely around here without her."

"Lonely?" He grinned. "That can be corrected. You know Lindsay, together, we're pretty good at solving crimes, and, we're pretty good at some other things too."

She blushed as he took her in his arms, gave her a long passionate kiss and carried her through the hall and into the bedroom.

And the body moved closer to shore, with each succeeding wave.

"Yea, though I walk through the valley of the shadow of death,

I will fear no evil: for thou art with me…"

Psalm 23

"I am a part of all I have met."

Telemecus